Dear Diary,

Disaster has struck our beautiful day care. Little Lily Marshall has been kidnapped—from the front yard! In broad daylight! Marilyn was the teacher in charge, and she's beside herself. She took her eyes off Lily and her friend Emily for only a matter of seconds—she went to investigate that homeless man who hangs around the fence. When Emily started screaming, she knew something was terribly wrong.

Once disaster strikes like this, somehow the world looks bleak. I'm frantic about Lily and I'm also worried about Alexandra. Her nightmares seem to be getting worse, and lately she's become obsessed with this homeless man.

But my prayers are all for Lily now, and for her mother, Faith. In the past twenty-four hours she's had more joy and heartache than most women could bear. For years she believed that Lily's father was dead, and now Ethan Dunn shows up alive on the very day his daughter disappears.

Faith must have so many questions that need answering. But right now the important thing is to find Lily. Ethan Dunn has a pretty-boy face, but I can sense a will of steel behind those baby-blue eyes. He looks like one determined man. I have no doubt he'll find his daughter—and then do everything in his power to forge a new family with Faith….

Till tomorrow, Katherine

DAY LECLAIRE

is the multi-award-winning author of more than thirty novels. Her lively, warmly emotional style has won tremendous worldwide popularity and many publishing honors, including The Colorado Award of Excellence, The Golden Quill Award, the *Romantic Times* magazine Career Achievement Award and five nominations for the prestigious Romance Writers of America RITA® Award.

Day's romances sparkle with humor and touch the heart; she makes you care about her characters as much as she does. In Day's own words, "I adore writing romances, and can't think of a better way to spend each day."

Forrester Square

LEGACIES . LIES . LOVE .

DAY LECLAIRE

KEEPING FAITH

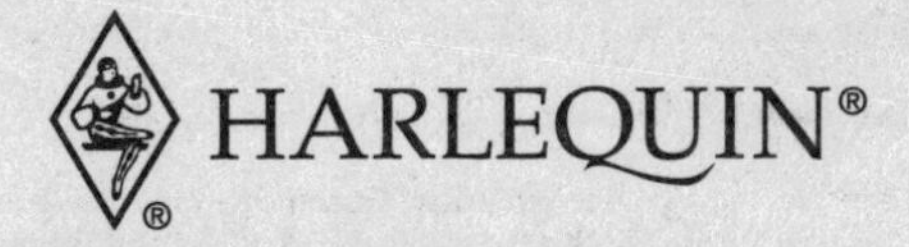

TORONTO • NEW YORK • LONDON
AMSTERDAM • PARIS • SYDNEY • HAMBURG
STOCKHOLM • ATHENS • TOKYO • MILAN • MADRID
PRAGUE • WARSAW • BUDAPEST • AUCKLAND

HARLEQUIN BOOKS
225 Duncan Mill Road, Don Mills,
Ontario, Canada M3B 3K9

ISBN-13: 978-0-373-61272-7
ISBN-10: 0-373-61272-9

KEEPING FAITH

Day Leclaire is acknowledged as the author of this work.

This edition published by arrangement with Harlequin Books S.A.

Visit us at www.eHarlequin.com

Printed in U.S.A.

Dear Reader,

This was such a fun book to write. *Fun?* A book about a kidnapping? I know, I know. Sounds rather grim. But it isn't when you're dealing with characters as special as Faith Marshall and Ethan Dunn and their daughter, Lily.

Faith appealed to me right from the start. I loved writing about a gutsy woman struggling to raise her daughter on her own, who takes charge of her own life and pursues goals, even in the face of hardship. She's the sort of woman who deserves a happy ending.

Then there's Ethan. Wow. I loved writing about a man who returns from the dead—and as far as Faith's concerned, that's precisely what he does. Here's a guy who's had to fight for everything he's ever had in life. He's a warrior. A protector. And he'll do anything to save the daughter he didn't know he had. What more could you want in a man?

As for the poor little kidnap victim… Well, don't feel too worried about Lily. She's got her mother's brains and her daddy's fighting spirit. This little girl takes no prisoners. Besides, it's Christmas. A time for miracles. And this book offers you the best kind of Christmas—one where Santa brings the perfect present for all concerned.

Please visit me at www.dayleclaire.com or write me at day@dayleclaire.com. I wish you all a joyous holiday season filled with peace, health, love and happiness.

Day Leclaire

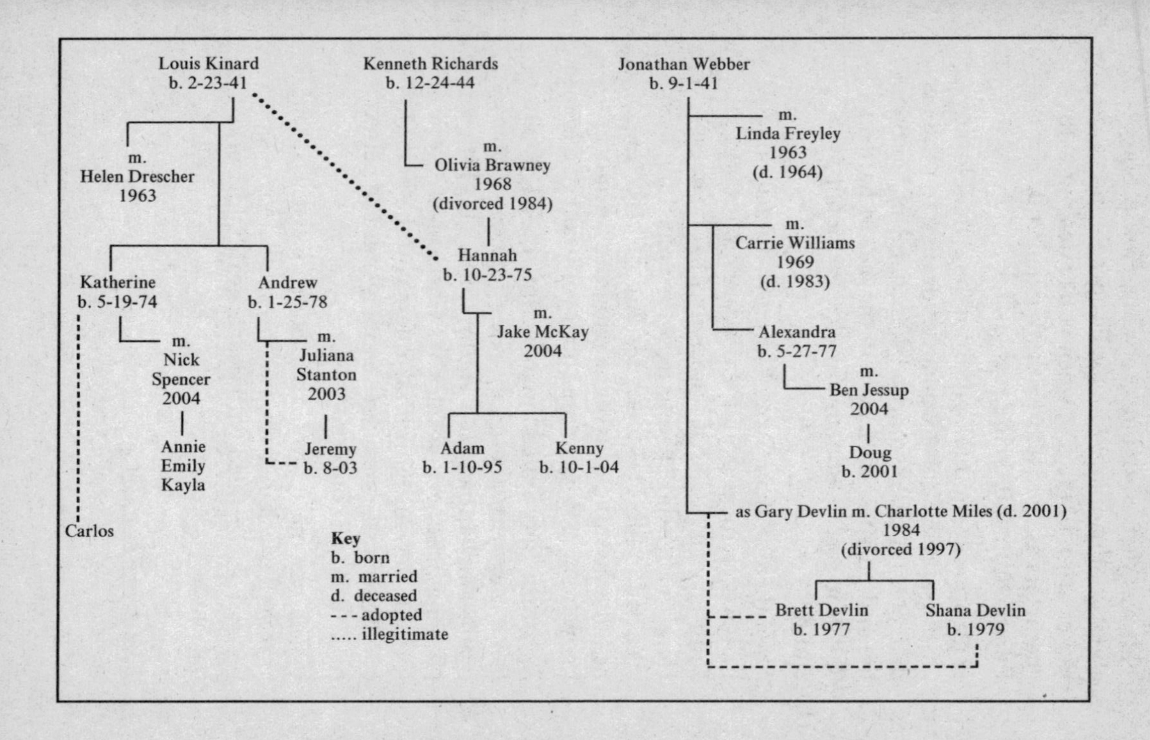
Louis Kinard
b. 2-23-41
m.
Helen Drescher
1963
Katherine
b. 5-19-74
m.
Nick
Spencer
2004
Annie
Emily
Kayla
Carlos
Andrew
b. 1-25-78
m.
Juliana
Stanton
2003
Jeremy
b. 8-03
Kenneth Richards
b. 12-24-44
m.
Olivia Brawney
1968
(divorced 1984)
Hannah
b. 10-23-75
m.
Jake McKay
2004
Adam
b. 1-10-95
Kenny
b. 10-1-04
Jonathan Webber
b. 9-1-41
m.
Linda Freyley
1963
(d. 1964)
m.
Carrie Williams
1969
(d. 1983)
Alexandra
b. 5-27-77
m.
Ben Jessup
2004
Doug
b. 2001
as Gary Devlin m. Charlotte Miles (d. 2001)
1984
(divorced 1997)
Brett Devlin
b. 1977
Shana Devlin
b. 1979
Key
b. born
m. married
d. deceased
- - - adopted
..... illegitimate

PROLOGUE

Portland, Oregon
June

"THIS IS A BAD IDEA, man."

Ethan Dunn didn't bother to reply. He focused his full attention on the small white church with its single spire and wide-flung doors. It wasn't Sunday, so what was Faith doing in there? A bible study, perhaps? Or maybe she'd simply needed the solace after he'd gone missing. He frowned. A year was an awfully long time to be needing solace. "Did the neighbors say why she was at church?"

"Yeah, they said." Jack shifted behind the wheel of the black Yukon, his muscular bulk causing the springs to ping in protest. "You look like hell, Dunn. Let me take you someplace. Someplace with good food and an even better supply of alcohol. You could use more healing time before we move forward with this."

Something in his friend's tone alerted Ethan. He slowly turned to face Jack. "What's that supposed to mean? Move forward with what?"

Jack lifted one massive shoulder. "You know. The whole, hey-honey-guess-who's-back-from-the-dead scene. You're still weak. One good lamp tossed at your head and you'll be laid up for another six months. After what you've been through, you don't need that. Why don't you take off for a few weeks, just until you get your strength back? Give your dodging skills a chance to come up to par."

Ethan didn't intend to wait even one more minute to see his woman, let alone a few weeks. And anyone who got between him and his goal was going down. Hard. Or as hard as he could manage in his current condition. One single thought keeping him alive during the six months he'd been imprisoned—getting back to Faith. And then he'd spent the next six months healing from the injuries he'd sustained, going quietly insane while he waited to see if he'd ever walk again. Now that he was whole, or as reasonably close to whole as he could get after a six-month stint riding a hospital bed, he planned to take Faith into his arms and never let go. The second he'd been released he'd limped straight here.

"I can heal some more once I've seen Faith." Ethan's eyes narrowed. "What's wrong with you? Why the attitude?"

"No attitude." Jack held up his hands, which were surprisingly delicate for such a big man. But in his line of work—getting past locks and alarms—delicacy came in handy. So did the amazing speed and agility he'd frequently demonstrated, his fingers a mahogany blur when throwing knives or fieldstripping a rifle. "Just thought... You might want to give it some time before you go surprising her. Women can react kinda funny when a dead man walks up on 'em."

"You shouldn't have told her I was dead."

Jack nodded, his face falling into a hangdog expression. "Yeah, you got me there. I guess it was finding your jeep all blown to bits with that burned-up body inside that had me fooled, especially since it sat there smoldering with your ID tags around its neck. Still, I should have known better. You're the best, Dunn. Most men don't last a week in unfriendly hands, let alone six whole months. My bad, man."

Ethan closed his eyes, fighting off a flash of memory. The stink of a cheap cigar. A torn photo of Faith tumbling to a dirt floor. A leather strap. Pain. A voice—slick, accented and cold. He clenched his hands as he fought for control. "I have to see her. Explain—"

"Explain what?" Jack snorted. "Honor? Loyalty? Brotherhood? Or were you hoping to explain the men you've had to kill over the years?"

"I told her all about that. She understood." The lie came with surprising ease.

Not that he fooled Jack. He zeroed right in on it. "Is that what she told you? That she understood?"

"She said—"

"Let me guess. She said, 'It's okay, sweetie pie. I don't mind that you're a mercenary.'" In other circumstances, the girlish inflection in Jack's gravelly voice would have provoked a laugh. "'All that danger and excitement makes me horny. Take me, lover. Right here and right now.'"

Ethan winced. Actually, their conversation hadn't come anywhere close to that. No gasps of wonder. No giggles. No trills of excitement. And there sure as hell hadn't been any taking. Instead, it had gone along the lines of "Have you lost your damn mind? You sorry son of a bitch! You said you were a businessman."

"I am. Granted, the business part is open to a bit of interpretation."

"Interpretation? You lied to me." Her glare had been as deadly as an M4 carbine spitting brass shells. "I don't want to have anything to do with someone who makes his living killing people for money."

"I don't kill people," he'd protested. "Much. Every once in a while there might be a bullet or two fired. Maybe a few people fall down and forget to get up. But that's only when I'm absolutely forced to, and only if they really deserve it."

"Forget to get up? You think this is funny? A game? A scene out of *True Lies?*" Her golden brown eyes had glittered with outrage. ‘‘I don’t find anything the least amusing about your…occupation.’’

She spat the word as though it were a hideous curse. He worked hard not to feel insulted. ‘‘It’s the only thing I’ve ever done well,’’ he tried to explain.

‘‘Great. I can’t tell you how delighted I am to discover that my fiancé is the best killing machine since Schwarzenegger.’’

‘‘Uh…I’m pretty sure he’s an actor. I don’t think he kills for real.’’

‘‘You know what I mean.’’ She began pacing, her hands moving faster than her legs. It was one of the qualities he’d always found privately amusing. The woman couldn’t talk without her hands motoring at twice the speed of her mouth. Somehow, it was less amusing watching them buzz like angry hornets. ‘‘When you said you were a businessman, I assumed that meant you pushed papers around a desk and spent half your life with a cell phone glued to your ear. The worst thing a businessman is supposed to do is take down other businesses or maybe play a rough game of racquetball every once in a while. It never occurred to me that your business was overthrowing governments and assassinating people for pay and—’’

‘‘Rescuing American hostages in foreign countries or taking out drug cartels or recovering kidnapped children,’’ he interjected evenly.

‘‘How noble. I’m all aflutter.’’ He dodged a hand demonstrating some seriously impressive flutter skills. ‘‘Maybe other women you’ve known find that sort of lifestyle exciting—’’

‘‘But not you.’’

She shook her head, pale blond curls bouncing against her cheek. ‘‘Not even a little. I told you from the start that I was a white-picket-fence sort of woman. I explained about my father—Mr. Missing in Action. He was all charm and no staying power, and he broke my mother's heart. Well, I won't repeat her mistake. I won't trade a husband who's banker-boring for a man with charm, good looks, but one foot out the door. I just won't. I want my husband at home demanding dinner at six for every night of our fifty-year marriage."

Fifty years? Didn't she understand how he hungered for that? "I have staying power," he argued. "And I told you, I'm all over a white-picket-fence lifestyle, not to mention banker-boring. It's what I want, too. I'm not your father, Faith. I don't have another family stashed on the side or a first wife that I neglected to divorce before marrying a second."

Her hand stopped fluttering and took up a poking motion. Her index finger slammed against his chest. She'd never been the least intimidated by him, not his size, the power of his body or the aura of toughness that held most men at bay while drawing women like proverbial moths to a flame. That lack of intimidation was something he'd admired about her…until now.

"No, what you have is worse—you have warrior buddies who'll always come first," she informed him. "Don't you get it? I want safe. I want boring. I want a man I can count on, not some crazy Rambo who's going to disappear at a moment's notice, chasing foolish causes while shouting, 'All for one, and one for all' as he's shooting up third world countries. And don't bother telling me Rambo's an actor. I already know that."

"Rambo's a character," he offered humbly. Man, she had a lot of strength in that little finger of hers. He surreptitiously rubbed his chest. "Stallone's the actor. And it was *The Three Musketeers* where they shouted, 'One for all—'"

"Can the wisecracks, Dunn, and give me some straight answers," she snapped. "I'm dead serious about this."

So was he, but wisecracks were his way of dealing with

tense situations. That's how he and his company had survived the atrocities they'd seen...and experienced. It really was "one for all and all for one." He searched for a way to explain that to her, to explain an existence as far distant from the life she led as it was possible to get. To explain, horror by horror, the steps that had taken him from being an average, congenial ten-year-old to a twenty-nine-year-old hired gun.

Words failed him and he found himself at a total loss. Damn it! He couldn't summon so much as a single glib comeback. How could he justify to her what he'd never been able to justify to himself? How could he share emotions he'd spent years stuffing down into the deepest, darkest part of his soul just so he could get through another day? Simple. He couldn't. Instead, he fell back on one of his oldest self-defense techniques.

He allowed his most winning smile to build across his face, the one that had bowled over every woman since he'd first tumbled from his cradle. "Now, honey—"

"No, Ethan." She stepped away from him, growing frighteningly still. "Don't you dare play me."

It was then that he realized how close he was to losing her, and that he'd do anything—*anything*—to prevent that from happening. His smile faded and he inclined his head. "Okay, no games. What do you want from me?"

"I'll make it simple." She folded her arms across her chest. "You have a choice. You can have your career or me. But not both."

"I made that choice the moment I met you," he stated roughly. "It's you I want. Only you."

"You'll give up soldiering?" she demanded. "Forever? You promise you'll never go back again?"

"I quit three months ago." He'd put through the call the day after he'd met her and first recognized the disparate choices yawning before him. ''No more missions. I swear to you....''

The long-ago memory of his conversation with Faith faded and Ethan returned to the present. He rubbed a hand across his face, exhausted beyond measure. No more missions, he'd told her. Except, of course, for the one that had culminated in an endless captivity.

''Faith understands,'' he insisted now to Jack. Or was he trying to convince himself? ''She wasn't happy that I had to go on that final mission, but she swore she'd wait for me. They were the last words she said before I left.''

''You mean, before you died,'' Jack said with surprising gentleness.

It was times like this that Ethan wished he still smoked. ''It won't matter. She promised,'' he repeated doggedly.

''Who was she supposed to wait for? A dead man?'' Jack shook his shaved head. ''Promises made to a dead man don't count. What was she supposed to wait for? A broken man? A man who still can't get through the night without screaming?''

Ethan jerked. ''You don't know what you're talking about.''

''Don't even try that crap on me. You think I don't know about the dreams? I've been there, man. Believe me, I know.''

Ethan clamped his teeth together. ''They're getting better.''

''Bull. They're getting worse.'' He waited a beat before adding, ''She's not for you, Ethan. Forget her.''

A cold, slick voice, both frightening and familiar, whispered in his ear. *Forget her,* hombre. *That* chica, *she is not for you. She is* elegante. *Classy, you know?*

Ethan thrust open the door of the SUV and stumbled onto the picturesque street, uncertain whether he was attempting to escape Jack or the voice in his head. The residential area on the outskirts of Portland looked like something out of a Thomas Kincaid calendar, the sort of neighborhood he'd always longed to live in, filled with the promise of normalcy.

He glanced around, inhaling the scent of freshly mowed grass and the indefinable odor of nature's rebirth. He'd left in early summer, and was now returning exactly one year later, recognizing this as a time of limitless hope and potential. Big leafy maples, spaced evenly down the street, canopied a tidy sidewalk. Nearby, a bed of geraniums exploded in a riot of flaming red. Dahlias and lilies vied for attention, poking up in regimented rows from each orderly garden. After so many months of darkness, the sheer beauty of the setting threatened to unman him.

And then there was the church, the centerpiece of the scene. Ethan walked toward it, step after painful step, drawn to the welcome implicit in the wide-open doorway. As he approached, he caught the distinctive sound of Handel's *Menuet* coming from inside. How long had it been since he'd heard a pipe organ? Not since he'd last attended services with Faith and her grandmother, Elizabeth. Before that… Hell. Not since those brief magical years when he'd gone with his own grandmother.

He reached the door and stepped into the foyer. It took a moment for his eyes to adjust to the gloom, and he waited patiently. Being imprisoned in a foreign country had taught him more about patience than he'd ever wanted to know, and he'd learned the lesson well. As soon as his vision cleared, he slipped into the sanctuary and took a seat in the back pew.

At first he didn't realize what was happening. Too much sensory input was coming at him too fast. Sunlight set fire to the stained glass windows, shooting flames of color across the wooden benches before leaping onto the small congregation. The organist continued to play, more softly now, switching to Pachelbel's *Canon in D.* A dozen people were crowded around the altar, bunched tightly together and talking excitedly. The minister stood in front, laughing as he attempted to bring order to the group.

Next, Ethan noticed Elizabeth, seated in the first pew, directly in front of him. She'd raised Faith after her parents had died. A brief smile touched his face. He'd missed the old gal. Missed her wisdom and her kindness. Missed the relationship he'd had with her, a relationship similar to the one he'd shared with his own grandmother before she'd died. He continued to search the gathering for Faith, finally spotting her pale blond hair. She stood in the middle of the crowd of people, tucked in close to a tall, slender man dressed in standard white-collar businessman issue—a pinstriped suit and sedate tie. Ethan frowned.

What the hell was she doing?

The organ music swelled just then, pounding out the opening strains of Beethoven's *Ode to Joy.* The minister lifted his hands and said something and the people surrounding Faith burst into laughter and applause. On some gut level Ethan understood what was happening—understood, but refused to accept. He couldn't seem to grasp the full significance until the suit-and-tie swept Faith into his arms and kissed her.

''No,'' Ethan whispered. He exploded from the pew, stopped in his instinctive rush toward the altar by a heavy hand on his shoulder. Still too weak to fight free of the hold, he was literally dragged backward into the foyer.

''I told you to let it go.'' Jack spoke softly, his voice a quiet rumble close to Ethan's ear. ''I told you to give it up. But you wouldn't. So I let you walk in on this—knew that you wouldn't be satisfied until you saw the truth for yourself.''

Ethan shook off the restraining hand, succeeding only because Jack chose to release him. ''She can't be marrying that bastard. She wouldn't. Not after what we meant to each other."

"She can and she will."

"Will?" His head jerked up, hope reigniting. "Then she's not— This wasn't a real wedding?"

"It's just the dress rehearsal. The real deal's scheduled for tomorrow at noon."

Ethan's hands curled into fists. "Then there's still time to stop it."

"Is that what you plan to do? You gonna bust in there and mess up her wedding? Screw with her life?" Jack released his breath in a slow sigh. "No, man. Your chance at a future with her ended when you went on that last mission. Don't you remember? She told you to choose. And you did."

"It was the last one. She agreed with my decision. Understood why it was critical that I go. Davis would have died if I hadn't gone."

Jack shrugged. "So you made your decision and Davis lived." He inclined his head toward the altar. "But in the meantime, Faith's moved on. It's time for you to do the same."

"*No!* Not after all I've been through."

"Let her go, Ethan. Men like us...hell, all we have is our honor. And messing with that..." He stabbed a finger in Faith's direction. "That ain't honorable. She deserves better than what our sort can give her. You know it's the truth, man. Deep down, you know."

Every instinct Ethan possessed urged him to ignore Jack, ignore the voices from his nightmares and take what he wanted. He deserved it. He'd earned it. He'd paid for it, hadn't he? Paid with a full year of his life and with his very blood. The time had come to collect. For an endless moment he wavered, inches away from storming the sanctuary. But

Jack had used the one word he couldn't ignore, reminded him of the one possession he still retained.

Honor.

Without a word, Ethan turned and left the church. He made his way to the Yukon, pain dogging his footsteps, a pain as much physical as it was mental. It was an ache that went so deep there was no bottom for it to hit, just endless, limitless space to expand into.

Once again, he was the odd man out, standing on the periphery, desperate to break through the barriers that kept him from his deepest desire. He'd had a single, delicious taste of the forbidden before he'd lost it, just as he had during the brief time he'd lived with his grandmother. But it wasn't nearly enough to sustain him. He stood gazing at a banquet, starving, and unable to take a single bite.

Life sucked.

Reaching the car, he snatched open the door and crawled inside. There was only one place he could go for sustenance. Only one place he'd ever been invited in, fed and clothed and treated decently.

''Drive,'' he ordered Jack.

Jack turned over the engine. ''Where to?''

''Does it matter?''

By noon tomorrow Ethan planned to be up to his eyeballs in the Three Wisemen—Jim Beam, Jack Daniels and Johnnie Walker. Maybe one of those gentlemen would help ease the pain, if only for a few short hours. Once he was done feeling sorry for himself he could decide what he'd do next. Not that it would take much thought. There was always his old company and one more mission. He leaned back against the seat and closed his eyes.

Hell, there was always one more mission.

CHAPTER ONE

Seattle, Washington
Four and a half years later

JULIAN BLACK SAT in the car watching the chattering children being led from Forrester Square Day Care by their exhausted parents. A keen sense of anticipation gave him an almost sexual rush. The anticipation built, heat pooling in the pit of his stomach and churning outward in delicious waves. Any moment now they'd appear, totally unaware of what fate— Oh, why be modest? What *he* had in store for them.

He stared at the arched doorway, fixating on it, willing his quarry to appear. And then she did. The woman in question was slender, brunette, and could be considered beautiful if the quiet, understated type appealed—which it didn't. His tastes ran toward elegant brunettes, sure. But he preferred them with long legs, plump breasts and questionable morals.

Unlike some of the other parents, the woman didn't rush along. Oblivious to his presence, she slowly descended the stairs, bypassing the iron park benches on either side of the steps. She moved as though she had all the time in the world, her stride shortened to match that of the little girl she held by the hand. He'd been vaguely aware of her over the past several months, but hadn't paid much attention to her—until recently. Until she'd interfered with his business.

Julian kept his attention fixed on the woman, narrowing his eyes in the gathering darkness as he watched. He'd thought her docile. Soft. Easily intimidated. He realized now that he'd underestimated her. He hadn't noticed the hidden strength, though he saw it now. It was there in the stubborn thrust of her chin, the directness of her gaze, the self-confident carriage. How could he have missed something so obvious? It was a stupid mistake to make. Unless…

Perhaps the strength was a recent acquisition. Perhaps it was no more than a pale reflection of the man in her life, a softer version of his brute power. Yes, that's why Julian hadn't noticed it. It had nothing to do with an error on his part. The woman wasn't strong. She was little more than a sponge, absorbing another's more forceful essence. Well, he knew precisely how to handle a sponge. His hand curled into a white-knuckled fist. Squeeze it hard enough and it would run dry, leached of all potency.

Satisfied with his assessment, he switched his attention to the little girl. She clung to her mother's hand, chattering excitedly about her day. She looked like a hundred other little girls and that annoyed him, perhaps because all little girls annoyed him. It reminded him of the childhood he'd shared with a litter of strident younger sisters. Little girls. He shuddered. Their voices were high and demanding, their features as soft and round and unmolded as a doll's face, their bodies a compilation of brittle twiglike arms and legs that threatened to snap if you gripped them too hard.

And they never shut up.

He glared at the child. This one looked like every other four- or five-year-old girl he'd ever had the displeasure of meeting. The only distinctive thing about her was the shade of her hair. It hung in two pale gold pigtails that bounced against her narrow shoulders as she skipped alongside her mother. How he despised the little creature, despised her shrill little voice and dancing little step and little pug face. He'd be doing the mother a favor when he took her. Hell, he'd be doing the world a favor.

A soft laugh escaped him. He was actually being altruistic, if the truth be known. He was ridding the world of a bit of vermin. One less rat in an overflowing nest. He directed his driver to move on, and leaned back against his seat, keeping his face carefully expressionless as he thought through the various possibilities and contingencies of his scheme. Checking, examining, rechecking. He couldn't see any flaws. It was quite, quite perfect. Naturally. He smiled in satisfaction.

Time to set his plan in motion.

Soon. Soon the mother would pay for what she'd done to him.

Portland, Oregon
The same day

ONE LAST LOOK.

That's all he wanted. Just one final look at Faith before he put the past where it belonged—in the past.

''Yeah, right,'' Ethan muttered to himself. ''You were supposed to close that door four and a half years ago. Yet here you are again, unbolting the locks, ripping off the padlock and tearing down a door you have no business touching. Smart move, Dunn. The kind of move guaranteed to rip the heart right out of your chest.''

He thought he'd put all this nonsense behind him on the eve of Faith's wedding. But in the years since, he'd been unable to cut the invisible bonds that kept him tied to her. And he'd tried. Heaven help him, he'd tried. He'd thrown himself into mission after mission, each time thinking that after he'd completed this next assignment, his suffering would end. That he'd return and no longer want her, no longer ache for a simple touch, a single word, a final kiss.

But it hadn't happened. He still ached. He still longed. And he still wanted with a single-minded desperation. Hell, he hadn't even managed to put himself out of his misery by stepping in front of a stray bullet, though on some of the crazier missions he'd accepted, he'd come close. This last time he'd come dangerously close.

Ethan Dunn parked his car, a vintage Trans Am that went by the incongruous name of Lil. He surveyed the house Faith shared with her grandmother and husband, looking for changes. There were none. It hadn't altered a lick since he'd last climbed the porch steps and swept Faith into his arms, giving her a final kiss before going after Davis. His leg twitched in protest at the prolonged time he'd spent in the car, and he dug his fingers into the muscles just above his left knee, absentmindedly massaging them.

The three-story Victorian was alive with sound and activity. Along the graceful lines of the porch and steps, red, white and green strings of lights twinkled a merry Christmas greeting. A huge wreath hung in the middle of the door, a door that kept opening to welcome a steady stream of partygoers.

He couldn't see Faith's grandmother, Elizabeth. But Faith and her husband were both there, apparently living with Elizabeth, and entertaining for the holidays. Another group arrived at the door, and this time he had an unobstructed view of the host and hostess. Faith stood in quarter profile, looking up at her husband, one hand on his arm, the other splayed across her expanding middle. That was all it took. One glimpse of a heavily pregnant Faith and the waking nightmare swept over him.

Ethan gripped the steering wheel, fighting with every ounce of strength to keep the memories from overtaking him. It didn't work. It never worked. The memories came anyway. In the five-plus years since his rescue, they'd grown gradually stronger and more all-consuming in their frequency. He could swear the stench of cigar smoke filled the car, the scent thick and heavy and cheap. Definitely not Cuban.

He saw the glow from the hand-rolled stub. The cigar was clenched between the Colombian's teeth, and he held a photo in dirt-encrusted fingers, studying it with a combination of appreciation and derision. With a flick of his fingers, he sent the tattered scrap flipping to the ground.

It landed photo side up, and Faith's fine-boned face smiled up at Ethan from the filth littering the dirt floor of the shack where he was being held. A jagged tear left only a hint of her blond hair. Half of her torso was also missing. She'd been lounging on the steps in front of her grandmother's house, her arms braced against the risers and one knee bent toward her chest when he'd taken the photo. He'd snapped it right before he'd accepted this final mission. The fact that the picture had turned out so well was more a credit to Faith's skill as a photographer than any expertise on his part. He'd simply followed her instructions.

The Colombian peered down at the photo before lifting his gaze to Ethan. There was even a hint of sympathy in the cold, black depths. But only a hint. "Forget her, hombre. *That* chica, *she is not for you. She is* elegante. *Classy, you know? She belongs with a rich, fat banker, using her charm to entertain his important clients during the day and her body to entertain her husband at night. Or maybe she is now the wife of the local* pastor, *visiting invalids and doing good deeds. But she is not for a man like you."*

Planting his boot heel on top of the photo, he took his time grinding it into the dirt. "Rest easy, amigo. *By now she will have forgotten all about you. She is married to her rich banker and this very minute has his son growing fat and heavy in her belly."*

"Not Faith." It hurt to talk, but Ethan didn't care. He forced the words past his swollen jaw and parched lips. "She'll wait."

The Colombian shrugged. "No woman waits for long, not even one named Faith. Forever is not in a woman's nature. And that is how long she will have to wait for you. Forever." He picked up a leather strap from a nearby table. "It is regrettable, but now we must get back to business. You have held out well, amigo. *You have proved how strong and brave you are. But it is time to give me the information I need."*

"I have no information."

The jailer ignored Ethan's comment. "I do not believe you are working for any of your government's agencies," he mused, testing the pliability of the strap. Satisfied, he snapped it in the direction of the table. It whizzed through the air, exploding against the rough wooden surface with an earsplitting crack. "A mercenary, perhaps. A hired gun paid handsomely by some capitalist bastard to come into my country and cause dissidence and upheaval. Tell me who sent you and why, and the pain can end. Otherwise—"

A car horn blared nearby and Ethan jumped. He ran a hand across his face. Hell. If the flashbacks didn't stop soon, he'd totally lose it. As it was, he stood inches away from plummeting into the sort of black pit men rarely crawled out of with their sanity intact. He'd hoped seeing Faith again would put an end to the dreams. Instead, it had provoked the most intense one yet.

Perhaps it was seeing her pregnant—seeing his captor's provocation turned into a bitter reality. Ethan grimaced. Or perhaps it was just watching her stand within calling distance, so close he could almost smell the tantalizing hint of Obsession wafting from her skin. God help him, he wanted her with a desperation that ate into what little remained of his soul. Once again he was hit with the full realization of all he'd lost when he'd gone on that mission. The knowledge threatened to drag him into the yawning black pit. It inched closer, tempting him with sweet oblivion.

Ethan pulled in a deep breath of winter-chilled air. Then another. He tumbled his car keys between his fingers, rolling them from one to the next and then back again. He focused on the discordant jangle, finding that the familiar sound helped ground him. This was ridiculous. He needed to get on with his life. He needed to cut all ties with the past and find a new focus. A new direction. With a swift twist of his wrist, he flipped the keys into the air, caught the appropriate one for the ignition and slid it home.

"Come on, Lil. Let's get out of here."

The Trans Am turned over with a muted roar, as though endorsing his suggestion. He was on the verge of spinning away from the curb when Faith swiveled toward the front door, greeting another couple who'd arrived on her doorstep. For a full second Ethan couldn't move. Couldn't breathe. His foot slipped off the clutch and the vintage car bucked in protest before the engine died. He swore beneath his breath.

It wasn't Faith. Son of a bitch. It wasn't her. The woman had the same pale blond hair, but that was the extent of the resemblance. Where Faith's features were more delicately drawn, this woman's face had been assembled along strong, bold lines. Instead of classic beauty, she possessed little more than a vague handsomeness. Examining her with a more discerning eye, Ethan could also see that her figure was all wrong, as well. She was too tall and large boned. Even pregnant, Faith wouldn't have such broad hips or be quite so well-rounded.

He frowned in concentration. If this wasn't Faith, who the hell was she, and why was she living in Elizabeth's house? There was only one way to find out. Ethan climbed from his car and crossed the street, fighting the debilitating limp that had put paid to his career—such as it was. He walked up to the open door and waited until the most recent guests had disappeared into the spacious interior before addressing the husband and wife.

"Are you the owners of this house?" he asked.

The abruptness of the question caused the husband to step forward in front of his wife, while the sheer power of Ethan's demeanor compelled him to respond. "We bought the house this past August." He swallowed before thrusting out his chin. "And you are?"

"Ethan Dunn. What happened to the previous owners?"

The wife shifted to stand beside her husband and blinked up at him. Where the husband saw an intimidating stranger and reacted instinctively to the scent of danger, the wife saw startling blue eyes set in a too-pretty face, and reacted instinctively to the scent of pheromones. She fluttered while he fretted.

"Elizabeth Marshall died last spring." She offered the information with a brilliant smile, belatedly imbued with regret. "Her granddaughter sold the house to us four months ago."

Elizabeth had died? Ethan fought to keep his face expressionless, but his hands tightened into fists in response to the flash of pain. Well, what had he expected? That life would remain in some ideal holding pattern? That old women would somehow escape the aging process and defy death? He glanced at the wife's protruding belly. Or perhaps he'd thought that the cycle of life would pause when he wasn't looking. This woman could easily have been Faith. Four-plus years of wedded bliss gave her plenty of opportunity in which to have a child.

"Where did she go?" Ethan's voice sounded raw, even to his own ears. "The granddaughter. Faith."

The wife reached out to touch his arm, thought better of it and leaned into the protective embrace of her husband. "You knew them, didn't you?"

Ethan nodded. ''From long ago. I was in the area and thought I'd look them up.''

''I'm sorry we had to give you the bad news about Mrs. Marshall.'' Her voice turned encouraging. ''But last we heard, Faith was doing well. My understanding is that she moved to Seattle right after the sale. I'm afraid I don't have an address. Perhaps the broker would—''

''Do you happen to know her husband's name?'' Ethan interrupted.

The wife looked momentarily bewildered. ''We never met him.'' She checked with her husband. ''Did we?''

''The one helping her move, maybe?'' the man replied. ''I guess that was him. A banker, I think.''

Ethan absorbed the blow with only the slightest flinch. A banker. Hell. It was his nightmare come true. Faith had moved on without him, her life full and rich and complete. Well, what had he expected? That she'd be divorced? That she'd be waiting for him to ride up in Lil and carry her off into the sunset? That was a dream, not reality. And he knew all about the pain of reality, with its accompanying knocks and bruises and bitter ironies. A banker husband had to be the most bitter irony of all.

''Anyway, they moved right after we bought the house.'' The husband lifted an eyebrow. ''I hope that helps.''

It was clearly a dismissal. ''Yeah, thanks.'' Belatedly, he added, ''Have a merry Christmas.'' The pleasantry felt strange on his tongue. When was the last time he'd celebrated Christmas? He couldn't remember.

The husband nodded brusquely. ''Same to you.'' Ethan had barely cleared the threshold before the door was slammed closed. In other circumstances, the expression of relief on the man's face would have been amusing.

Ethan limped slowly to his car. So Faith was living in Seattle with her husband. That put paid to that. Time to close the door and get it safely padlocked and bolted once again. Maybe he'd head south to California, check out the Bay Area. Or take the coast road to L.A. and soak up some sun. It didn't matter where he went so long as it wasn't north.

"What do you say, Lil?" he asked as he climbed into the Trans Am. "How does California sound? Or we could shoot over to Sin City, catch a few shows and spend some time shooting craps. Does Vegas appeal?" Fortunately, the car didn't answer, which Ethan found immensely encouraging. At least he hadn't gone totally over the edge.

Yet.

After twenty minutes of breakneck driving, he slowed as he hit the entrance to Interstate 5. He idled in the middle of the road, considering his choices. The first entrance ramp headed south toward California and a future filled with possibility. The second led north toward places he should avoid and into the lives of people to whom he was little more than an unwanted ghost from the past. There wasn't any question which road was his.

Thrusting Lil into gear, Ethan took the second ramp.

Seattle, Washington
The next day

"UH-OH."

Faith removed a stack of plastic containers from the box she'd been unpacking and glanced at her daughter. "What's wrong, Lily?"

"Look." The little girl could barely be seen over the pile of crumpled newspaper that surrounded her. Holding a framed picture aloft, she showed it to her mother. The glass had shattered, the cracks spreading across the photo like a huge spiderweb. "It broke."

Faith abandoned her box and carefully plucked the damaged picture out of Lily's small hands. "Careful, sweet pea.

Broken glass can give you a bad cut. Why don't I take care of this box and you can pull stuff out of the one I was working on? No glass there."

"'Kay."

Lily ducked down, disappearing into the mountain of newspaper, and tunneled across the room. Faith grinned. Every few yards her daughter would poke her head up through the paper and Faith would catch a fleeting glimpse of pale golden blond hair or laughing blue eyes. Eyes that were the exact same shade as her father's.

At first, the similarity had caused unbearable pain. She'd missed Ethan more than she'd thought possible. The longing had never truly gone away, even after all these years. In the early days it was hideous, and would intensify every time she looked at her baby. She saw Ethan whenever Lily's dimples would flash, or she'd offer a crooked grin. His face lived on in hers—the high cheekbones that became more pronounced with each passing year, the way she'd tilt her head to one side while she puzzled through a problem, as well as the prettiness that showed every sign of growing into true beauty. Even her laugh held an echo of his.

And it hurt; it reminded Faith of all they'd lost with Ethan's death.

But then, so slowly and subtly she'd scarcely noticed, something had changed. She'd changed. She'd begun to celebrate the similarities Lily shared with her father, to celebrate that some small part of him had lived on after his death. She'd been filled with a bone-deep gratitude that she had Lily in her life. Ethan had given her a gift she treasured more than anything in this world.

Only one regret continued to bother her. She'd never told Ethan she was pregnant before he'd gone on that last mission. And she wished with all her heart that she'd shared her joyous discovery with him. Maybe she would have if she hadn't been so furious with his decision to rejoin his unit for one final foray. Anger had propelled her to keep the news from him. Still, she couldn't help wondering.... Would it have made a difference in those moments before his death? Would he have done something different? Fought harder? Been more careful? Not gone at all? The possibility frequently troubled her.

Discarded newspapers rustled from across the room, and Faith smiled as Lily kept tunneling. Ethan would have adored his daughter. He'd have gotten such a kick out of her sense of humor and her playfulness, no doubt encouraging her sharp wit and intelligence. He'd also have helped direct her adventurous nature into pursuits more appropriate to a little girl fast approaching her fifth birthday. Faith's mouth pulled to one side. At least, she hoped he would have.

Halfway to the box, Lily glanced over her shoulder. "Mommy, what does a mole say?"

"Is that what you're being? A mole?"

"Yes, but I don't know what it says when it makes tunnels."

Faith gave the question a moment's thought. "It says, 'Where are my glasses? I can't see a thing.'"

Lily tipped her head to one side in consideration before nodding decisively and disappearing beneath the crumpled newspapers once again. In a high, squeaky voice she said, "Where are my glasses? I can't see a thing." Arriving at one of the boxes, she repeatedly bumped her head against it. Finally, she came up for air and crawled inside, tossing packing material and plastic storage containers in a wide arc around the box. "What are you doing in a mole's house?" she demanded as she worked. "Out, out."

In truth, Lily was often more hindrance than help. Not that Faith cared. Her little girl had brought joy and laughter into a barren life. What did it matter if she also brought chaos and craziness? Not to mention mischief. Faith grinned. Endless, frustrating, delightful, hilarious mischief.

Faith glanced again at the shattered photo she held. It had been taken last spring, shortly before her grandmother's death. The three of them were piled together in the garden, surrounded by jonquils, irises and a profusion of tulips. It was one of her favorite pictures and one she wanted to add to her wall of family photos as soon as possible.

She examined the box and grimaced. All the most recent photos had been damaged, the frames broken or the glass cracked. When they'd first moved to Seattle four months ago, she'd put everything into storage while she'd waited for escrow to close on the house she'd purchased. This box must have been crushed beneath a stack of books or other heavy items, despite the Fragile labels stuck all over it.

Lifting out the rest of the pictures, she glanced at the entryway wall. She'd already hung the baby pictures. They extended halfway to the living room. These more current ones would have to be fixed before they joined the others. Removing the photos from the damaged frames, she slipped them carefully into a protective case. Tomorrow, after she dropped Lily off at Forrester Square Day Care, she'd take these to a nearby shop for framing.

The phone rang from somewhere beneath a pile of garbage bags stuffed with discarded packing material, and Faith scrambled to locate it. She found it on the fourth ring, emerging from her tussle with the bags, phone in hand. "Hello?"

"Are you all right? You sound out of breath."

Faith grinned. "Hi, Abby. Just had a time finding the phone. You should see this place." She surveyed the room and winced. "It's a disaster."

"Emily and I can come over after dinner and help with the unpacking, if you'd like. Or rather, I can help with the unpacking and Emily can help keep Lily out of your hair."

Faith laughed. She'd met Abby at the day care center shortly after moving to Seattle. Her daughter, Emily, had quickly bonded with Lily, the two becoming instant best friends. Faith and Abby had also hit it off, frequently chatting over coffee while their daughters enjoyed a play date.

"Actually, we'll be decorating our Christmas tree after dinner," Faith said. "If you'd like to come over for some cookies and eggnog, the girls can take care of the tree. Bring Luke along, if he's interested."

Luke Sloan, a Seattle police detective, was Abby's fiancé. The two had met when Luke had posed as a carpenter working at the day care center. In truth, he'd been investigating a fencing operation at the Emerald City Jewelry Exchange, where Abby worked. The day care center, directly across the street from the jewelry exchange, had provided the perfect surveillance spot for the operation. Initially, Luke had suspected Abby of being involved in the thefts. But it hadn't taken long for the hard-edged detective to uncover the truth and arrest the true mastermind—the store manager, Bettina Carlton.

"Cookies and eggnog sounds great," Abby said. "Is seven a good time?"

"Perfect. Lily will be thrilled. They've become such good friends."

"Two peas in a pod, I'm sorry to say," Abby said dryly.

Faith chuckled. "They are a handful."

"And then some." There was a crash in the background and Abby groaned. "I've got to run. Emily's pretending to be a puppy and just chased down a stuffed cat."

"I didn't know stuffed cats made crashing noises."

"They do when they're next to a lamp."

"Gotcha. Then I won't keep you any longer. See you at seven."

She hung up and went in search of Lily to tell her about the planned activities for the evening. Her daughter was nowhere to be found. Five minutes of searching ensued while Faith fought to stem a rising feeling of panic. Lily couldn't have gotten outside. No matter how ingenious her daughter often proved to be, all the doors were locked and she was too short to reach the latch. *Unless she used a chair.* The thought was distressing. Finally, Faith walked to the middle of the living room and stood perfectly still.

"Okay, I give up," she announced to the house at large. "I need a clue."

Almost immediately a tiny mewling sound came from the direction of the unadorned Christmas tree. Faith turned and finally spotted her quarry. She closed her eyes, encroaching panic giving way to exasperation. "Lily Elizabeth Marshall. What am I going to do with you?"

"Meow! Call the fire department. I'm stuck in the tree."

Faith pushed aside the branches of the spruce and plucked her daughter from her perch. "Not smart, kitty. Be glad I tied the tree in place. Otherwise it would have tipped over and you could have been hurt."

Her observation made no impression whatsoever. Lily beamed in delight and wrapped her arms tight around Faith's neck, nearly strangling her. "I climbed it, Mommy. I climbed a tree."

Faith hugged her close. "Yeah? Well, you scared me half to death. I thought you were lost. What would I do if I ever lost you?"

"That's easy, Mommy," Lily said with a child's impeccable logic. "You'd find me."

The final remnants of her distress faded and Faith chuckled. "You're absolutely right. Find you, I would."

CHAPTER TWO

Seattle
The next day

BETTINA CARLTON WAS was in an exceptionally good mood, especially for someone who, until just ten minutes ago, had been in the custody of the police with little hope of being released any time soon. She had no idea how or why that had changed, but who was she to question providence when it dropped a miracle in her lap?

A lawyer she'd never met had shown up at her bond hearing late yesterday afternoon. He'd said a lot of mumbo-jumbo to the judge, who'd been foolish enough to opine that since her crime involved property loss without injury to the general public, he would set a reasonable bail. The lawyer had promptly posted it, courtesy of a company she'd never heard of before. First thing this morning, Bettina had dropped her ugly red prison garb in a heap, collected the few possessions she'd had on her at the time of her arrest, and out she'd walked, free as the proverbial bird.

Now she intended to take full advantage of the judge's kind, if imprudent, assistance. She took to the street with a determined stride. It was time to start a new life and make some serious changes. Maybe she'd even go straight. Maybe she'd find a man who'd treat her decently and get married. Maybe—

Just as she reached the corner of James, a car slowed, easing close to the curb beside her. Bettina glanced at it and missed a step. She should have known. Damn it! She should have at least suspected. Get-out-of-jail-free passes were never truly free. They always came with strings attached. And this particular string was becoming more like a noose.

The two-tone Rolls-Royce Seraph pulled a few feet ahead of her and came to a stop. The back door swung open in clear invitation. For a brief, insane moment, Bettina considered turning around and making a beeline for the jailhouse. It would be safer. Smarter. Healthier. Curiosity got the better of her. She climbed into the Rolls. "Hello, lover," she greeted her former employer and bedmate. "I was just on my way to my apartment to change."

"Not necessary." Julian Black offered a smile. It was a charming smile, one that came as naturally to him as breathing, and successfully disguised his true nature. It had taken Bettina months to see the truth hidden beneath that swift, friendly quirk of his mouth. "I took the liberty of sending Crock to pick up some things for you."

She spared a quick glance toward Julian's driver. That didn't sound good. What was going on? "Why would you do that?" she asked.

Julian dismissed the question with a shrug. "We can discuss that later. But first…how have you been, my dear?"

Considering the circumstances, it was a bizarre question. "Not so good. How about yourself?"

"I've been terribly worried about you."

"Really?"

He frowned. "I'm serious. All this business with the police." He swept a fine-boned hand through the air. "It's very distressing."

He thought it was distressing? That was rich. "You might say that, considering I was the one sitting in jail."

"You *were* sitting in jail. Now you're out." He cupped her knee, sliding his hand upward toward the edge of her skirt. "If you thank me nicely, I'll make certain my lawyer keeps you out."

It was stupid of her not to have made the connection earlier. Clearly, being locked up didn't agree with the normal functioning of her brain cells. "That was your lawyer? You paid the bond?"

"He's a recent addition to my staff. And a dummy corporation fronted the money so it can't be traced back to me." He stroked the inside of her knee. "You must have known I'd take care of you. I wouldn't have let you remain in jail for long."

"No, of course not." Understanding dawned. "After all, you wouldn't want me implicating you in any of this. How would that look to all of your society friends? Julian Black, owner of the exclusive Emerald City Jewelry Exchange, the mastermind behind a tawdry fencing operation. It's so... common."

She shouldn't have taunted him. Anger flared in his eyes, turning the color from a soft powder blue to a sapphire hardness. His fingers dug into her thigh. "What have you told the police?"

Bettina swallowed. "Nothing. I swear, Julian. I haven't said anything at all."

"I haven't been mentioned?" He squeezed a little tighter. "Are you certain?"

She squirmed beneath his hold. "As far as they're concerned, they have the person responsible. Me." His grip eased and it was her turn to send a cold look. "What are you going to do about that, Julian?"

He released her and relaxed against the plush leather seat. "Why, you're going to skip bail, and I'm going to make you comfortable in the country of your choice, of course. It's the least I can do after all your hard work."

He'd caught her by surprise. She hadn't expected such generosity, and she offered her first genuine smile. "Sweetheart,'' she murmured, shifting closer. She now understood Crock's trip to her apartment. ''How can I thank you?''

It was the wrong question to ask. A hint of satisfaction touched his elegant features. ''As a matter of fact, I have one small job I need you to do before you leave.''

''Another job?'' She should have known. ''Julian, the district attorney isn't going to let me wander around loose forever. What happens if my bond is revoked? It could happen. That detective—Sloan—he said he'd make sure it would. If I'm going to leave, I need to go *now.*''

''Don't worry. We have time. Besides, if they revoke your bond, you won't be anywhere they're likely to look.'' He nodded toward the driver. ''Crock will keep you out of harm's way.''

She didn't like the sound of that. Despite his bland outward appearance, Crock had two settings: crush and destroy. When he wasn't driving Julian around the city, he was busy smoothing over untidy problems and tying off loose ends. A sudden realization seized her, making it difficult to think straight. *She* had become an untidy problem, a loose end in serious need of a good solid knotting. She lifted her hand to her throat, feeling the noose tighten with each passing minute. ''What's this job?'' she managed to ask.

''I want you to pick up a package for me. A cute little pigtailed package. She won't give you any trouble at all.''

''A kid? You want me to pick up a kid?'' It took Bettina a minute to catch his drift. ''You want me to *kidnap* her? No way, Julian. Fencing is one thing. This is beyond serious. The cops will be all over me if I take a child. We're talking Feds and hard time in a hellhole. That's not my idea of a small job.''

''No one will know you're responsible. You can wear a disguise. And Crock will be there to protect you.'' Julian's smile terrified her, the deadly intent clear beneath the surface charm. "After all, we wouldn't want the police turning up at an inopportune moment."

Bettina turned and stared out the window. She could see her reflection in the tinted glass. Dark hair framed a pale face, the elegant angles of her features flattened into distressing commonness. Only the painful red of her mouth and the bitter darkness of her eyes stood out. Hell. She'd thought she was in serious trouble when she'd been arrested for fencing stolen jewelry. But this...

She might be a lot of things, but she wasn't a kidnapper. Even she had her scruples. Unfortunately, a sudden bout of morality wouldn't go over well with Julian. Her gaze flickered toward Crock and then away. If she balked now, she'd have Julian's fix-it man to deal with—and people rarely walked away from their dealings with Crock. They didn't even crawl away. Usually they simply vanished.

Well, she had no intention of vanishing. Forcing her mouth into her most seductive smile, she turned back to Julian. "I'd be happy to help you with your little problem. Tell me your plan." She slid closer, pressing herself against him, praying he didn't sense her sudden aversion. "Knowing you, it's a good one."

A hint of warmth returned to his eyes. "Of course it's good. My plans are always excellent."

Except for the one that ended with her in a jail cell. She moistened her lips and whispered close to his ear, "Tell me about it. Dazzle me with this excellent plan of yours." With any luck, she'd find a flaw somewhere that she could turn to her advantage, anything that would allow her to get out of this with her skin intact.

"COME ON, LILY. We're already late. You're going to make us later."

"But, Mommy... Emily and me are turtles today. We're both dressing in green and going very slow."

Faith thought fast. ''You can be slow when you get to school. Do you think you could be a bunny rabbit until then?''

Lily's brow crinkled. ''Bunnies aren't green.''

''Bunnies who have been rolling in the grass might be.''

Lily tilted her head to one side and thought about it. Finally, she nodded. Dimples flashing, she hopped her way to the car. Faith put the photos she needed to have reframed on the back seat and then turned to speak to her neighbor, Mrs. Thorsen. ''Thanks for house-sitting for me. Thomas promised he'd stop by first thing this morning to take care of the chimney.''

The older woman smiled. ''I don't mind a bit. I'm just so relieved you bought Ruth's home when she moved to Florida. I was hoping we'd get a nice family.'' She tugged on Lily's braid, beaming down at the little girl. ''And we got the very best.''

Lily gave Mrs. Thorsen a quick hug before clambering into the car, and Faith smiled in pleasure. They'd only met Mrs. Thorsen two weeks ago, when they'd moved in, but already she was proving to be an absolute treasure—an absolute treasure with impeccable timing. On three separate occasions she'd shown up at the end of what for Faith had been an exhausting day, bearing casseroles and rhubarb pies, or, for one memorable meal, a delicious dish featuring yellow Finn potatoes, cheese and Walla Walla onions. Lily had adored her great-grandmother, Elizabeth, and though Mrs. Thorsen couldn't replace her, having another grandmother figure in her life should help ease the loss ever so slightly.

''I shouldn't be gone for more than an hour or two,'' Faith said, handing her neighbor the key to the front door. ''I just don't want to risk missing Thomas again.''

Mrs. Thorsen slipped the key into her pocket. ''I'm happy to help. That's what neighbors are for.''

With a final smile and wave, Faith climbed into the ancient Honda and backed out of her driveway. As she headed east on NW 75th Street, a low-slung red Trans Am crept past her and she gave it a curious glance. She lived in an older area of Ballard, just north of Seattle. Most of her neighbors were elderly Scandinavians or young professional couples. Neither set had a propensity toward Trans Ams, particularly bright red vintage models. She caught a glimpse of dark wavy hair and a square jaw as she turned south onto 15th Avenue toward Seattle.

"Ethan," she whispered. The minute she realized what she'd said, she groaned.

"What, Mommy?" Lily asked.

"Nothing, Lily. I was just thinking about your daddy."

Her daughter's little face pulled into a sympathetic frown. "Are you missing him again?"

Faith had always made it a point to talk to Lily about her father, to make him a natural part of their family. "Yeah," she admitted. "I'm missing him bad." Lily reached over and patted her arm while Faith fought back tears. "Thanks, baby. That helps a lot."

Why, oh, why couldn't she put the past where it belonged—in the past? It had been five and a half years since she'd last seen Lily's father and *still* he jumped into her thoughts at the oddest times. She'd catch a glimpse of a stranger driving by with an appearance similar to Ethan's, and the pain of losing him would return, as strong and fresh as the day Jack had showed up on her doorstep with the horrible news.

This had to stop.

She deliberately turned her attention to the traffic on 15th. A heavy stream of cars headed toward Seattle. If she were lucky, she'd make it into the city and back in the allotted hour. As she approached the Ballard Bridge, she saw that the spans of the drawbridge were up. Not good. She checked her watch. Eight-thirty. Not good at all. They only raised the bridge during rush hour if the boat was large, commercial or both. That meant it could take awhile. Faith released her breath in an exasperated sigh.

This did not bode well for her day.

"PARK THE CAR, Crock. We don't want to attract unwanted attention to ourselves by constantly circling the block."

Bettina yanked at the harsh purplish-blue wig, struggling to seat it more comfortably on her head. The bloody thing was cheap and hot, with shiny synthetic fibers that brushed against her cheeks and neck and made her skin itch. She resisted the urge to scratch. Maybe she was allergic to it. "I look ridiculous," she complained to Julian. "Why did you choose such a demented shade? I look like a blue-light special."

"It'll draw attention to your hair. Anyone who looks at you will be so busy staring at the wig, they won't notice your face. Here." He thrust a huge pair of sunglasses into her hands. "With these on, even your own mother won't recognize you."

"That old lush wouldn't recognize me if I pasted a bull's-eye on my backside and wore a sign around my neck that said, Daughter Here." Bettina slid the glasses onto the bridge of her nose and peered over the garish rims. "They're too dark. I can't see a thing."

"They won't be too dark once you're outside." An impatient edge entered his voice. "You're clear on the plan?"

"I'm clear." She stared out the window, fighting to remain calm. She'd wanted out of this situation from the moment Julian had explained it to her. Unfortunately, Crock hadn't given her the opportunity. He'd stuck to her like the leech he was, draining her of every scrap of hope. "I wish it had rained today. It rains almost every other day. Why not today? If it was raining, I could hide under an umbrella."

''You can't hold an umbrella and snatch a kid at the same time. Besides, this is the perfect opportunity. Abby always drops her daughter off late on Fridays. Late means fewer parents coming and going. Everyone's already inside the center and not paying attention to the street. Best of all, the local shops aren't open yet. Now, let's go over the plan again.'' Bettina waved aside his request and he grabbed her arm in a punishing grip. ''Let's go over it, I said. When Abby walks from the parking area to the front door, you hit her—''

''*Hit* her? You can't mean *hit* her, hit her.''

''Of course that's what I mean. From behind. Knock her down. Take her out.''

Damn it! He hadn't said anything about hitting. Now Bettina was supposed to attack the woman? This just got better and better. ''You must have forgotten to mention that part, Julian.'' She couldn't prevent the sarcasm in her tone. ''How am I supposed to do that? I don't know how to fight.''

''I'm not asking you to get in a boxing match with the woman. We need her indisposed long enough for you to escape with the little girl.''

''You can't honestly expect me to attack someone.''

''What did you think? That she'd simply hand over her precious baby without a whimper? You know how protective she is.'' He didn't wait for a response, which was probably just as well, since the only reply that occurred to Bettina would have earned her a smack in the mouth. ''Just shove her to the ground hard enough that she'll have trouble getting up.''

''I thought that was Crock's province. Make him do it.''

''Crock has a job. He'll be getting us out of here afterward.''

From the front seat, Crock tossed a small palm-size canister toward Bettina. She caught it automatically. ''Pepper spray,'' he said, glancing at her in the rearview mirror. ''Make sure you aim it in the right direction. You don't want it coming back at you. Get within six feet and spray her face. It'll blind her for fifteen minutes. Half hour if you do a good job of it. The stuff'll also make her gag so she won't be able to scream.''

''Excellent work, Crock,'' Julian said approvingly. He returned his attention to Bettina. ''Once she's incapacitated, grab the kid and get back here. Are we clear?''

She closed her eyes. What had she gotten herself into? The cops would never believe she wasn't a party to the attack if she hurt Abby. Bettina moistened her lips and used her most persuasive tone of voice. ''Are you sure you want to go through with this, Julian? I can't help but think it's a bad mistake. What if someone notices your car, or sees me get in it with the kid? A Rolls is pretty distinctive.''

''That's what makes it so perfect. Emerald City is directly across the street. I often have Crock wait for me here if I'm running into the store for a moment.'' He shrugged. ''It's like having a burglar driving a UPS truck or FedEx van. It's such a common sight, a thief could unload the contents of the Federal Reserve into the back of the truck and no one would notice.''

''So now a Rolls is the Belltown equivalent of UPS,'' she muttered. ''Yeah, that makes sense.''

He ignored her. ''I want Abby Douglas to get my message loud and clear. If she testifies about the fencing operation, she loses her kid. We'll keep her daughter long enough to terrify her, and then we'll ditch the brat—with a small warning.''

''What kind of warning?'' Bettina asked uneasily.

''A note. Just a note. 'Shut up or else.' Something like that.''

Her uneasiness grew. ''They can trace stuff like that these

days. I've seen it on TV. Forensic science or something. It's all the thing.''

''I have it planned. There won't be any evidence to trace, forensic or otherwise.''

She couldn't stand it any longer. ''You're not doing this to keep Abby quiet.'' The accusation burst from her. ''There's only one reason you're doing this—for revenge. Because you're furious that Abby interfered with your operation.''

''So what if I am?'' His eyes were crazed, revealing just how far over the edge he'd fallen. ''Abby Douglas deserves what she gets. She's a nobody. Less than nothing. How dare she turn on me? I gave her a job. I helped her enroll that spawn of hers into Forrester Square Day Care. She should have warned me that the cops had set up a reconnaissance operation there. That bitch even helped them. Do you have any idea how much money this will cost me?'' He thumped the seat, his fist sinking into the plush Connolley leather. ''She's going to pay. And she's going to pay in the type of coin she understands best.''

Bettina shivered. Julian was obsessed. And obsessed people were dangerous because they didn't think clearly and would do anything, no matter how irrational, to accomplish their goal. Kidnapping Abby's daughter definitely qualified as irrational. ''Julian, think. There won't be a trial, not if I'm out of the country. If we kidnap this little girl, the cops will be all over us. That won't help you get your fencing operation up and running again. All it will do is cause them to look more carefully at us.''

He leaned forward in his seat, ignoring her. ''Circle the block again, Crock. Then park a couple doors down from the day care center.''

Bettina fell silent. So now what? The answer didn't take much thought. It was time to do whatever was necessary to get herself out of this. She leaned back against the cream-colored leather. It was baby-soft and helped her relax. Helped her think. Helped her consider the possible angles that might get her out of this mess with her skin intact.

She needed a plan.

ETHAN DROVE SLOWLY along the residential streets, checking house numbers. Finding the one he wanted, he eased Lil into an open parking space on the street and killed the engine. He compared the numbers neatly lined up on the side of the house with the information scrawled on the slip of paper he held. It matched.

The house was far different from the huge old Victorian in Portland. This one was a small two-story affair with crisp white trim and pale gray clapboard siding. The design was one he recognized from the years he'd lived in Seattle. It was an arts-and-crafts cottage that had enjoyed popularity at the turn of the century. A shingle roof rambled downward from the second story, its slide abruptly halted by a dormer jutting toward the street from the left half of the house. The front door was set to the right of center on the opposite side, while a bow window squatted beneath the dormer, protruding from the house like a pregnant woman's belly. The overall result was delightfully asymmetrical and made Ethan smile just looking at it.

So now what? Did he go up and knock on the door? Yeah, that would work. Faith would take one look at him and either sock him in the jaw or faint dead away. Or maybe, after five-plus years, she wouldn't even remember him. Then there was the husband. How did Ethan plan to handle the situation if the man of the house answered the door? Easy. Walk away.

He shifted in his seat, aware of the minutes ticking by while he sat procrastinating. If any of his former unit could have seen him dithering like an old woman, they'd be laughing their asses off.

Okay. Decision time. If she was happily married, he'd wish her well and leave. And if she wasn't? What would he do if the marriage was on the rocks? Help finish it off? Beg Faith to leave her husband for him? Grab her and run?

Come on, Dunn. Make your decision.

He had two options. He could confront or he could drive away. Shoving open the door, he climbed from the car. There'd never been any question about what he'd do. He hadn't trailed Faith from Portland to Seattle only to leave matters unsettled between them. If the husband answered, he'd say, "Sorry, wrong number," and then hightail it out of there. But if Faith answered, he'd...what?

It didn't take any thought. He'd pull her into his arms and kiss her like there was no tomorrow. Then her husband would punch him in the face. He'd put the husband down—hard—then throw Faith over his shoulder, dump her into the car and point Lil's hood due east and drive off into the sunset— Rise. Sunrise. Driving into the sunset from Seattle was definitely not advisable without some serious flotation devices. Driving into the sunrise might not be in line with tradition, but what the hell.

He hesitated outside a picket fence that embraced an expansive yard. He could still change his mind about seeing Faith. It wasn't too late to choose the honorable path. It's what his grandmother would have expected. No doubt it was what Elizabeth would have wanted, as well. Both had loved him dearly. And both had always had the uncanny knack for seeing right through him, seeing the wild, volatile spirit beneath the pretty-boy looks. Both had also expected only the best from him, never letting him compromise his integrity by trading on those looks.

His decision was made. He couldn't leave. Not without seeing Faith. "I'm not that honorable," he whispered.

Shoving open the gate, he entered the yard, walked past a tidy garden bedded down for the winter, and climbed the steps to the front porch. Without hesitating further, he banged on the door. It was opened almost immediately, but not by Faith. An elderly woman stood there, her white hair pulled back tightly from a round, cheerful face.

"Come right in. I've been waiting for you." She beamed. "Aren't you a fine-looking young man."

He allowed himself to be ushered into the house. "You were expecting me, Mrs...?"

"Thorsen. I'm Faith's next-door neighbor. It's Thomas, isn't it? She said you'd show up this morning to sweep her chimney, and here you are. Right on time." She looked him over. "How clever of you to wear all that black so the soot won't show. I'd stash that leather jacket somewhere safe before you begin, though."

"I'm not Thomas, Mrs. Thorsen." Ethan offered a rueful grin. "I'm not even a chimney sweep. I'm—"

Mrs. Thorsen gasped. "Of course. You must be Faith's husband. Did you lose your key? I haven't seen you around, but then you and your family only moved in two weeks ago. Have you been away on business all this time? I must say, your daughter is the very image of you."

It took every ounce of self-possession not to react. "My daughter?"

"Such a cute little thing," Mrs. Thorsen continued. She swept around him and paused in front of a wall covered with photographs. "You must be so proud of her."

Ethan followed the elderly woman, his limp more pronounced than before. He stopped in front of the wall and forced himself to look at the pictures. There were dozens of photos, all of a little girl delighting in her first year of life. Elizabeth was even in a few, holding the tiny bundle in her arms, a tearful smile on her heavily lined face. At least she'd lived long enough to know her great-granddaughter. She'd often expressed that hope to Ethan.

He focused on Faith's daughter, a fierce pain ripping

through him. Faith had given birth to a baby. A beautiful baby girl with a headful of golden curls and a killer smile. If life had taken a different turn, Faith would have been his wife and that baby could have been his. One reckless decision. One road taken instead of ignored, and a taunting wall full of might-have-beens stretched before him, showing him in graphic detail all he'd missed.

His hands folded into fists as he stared at the pictures. He could see why Mrs. Thorsen had made the mistake of connecting him with the baby. She did share a passing resemblance to him, despite her gold curls. She had his dimples and blue eyes, though the color was a darker shade than his own. She was a striking child, her baby features suggesting the potential for true beauty.

His brows drew together as his attention shifted from picture to picture. Something about them troubled him, but he couldn't quite put his finger on the elusive detail. It was an element he should pick up on, an important aspect that should be frustratingly obvious. An expression came to mind, one that he and his men lived by—one that had saved their hides on more missions than he could count. *There were details missing. And knowing the details was what kept you alive.*

Mrs. Thorsen interrupted his line of thought before he could grasp the missing element. ''I just love old-fashioned names. I understand Faith named your daughter after her grandmother.''

''Elizabeth,'' he said absently.

''Elizabeth?'' Her brow crinkled. ''I thought it was—''

''I'm sorry, Mrs. Thorsen,'' Ethan interrupted. He took a step back from the wall. He'd seen all he needed to. ''I'm afraid I have to leave now.''

''Do you want to wait for the chimney sweep?''

He forced himself to turn his back on the photos. This changed everything. He could fantasize about stealing Faith from her husband. But coming between a husband, wife and baby… No way. No way could he destroy a family unit. "Would you mind waiting for the chimney sweep until Faith returns?"

Her confusion grew, along with her curiosity. "Not at all. I promised her I would."

He didn't waste any more time. With a gruff farewell, he turned and left the house. He'd made a mistake attempting to resurrect the past. *Forget her,* hombre, an insidious voice whispered. *By now she will have forgotten all about you. She is married to her rich banker and this very minute has his son growing fat and heavy in her belly.*

His jailer had gotten the banker part right. But her baby had turned out to be a daughter instead of a son. And judging by the expression in the various photographs, Faith was delighted with the life she'd created. She'd looked so happy holding her daughter, so contented. Ethan hunched a shoulder against the winter chill as he limped to his car.

Well, he'd gotten the answer he'd come for, without disturbing the even tenor of Faith's life. She was married, had a child and was clearly happy. She didn't need an old lover in her life dredging up a lot of pain and misery. She deserved better than that.

He paused by the driver's door, casting Faith's house a final long look. Once upon a time they'd discussed moving to Seattle, mainly because it was his childhood stomping ground. They'd talked about buying a small cottage, complete with a white picket fence. Returning to his hometown with Faith had seemed right, somehow. A circle completed. Now he felt more alienated than ever, Seattle a place he'd have to avoid from now on. The wind picked up, carrying a bitter sting straight from the arctic. Opening the car door, he climbed in, his knee protesting at his lack of care.

He headed east on NW 75th Street, working his way over a network of side streets toward the freeway. Once on I-5, he'd escape the city with all due speed. Then he'd do what he should have when he'd left Portland. He'd point Lil south and eat up as many miles as there was road. The destination didn't matter, so long as it was as far from Seattle as he could get. But as he drove, one thought kept churning through his brain.

There were details missing.

CHAPTER THREE

FAITH PULLED INTO the parking lot of Forrester Square Day Care and helped Lily from the car. A brisk snapping sound drew her attention to a banner hanging vertically from the top of the three-story building, a chilly breeze causing it to unfurl against its anchors like a wave on a stormy ocean. The banner had been designed to look like an elongated house, complete with peaked roof, and even had a spiral of gray smoke escaping from a redbrick chimney. The name of the day care was spelled out in the type of crayon letters a child would draw, and gave the overall impression that this was as much a home as a business, and one that catered to the express needs of the children it took beneath its roof.

The wind gusted again and Faith picked up her pace. Just ahead of her, Abby was entering the fenced-in yard of the day care center, with Emily skipping along beside her. Pushing through the wrought-iron gate, Lily hopped over to join her friend, and the two, outfitted in similar green dresses and windbreakers, put their heads together, chattering urgently. An instant later, they hopped over to one of the benches positioned beside the front steps of the center.

Abby paused, waiting for Faith to catch up. "We started out as a turtle," she said in mock horror. "I thought we'd never get here."

Faith grinned. "You, too? Were you able to convince her to give a rabbit a try, instead?"

"Didn't even think of it. Did it work for you?"

"We're here, aren't we?" The two laughed, and Faith

gestured to the bench on the opposite side of the steps from the two girls. ''Do you have a minute? I wanted to talk to you about the girls' costumes for the Christmas play.''

Marilyn Albee, the girls' teacher, exited the front doors just then. She waved at the mothers, indicating that they could continue talking while she watched the two girls. Faith mouthed a quick thank-you before turning back to Abby.

Beneath Marilyn's amused gaze, the girls hopped off the bench and began lumbering like turtles across the yard toward the fence fronting the street.

''THERE SHE IS,'' Julian said. ''Are you ready?''

''You said all the parents would have dropped off their kids already and Abby would be alone.'' Bettina pointed toward the front of the day care center. ''I count three adults plus two kids.''

''Give it a minute.''

''No way. I'm not doing this in front of witnesses.''

''I said give it a minute. Look. The kid's coming right toward us. If we time this right, we can get our hands on her before they even realize what's happening. Put your gloves and sunglasses on. Remember not to run. Once you have the kid, pick her up like she was your own. Just make sure you cover her mouth. We're going to roll forward, out of sight of the day care. The minute you have her, catch up with the car and get in. Fast, but not frantically enough to draw attention to yourself.''

He was nuts. Chock-full of nuts, all of them shelled, salted and roasted to a crisp. ''I don't think I can do this.''

''You'll do it.'' Julian turned toward her. ''You'll do it…or else.''

There was no mistaking the threat in his pale blue eyes. Bettina turned away with a shudder and gazed at the two girls. They crept across the front yard toward the wrought-iron fence enclosing the property. Bettina wanted to shout at them to turn around and run. Her hands twisted together as she willed them away.

They kept coming.

As they approached the fence, she stared at them, her brows pulling together. Damn, but the girls looked similar. Both had pale gold hair hanging in neat braids. The taller of the pair had hair slightly lighter than the other, true. But the two could be sisters, they looked so much alike. She hoped she'd be able to tell which was which. She hadn't paid that much attention to Abby's daughter the few times the kid had been in the exchange.

Beside her, Julian cursed, the single word enough to make Bettina wince. Were people even allowed to say that when riding around in a Rolls? It felt blasphemous somehow. "Look at them." He gestured toward the two girls, frustration eating at his voice. "They look so alike."

Hope bloomed. "That could be a problem." She attempted to sound offhand. "Maybe we should reconsider this."

He turned on her, snarling like a feral animal trapped in a corner. "Or maybe I should reconsider getting you out of the country. You know the kid. Now, which one is it?"

She stared at the two girls, her gaze settling on the smaller of the pair, the one whose hair was a shade darker. Ten to one she'd have eyes like Abby. But if Bettina snatched the kid, what then? *She'd* be on the hook for kidnapping, not Julian. He could claim he didn't know what she'd intended. Or that *she* was the one threatening *him.* And Crock would back him up. Oh, man. This was *not* good.

A sudden idea occurred to her, one born of sheer desperation. Would it work? Could she pull it off? She spared a swift glance in Julian's direction. When it came to gems and jewelry, he was the best. He could grade a diamond with better accuracy than anyone she'd ever met. Time after time she'd seen the lab tests verify his assessment. His powers of observation when it came to his speciality couldn't be matched.

But kids clearly weren't his area of expertise. She thought fast, trying to put together a plan of action in the short time she had available. Fear seemed to clog her brain, slowing it and making it difficult to consider all the angles. Still, her idea held merit. Of course, if Julian realized what she'd done—or that it had been deliberate—her last conversation in this world would be with Crock.

MARILYN ALBEE WATCHED Lily and Emily pantomiming the movements of a pair of turtles as they crept across the front yard of the day care center. They were actually quite good, born actresses the both of them. She absolutely adored this age group, loved all the ''little people'' in her care and received a wealth of affection in return. But she had to admit that these two in particular had stolen her heart. While her class was occupied watching the older children rehearse a Christmas play, she'd come out to collect her last two ducklings.

A small movement along the far side of the day care property caught her attention and she turned to look. A scruffy man in his early sixties stood near the fence, staring at her. He wore the signature clothing of the homeless—ripped jeans, a plaid wool shirt and an ill-fitting coat—the getup hanging from his emaciated frame. Deep-set blue eyes gazed at her from beneath a mop of long, scraggly gray hair, and he lifted a trembling hand to tug at his beard. He opened his mouth as though he wanted to say something, then his gaze darted to the two little girls. A perplexed frown creased his brow and he approached the fence, wrapping his hands around the wrought-iron bars, his attention fixated on Lily and Emily.

He called out a name, but Marilyn couldn't quite catch

it. She frowned. There'd been a lot of discussion among the owners of the day care center—Katherine, Hannah and Alexandra—about this man. Despite the raw December weather, he'd been seen hanging around on a fairly regular basis. Several of the teachers wanted to call the police, but Alexandra had insisted they hold off.

Marilyn thought it was a mistake. A strange man watching the comings and goings around the day care was dangerous. It put the children at risk, and she, for one, refused to sit still for it. She spared a quick glance at the two girls. They were crouched between a pair of rhododendron bushes by the front fence, growling and snarling like a pair of tigers, their tiny hands curled into swiping claws.

''Keep your hands inside the fence, girls,'' she called to them. Then she returned her attention to the homeless man. Some issues in life were clear-cut, the right and wrong unquestionable. This was one of those issues. Every aspect of her training told her this situation should be aggressively addressed. Her mind made up, she strode over toward where the homeless man stood.

''NOW,'' JULIAN ORDERED. ''Go get her.''

Bettina sucked in a deep breath and thrust open the passenger door. A brisk wind stirred the violent blue strands of her wig and she flattened her hand against the crown to hold it in place. Hurrying up to the fence, she spared a swift look around. A few pedestrians scurried along the street, but they were eager to escape the chilly wind, and none of them paid any attention to her. She stooped down in front of the girls and smiled at them.

''Hey, there.''

To her dismay, the smaller girl pulled back from the fence, surveying Bettina with deep suspicion. ''You're a stranger,'' she said clearly. ''Mommy said never, ever talk to strangers.''

''I'm not a stranger,'' she replied. ''Your name is Emily. See? I know you.''

Emily took another step backward, while her friend watched, puzzled. Okay, that settled that. No way could she get her hands on the right kid. That left the other one, who continued to switch her attention between Emily and Bettina.

''What's the matter?'' the little girl asked Emily. ''How come you're not playing tigers anymore?''

''We're going to play a new game,'' Bettina announced brightly. ''Emily, you have to tell your mom exactly what I say, okay?''

''Mommy said never, ever talk to strangers.''

Bettina suppressed a groan of exasperation. ''Except this one time.'' Could she pull Emily's friend through the bars or would she have to lift her over? Over. If she stood on her tiptoes, she could grab the child's jacket and haul her out of the yard. Now to keep the message short and easy to remember. ''Tell your mother it's Bettina, and we're going to play a game of hide and seek. We'll be at Mary Lou's. You got that? Bettina's playing hide and seek at Mary Lou's.''

She didn't dare wait another minute. Reaching over the fence, she grabbed hold of Emily's friend and unceremoniously yanked her into the street. The instant the child was clear of the fence, Bettina covered her mouth and scooped her up all in one swift move. Behind her, Emily began to scream, and the child Bettina was holding flailed her arms, walloping Bettina on the side of her head. The wig slid down over one ear and she picked up her pace. The door to the Rolls swung open and Bettina tossed the kid toward Julian before leaping in behind her.

''Move!'' she shouted.

Crock didn't gun the car. Instead, he eased from the curb and rumbled down the street in stately elegance.

On the floor of the Rolls, the kid sat shrieking. Bettina closed her eyes, fighting for breath. Oh, man. They'd just kidnapped a kid. *They'd just kidnapped a kid!* And they'd done it in a damned Rolls-Royce. How bizarre was that?

Then she began to laugh.

AT EMILY'S SHRIEK, Abby came off the bench in a flash. Faith was a step behind and gaining fast. Emily raced across the front of the yard toward them, her braids bouncing against her narrow shoulders, and launched herself into her mother's arms.

It was at that instant that Faith realized she didn't see Lily. Her mouth went bone-dry and her stomach muscles spasmed. She'd experienced such an overwhelming jolt of fear only once before—the night Jack had arrived on her doorstep to tell her that Ethan had been killed.

"Lily," she whispered. And then her voice gained in strength, ripping from her lungs. *"Lily!"*

She ran toward the fence at the bottom of the yard and frantically scanned the sidewalk. Cars came and went, cruising along Sandringham Drive with casual indifference to Faith's desperation.

Lily was nowhere to be seen.

Faith raced toward the small parking lot on the side of the day care center and slammed through the wrought-iron gate. She stumbled into the middle of the street, shrieking for her daughter. She was vaguely conscious of the squeal of brakes and the unending blast of car horns.

As the cars slowed, she darted to their windows, peering in, weeping as she called out Lily's name over and over and over again. She had no idea how long she remained in the street, ricocheting from car to car. Time held no meaning. It wasn't until she heard the distant wail of a police car that she regained a spark of self-awareness. And with that self-awareness came an undeniable knowledge.

Lily was gone.

The pain hit again, harder than before, and she crumbled beneath it. Folding, she sank to the cold tarmac. And then she wept.

"DID THEY SEE?" Bettina's voice bounced around the leather interior of the Rolls-Royce, as high-pitched and hysterical as the kid's sobs. "Man, oh man, oh man. *Did anyone see us do it?*"

Julian responded by backhanding her across the face. The wig flew off her head and landed on the floor next to the little girl. The harsh bluish-purple fibers rippled outward from the crown like the probing tentacles of an octopus. In response, the kid pulled herself into a tight ball away from the wig.

"Shut up," he ordered. Stress gave his voice a dangerous edge, and that calmed Bettina faster than the slap. Julian, stressed, was capable of anything. "And shut that kid up, too, or I'll have Crock take care of it."

The threat had Bettina sliding off the seat and onto the floor next to the kid. "Hey," she whispered. "Take it easy. We're not going to hurt you. We're just playing a game."

In response, the Emily look-alike, inched toward the door. Her legs were bent close to her chest, her arms wrapped tightly around them. The only visible portion of her face was her eyes, and they were a brilliant sky-blue. "I wanna go home," she insisted through her tears. "I don't want to play with you."

Bettina closed in on her and spared a surreptitious glance in Julian's direction. He continued to huddle against the opposite door, as far from the little girl as he could get. His expression registered distaste, along with something else. Could it be…fear? How peculiar. What did Julian have to fear? She was the one who'd taken all the risks.

Turning back, she put her mouth close to the little girl's

ear and whispered, ''You see that guy behind me?'' The child nodded and Bettina continued. ''He doesn't play very nice. We don't want him to get mad. He hits when he gets mad and we don't want you to get hit like I did.''

The Emily clone nodded vehemently. Encouraged, Bettina eased closer, praying neither of the men could hear their conversation. The Rolls was roomy, but Crock had ears like a bat. ''And the guy in front driving the car? He's not nice, either. That means that in this game it's just you and me against them. The girls against the boys. Do you understand?''

A spark of comprehension gleamed in the kid's eyes. To Bettina's relief, the waterworks slowed and she nodded again.

''The boys think you're Emily, and I need you to pretend that's who you are. Got it?'' She waited for another affirmative response. ''If you need to cry some more, wait until we're alone. Then you can cry all you want. I don't mind. But when the boys are around, you have to be brave. Can you do that? Can you be brave?''

This time the little girl's head lifted. Where once terror had glittered within the tears, now the light of battle gleamed, along with a spark of anger. ''My name's Emily and I'm a lion,'' she whispered. ''Lions eat bad people.''

Bettina swallowed. Oh, man. Julian and Crock had no idea what they'd gotten themselves into. This kid was trouble.

''Mr. Black?'' Crock spoke from the front. ''I think we have a small problem.''

''Christ! What else can go wrong?'' Julian kicked the seat in front of him. ''What the hell's the problem? And you damn well better have a solution for me before you tell me what it is.''

''I think there was a witness.'' Cold brown eyes gleamed

in the rearview mirror. ''As for a solution, that's simple enough. Just leave it to me.''

ETHAN INCHED THROUGH the traffic jam leading from Seattle. Getting out of the city was proving more difficult than he'd anticipated. It seemed that everyone from Ballard east had decided to head for the freeway. Finally the snarl cleared and he reached I-5, only to have the traffic knot up again. Two accidents and a full ninety minutes later, he'd gotten only as far as Sea-Tac Airport. An hour after that, he'd worked his way through the traffic around Olympia and breezed into Tumwater just as Lil sucked up the last of the gas in the tank. Exiting the freeway, he grabbed an early lunch before pulling into the closest gas station.

Lil was a great little car, but she guzzled gas like a drunk guzzled cheap liquor. After Ethan finished filling the tank and cleaning the windshield, he walked into the station and handed the old man behind the counter a couple of twenties. A battered TV set was bolted to the ceiling above him and a reporter gave the noon report with unusual urgency. Ethan jerked his head in the direction of the set. ''What's going on?''

''Some kid got snatched.''

Ethan grimaced. ''A hell of a thing.''

''It's happening more and more these days. Sick. That's what it is. They snatched the little girl right out of the yard of her day care center. In broad daylight, no less, with her poor momma looking on.'' The old man rang up the sale and counted out the change. ''Animals oughtta be thrown in a hole and never allowed to see the light of day again.''

''I hear you.'' Ethan pocketed the money. ''Hope they find her,'' he said on his way out.

The reporter continued with her commentary and Ethan paused. He could have sworn she said, ''Marshall.'' He pushed through the door, shaking his head as he crossed to the Trans Am. He really had it bad. Even if it was Marshall, Faith wouldn't be using that name, not unless her husband was also a Marshall. And what were the odds of that?

There were details missing. And knowing the details was what kept you alive.

Ethan paused in the act of closing his car door, one foot still planted on the grease-splattered concrete. The missing piece hit him then. Hit him hard.

Her husband.

That's what was wrong with the photos. There hadn't been a single picture of the husband. Tons of the baby. Another slew of them with Elizabeth holding her great-granddaughter, and of Faith and her daughter. But not one single shot showed the proud daddy cradling his baby girl. Ethan climbed out of the vehicle and limped back to the station. Opening the door, he called to the old man. ''Hey, did they mention the kid's name? The one who was kidnapped?''

''Yeah. Give me a sec now. My memory ain't so good no more.'' The station attendant's brow furrowed. ''Marshall. Lily Marshall.''

Ethan's gut tensed. ''How old? Did they say? A year? Eighteen months?''

''Nah. Older than that.'' He glanced up at the set. ''There's a picture of her. What's she look? Four? Maybe five.''

To the attendant's surprise, he was talking to thin air.

THE '73 TRANS AM Super Duty 455 featured a special V-8 racing engine and ''header'' style ram air exhaust manifolds. Beneath the hood, three hundred and ten foaming-at-the-mouth horses strained at the bridle. One of only seventy-two standard models built that year, it contained a heavy-duty block, a Rochester Quadrajet 800 cfm carb,

4-speed transmission, and it could go from zero to 100 in twelve-point-eight seconds.

Ethan managed it in twelve-point-six. The white-as-a-sheet state trooper who pulled him over clocked him at 173 on a particularly long straightaway, which impressed the hell out of Ethan. According to all the specs he'd read, Lil topped out at 165. When he explained about the kidnapping—and dropped a couple of names from his past—he received a police escort back to Seattle.

One of the names he'd dropped turned out to be Assistant Deputy Chief of Police Griffith. As a kid, Ethan had jokingly called the then-beat cop ''Andy,'' though never to his face. The deputy chief had a son a couple years younger than Ethan, a geeky kid nicknamed ''Opie,'' who'd later made a mint working for Bill Gates. On one memorable occasion, Opie had been attacked by a gang of school yard bullies. Ethan, never one to miss out on a good fight, had gone back-to-back with the kid, and taken on all comers. Griffith had never forgotten the incident. Ethan would never forget this.

He rode the state trooper's bumper the entire way back to Seattle at a sedate 100 mph. With every mile that passed, he kept telling himself he'd made a mistake. Lily Marshall couldn't be Faith's daughter. It must be another Marshall. But he knew in his gut that it was the same Faith and the same Marshall. And that meant the little girl could be his. The suspicion went beyond wishful thinking. He'd seen Lily's face on the TV and there was no disputing one incontrovertible fact. The face shown was eerily similar to the one he shaved each morning. He also knew one other fact.

What had Mrs. Thorsen said? *I understand Faith named her daughter after her grandmother.* Mrs. Thorsen had been wrong. His daughter hadn't been named after Faith's grandmother, Elizabeth. She'd been named after *his* grandmother.

Lily.

''ARE YOU SURE you don't want us to stay with you?'' Abby asked.

Faith shook her head. ''I need some peace and quiet. I just want to get home.''

''Home isn't going to be all that peaceful or quiet,'' Luke said. ''The press are going to be at your door day and night.'' Luke, Abby's fiancé and a detective with Homicide and Robbery, had been one of the first police officers on the scene. The minute he'd heard about the kidnapping, he'd done everything possible to find Lily. Not that it had met with any success. Despite the abduction occurring in broad daylight on a busy street, the only witness had been Abby's daughter, Emily. And she'd been too hysterical to say more than that a woman had taken Lily.

''I won't answer the door without checking first.'' Faith twisted her hands together. ''Maybe the kidnappers will call. Maybe they'll want a ransom.''

She sensed the look that flashed between Abby and Luke.

''If that happens, we'll put an officer in the house and authorize a tap. But this doesn't feel like a ransom case. Plus, you don't have the sort of money most kidnappers are looking for in a situation like this.''

Faith fought for control. It was almost impossible. From the moment she'd realized Lily had been taken, her brain had stopped functioning. And she needed it to function. She needed desperately to think, to reason, to figure out what she should do in order to find her daughter.

She moistened her lips. ''Maybe—'' Her voice cracked and she tried again. ''Maybe they thought she belonged to one of the wealthier parents. When they find out she doesn't...''

''We're doing everything we can. We'll find her.'' Luke's voice held the sort of assurance she desperately needed—and didn't believe for one minute. He bypassed her street, circling to the next block. He pulled over to the curb in front of a neighbor's house, an elderly gentleman whose property was directly behind hers. "I've arranged to go through his yard and enter by way of your back door. I've also arranged for an officer to get your car to you. They'll park it here sometime in the next hour."

"I'll stay if you want," Abby offered for the twentieth time.

Faith shook her head. "Emily needs you. She's terrified."

"You could stay with us, instead."

It was another offer that had been made repeatedly. "I really appreciate the suggestion, Abby. But I can't. What if the kidnappers call? I have to be there to answer the phone."

Luke parked his SUV and the three of them cut through the yard. They entered Faith's house with no one the wiser. Luke took a quick look around before nodding in satisfaction. "It's clear."

The two stayed another ten minutes, offering food, offering comfort, offering suggestions Faith's brain couldn't seem to process. At long last they left and she was alone in the house. She wandered from room to room, trudging up and down the steps to the upper level a dozen times. Lily's bedroom drew her, but she couldn't bring herself to enter it. She also avoided the brightly decorated Christmas tree. Her emotions were still too raw for either one.

Periodically a reporter would come and bang on the door, or call to her through the sturdy oak wood. Then the person would disappear, only to be replaced by another. Faith made a point of keeping well away from any windows where movement might tip off the media that she was there. She did leave a message at the newspaper where she did freelance work, explaining that she wouldn't be available until the situation had been resolved. To her relief, the editor she spoke to kept her questions to a minimum, intent only on getting any pertinent information that might help find Lily.

Finally, huddling on the floor in front of the couch, Faith

picked up the remote control and flipped around the channels on the TV set. She'd given up answering the phone, and allowed the answering machine to get it, listening desperately to each incoming message for news about Lily. But there was never any news, just more reporters. In between calls, the doorbell continued to peal or someone would knock, and she'd tiptoe to the door and check the peephole. Assured it was no one she knew, she'd return to the television set.

When the evening news came on, Lily's grinning image flashed across the screen. It was the last straw. Faith crept toward the set and slid to the floor in front of it. She pressed herself against the cold screen, against the bigger-than-life image of Lily.

And then she wept.

A LOUD BANGING WOKE FAITH.

She opened her eyes, aware that she must have slept at some point, curled close to the TV. An old black-and-white film flickered across the screen, and Bogie growled something through a cloud of cigarette smoke. Above the TV, a clock glared the witching hour of midnight.

''Faith? Hurry and let me in before the reporters come back.''

The banging resumed and she struggled to get her feet properly situated beneath her. Her legs were a mass of pins and needles, throwing her off balance. The voice sounded like Luke's, and the minute she recognized that fact, all thoughts but one gripped her. *Lily!* Did he have news about her daughter? She ran for the door, belatedly checking the peephole before opening up. Catching a glimpse of Luke's muscular build and distinctive dark hair, she flung off the chain and ripped open the dead bolt.

"Luke? Have you found her? Have you found—"

It wasn't Luke. In fact, it was the last person she'd have ever expected to find on her doorstep.

"Hello, Faith," Ethan said.

CHAPTER FOUR

FAITH STUMBLED BACKWARD, staring in disbelief. ''Ethan?'' She bumped up against a small table. It crashed to the floor and she followed it down, landing hard on one hip.

Ethan was in the house like a shot, slamming the door behind him. He attempted to catch her as she fell, but his bad leg folded beneath him and he hit the floor alongside of her.

She scrambled backward, away from him. ''You're not Ethan.'' Her face was dead white, her lips the odd purplish-blue of a hypothermia victim. ''You can't be. Ethan's dead.''

He clumsily gained his feet and held out a hand. ''I didn't die.''

She stared at his hand as though it were a viper. Ignoring the offer of help, she continued to inch away from him. ''No.''

''Honey—''

''No!'' A thousand different emotions swept across her face. Denial. Joy. Relief. Confusion. After all the turmoil in the wake of Lily's abduction, he could tell she was fast approaching the point of overload.

Ethan started toward her, then stopped when she scuttled backward like a crab. She was rapidly passing from general overload to total system meltdown, and he kept a safe distance, afraid of tipping her over the edge. ''It's me,'' he said simply. ''I'm sorry to frighten you, sweetheart. But it really is me.''

She shook her head. ''Jack came.'' She struggled to her knees, and Ethan forced himself to watch instead of lending assistance. It was clear she didn't want him touching her, though the knowledge just about killed him. She planted her shoulder against the wall and used her legs to shove herself upright, while her arms remained weighted at her sides. After a momentary struggle, she managed to align her feet and legs sufficiently to stand. She appeared wobbly, but he didn't think she was in imminent danger of falling again. ''He said you'd been killed.''

''They thought I was dead. They didn't know I'd survived until five or six months later.'' He spoke dispassionately about events too hideous for words. Boxing off the memories gave him the best chance for survival. Unfortunately, it also made light of a time when darkness had nearly crushed the life from him. But every instinct told him to bury the darkness, to hide scars too hideous to bring into the light. ''It took another full month for the unit to organize and mount a successful rescue.''

She fought to take it in, and Ethan couldn't tell how much actually made it through. ''Jack said you'd been ambushed. Your jeep…'' Her chin quivered uncontrollably. So did her hands. They told a story all their own, sweeping the air in jerky, disjointed movements that lacked her usual grace. ''Your jeep. It blew up. I said it was a mistake. You couldn't be dead. I'd know. But they found your identification on the…on the body. They said there wasn't any question. We had a funeral for you. It was quite beautiful. You should have been there.'' A laugh broke from her. Then she started to cry.

He kept his voice low and soothing. ''The people who captured me set it up. They wanted everyone to think I was dead.''

Her mouth worked, striving to form a coherent string of words. "I don't understand," she managed to say through the tears. *"Why?"*

"So they could find out who I was working for without my employers realizing they'd been exposed."

Relief and joy broke through all other emotions. At least, he hoped he read her right. He wanted desperately to believe it was joy that lit her face. "You're alive?" she begged. "You're really alive?"

He managed a smile. "I'm alive, sweetheart."

She was in his arms then, practically bowling him over. She hugged him, kissed the sweep of his jaw, his mouth, his throat—anywhere she could reach. Her tears wet his face and he absorbed them into his skin, absorbed all of her. Her softness, her scent, the sweetness of her mouth, the urgency of her touch. It had been so long since he'd last held her in his arms, and he drank in her essence, instantly intoxicated after what felt like an endless drought.

He cupped her face and kissed her fully, shuddering at the intense pleasure. He couldn't get enough. It would never be enough, not after all they'd been through. Their bodies remembered each other, coming together with a delicious familiarity. She slipped into the juncture of his thighs just as she always had when they'd been a couple, leaning against him. He responded automatically, planting his hands low on her hips and tugging her close. Cupping her bottom, he lifted her up and into him. She shimmied closer, wrapping herself around him.

Their mouths moved in concert, joining, parting, rejoining, clinging. Slow. Then fast. Then hard and long, tongues entwining. They were kisses of reacquaintance. Frenzied kisses. Gentle kisses. Kisses that expressed an odd curiosity, as though comparing what they were experiencing now to what had once been.

For the first time in five and a half long, lonely years, Ethan felt hope stir.

The minute they came up for air, her words flowed, singing in his ear like the sweetest jazz, tumbling over themselves in a rhythmic staccato. "You have no idea. It's been awful. Awful! I needed you. Badly. Elizabeth helped, but it wasn't the same. It took years before I came to terms with—" The singing ended as abruptly as it had begun, the jazz fading from the air on a jarring note. "I hurt for years and years, Ethan. But you…you said you were only imprisoned for—"

She broke off, struggling free of his arms. She took a quick step backward, then another. He stood silently, waiting. He knew what she was thinking.

"Say it," he ordered.

She'd gone from joy to fury in the space of a heartbeat. "You son of a bitch," she whispered. "You said six months. You said they imprisoned you for six months. What about the rest of that time? What about all those years I thought you were dead? Where the *hell* have you been?"

"Staying out of your life."

"No sh—"

Lily. She shook her head, her thoughts muddled and confused. Too much was happening too fast. First Lily was taken. Then Ethan arrived. Lily, then Ethan. Lily. Ethan. Her brain made the connection, two pieces of a jigsaw puzzle locking together even though the colors looked wrong and the fit slightly off. It didn't matter. She'd found a possible passageway through the chaos and she seized on it, desperately following it to its irrational conclusion. It was something she could focus on, a possibility she could grab hold of, an avenue of hope. It was a road to Lily, no matter how skewed.

The timing of Ethan's return struck her as too convenient, too orchestrated. The minute Lily had disappeared, her father showed up on her doorstep. What were the chances that the two were unrelated? Somewhere between zero and none. She faced him down, half-crazed, exhaustion vying with a disorienting combination of fear and suspicion.

''Where's my daughter?'' The question exploded from her.

''That's what I'm here to find out.''

''No. *No!*'' She wouldn't let him get away with it. ''Where's Lily? Did you take her? Do you have my daughter?''

''Is that what you think?'' he asked. He stared at her with the sort of impassive expression she remembered from before. It meant that he'd stuffed his emotions into an unreachable pit. It meant he was hurting. Not that she cared. She was hurting, too. ''You think I'd snatch her like some sort of low-life thug?''

No. Yes. She pressed her hands against her temples. She didn't know anything anymore. The one fact she could state with any certainty was that her daughter had been taken. ''How should I know what you might do? You've lied to me before. You claimed you were a businessman, when in truth you were a mercenary. You promised you were through with all that, then went back the minute they called. Even your death was a lie.'' Her arms dropped to her sides, her hands balling into fists. ''Now answer me, damn you! Did you take Lily?''

''Are you asking…or accusing?''

She came at him, a lioness in defense of her young, fingers curled, teeth bared, frantic to protect what was hers. She slammed into him. It felt like running full force into a brick wall, not that it stopped her. She wrapped her fists in his shirt and held on for all she was worth. ''Did you take her? Is that why you're here? How could you do such a thing? Give me back my daughter!''

He didn't answer. He simply closed his arms around her and cradled her against his chest. "Calm down and think."

"I am thinking." She fought against his hold, but it was no use. He was too strong. Too hard. She didn't accomplish a thing, except to expend energy she couldn't afford to waste. The effort drained her, leaving her panting and exhausted. "It can't be a coincidence. It can't be."

"You know me." He held her tightly, speaking low and fast in her ear. "I may be a lot of things, but is this something I'd do? Ever?"

She refused to give up, flailing against him, weaker than before. "You have to have taken her. You have to have her somewhere safe. Someplace where no one can harm her. Tell me you have her, Ethan," she begged. "It'll be okay if you do. You're not a monster. You won't hurt her. And you won't let anyone else hurt her, either. Please. I just want to see her and make sure she's all right."

"I know," he said, rocking her in his arms. "I know. And we will. We'll see her again. I promise. I'll do whatever it takes to get her home."

Faith finally heard her own words, heard herself admit that Ethan would never hurt Lily or let anyone else hurt her, that he'd keep her safe, that he wasn't a monster. It was the simple truth. Even as a mercenary, he'd spent his life protecting others. He'd always had a clearly defined sense of right versus wrong. He didn't believe in shortcuts or gray areas or easy outs. He'd once explained that he had to do what he felt was right. Otherwise, he couldn't live with himself.

Her fear and anger died, along with her suspicion. Dear heaven, what had she done? What horrible thoughts and words had she allowed to come from this craziness? Ethan put honor ahead of everything. He always had. He wouldn't abduct Lily. He was incapable of such a cowardly act.

She sagged against him, her breath escaping in ragged

gasps. "I'm sorry," she said. "I'm so sorry, Ethan. I know you didn't take her. You'd never do anything so despicable."

He accepted her apology with a nod, his chin brushing the top of her head. And, as was so typical of him, that one simple nod put an end to the conflict. Permanently. He wouldn't raise the issue again, or accuse her of a lack of trust, or hold the accusation against her. That wasn't Ethan's style. He'd simply regard the mistake as just that. A mistake. Something he had to accept and put behind him, then move on.

"Can you answer some questions?" he asked after a moment.

"I'll try."

He was silent for a long while, no doubt organizing his thoughts. It was another characteristic she'd nearly forgotten. "I don't suppose there's any point in asking whether she's mine, is there?" His first question didn't come as any surprise.

"Not really." Faith attempted a smile. "She's definitely your daughter, right down to the way she tackles the world, rushing at it full tilt."

"She's…what? Four? Five?"

"She'll be five next month. On the twenty-fifth of January. She was two weeks late."

"You named her after my grandmother."

It wasn't a question, but a quietly satisfied statement. "Yes. It seemed—" she looked up at him and lifted a shoulder "—appropriate, somehow. I know how much you adored your grandmother."

"Thanks." Emotion tinged his voice, roughening the edges. "It means a lot to me."

"Lily looks a little like the photos I've seen of your grandmother. She has the same eyebrows and nose. I have pictures…." No. Come to think of it, she didn't. Not recent ones. She'd planned to have them reframed before— She flinched at the painful cascade of memories, images from that morning that would haunt her forever. ''The pictures are out in my car, wherever that is. I can show them to you tomorrow.''

''I'd like that.'' He hesitated, gathering himself in a way that had her tensing. ''I know this is going to be difficult for you, but you need to tell me what happened.''

''Simple.'' Not at all simple. ''Someone took her.''

''Who?'' he pressed.

''They don't know. A woman. She spoke to Lily and her friend Emily. Then she grabbed Lily and took off in a car. There weren't any other witnesses.'' Faith escaped from his arms. She was so exhausted, even her teeth ached. But she had questions, too. ''Why are you here? Why show up now?''

''I saw a newscast about the kidnapping. As soon as I heard the name and saw her picture, I put it together.''

''No, that's not what I mean. Why didn't you come yesterday? Or last week? Or last month?'' She locked gazes with him. ''Or five years ago?''

The muscle along his jaw spasmed. ''I did come back. It was spring, a year after I'd left. You were in the middle of a wedding ceremony.''

She closed her eyes, the breath escaping her lungs in a soft rush. ''Oh, no.''

Ethan crowded close. ''Who was he, Faith? Who did you meet and fall in love with while pregnant with my child? A banker, someone told me.''

''Christopher was…is…a friend.'' The words were soft. Bleak. She made a small gesture, a flutter of her fingers that resembled the movements of a wounded bird. The motion lacked the energy and passion he remembered from years ago. ''Just a friend.''

Christopher. Ethan fought against a flash of resentment.

Whoever this man was, he'd been there for Faith when Ethan hadn't. Christopher had helped her through a difficult time. He'd been willing to give Faith a home, a name, and care for a daughter he hadn't fathered. And Ethan hated him with a passion he hadn't realized he possessed.

"What happened to the marriage?" he asked.

"There was no marriage. I called it off the night before."

Shock held him silent for a moment. "Why?"

Her gaze lifted to his, her gold-tinted eyes two tarnished smudges of pain. "You know why. I didn't love him. How could I marry him under those circumstances? It wouldn't have been—" She broke off, shaking her head.

"Honorable?"

Her mouth twisted. "Something like that."

He knew all about honor. He also knew that when he got his hands on Jack, he intended to put a fist through him. But he could take care of that later. Right now, it was time to back off from all the emotional turmoil, to give them both a chance to catch their breath.

"When did you last eat?" he asked.

Her brow wrinkled. "I can't remember. Breakfast, I guess."

Not good. "That was eighteen hours ago. You need to refuel so you can keep up your strength."

"I'm really not hungry."

He didn't let her get away with it. Pressing her into the couch, he ordered her to stay put. "Close your eyes for a few minutes. I'll throw something together."

He made his way to the kitchen and poked around in her fridge. She must have gone shopping recently; it was fully stocked. Lots of fresh fruit and vegetables. Milk, eggs, cheese. Bottled water. Salad fixings and dressings. There were even natural fruit drinks with little plastic-wrapped straws stuck to the waxed cardboard boxes, the boxes neatly lined up on one of the lower shelves, where a child could reach them. No question who they belonged to. He removed one from the row and simply held it between his hands. He had a daughter. She drank fruit drinks. A groan rumbled in the back of his throat.

And she'd been stolen before he'd ever set eyes on her.

When he next checked the living room, Faith was out cold. He fixed himself some coffee and gave her an hour. He spent the time up in his daughter's bedroom, absorbing her presence, soaking her into his skin. He sensed an interesting dichotomy to her personality. A baseball mitt was tossed casually onto the floor beside a collection of dolls. Next to the dolls he found a huge plastic tray with a dozen different compartments. Barrettes of every possible shade filled one cubbyhole, sparkly hair bands another, a selection of pebbles in a third. The pebbles made him smile. Still another cubbyhole held a jumble of ribbons, while a fifth contained enough rings for a couple dozen fingers.

After a moment's consideration he removed one of the ribbons—a brilliant blue one—and a matching ring. He threaded the ring onto the ribbon and tied it around his throat. Now he carried her with him, felt her against his skin, sensed her with every breath he drew.

''Hang on, baby girl. Daddy's coming,'' he vowed to the room at large. ''I'll find you. No matter what it takes, I'll bring you home again.''

Back downstairs, Ethan threw together a couple of omelettes and toast, along with two mugs of steaming coffee. He filled his mug to the brim with the fragrant brew, but went a little easier on the second cup, topping it off with a generous portion of cream and sugar.

Returning to the living room, he crouched beside Faith. The day had left its mark on her. A deep furrow creased her brow, smaller ones bracketing her mouth. She'd always been fine-boned, but now she appeared downright delicate. Sooty semicircles marred the areas beneath her eyes, and dampness glistened along her lashes. Even in sleep tension gripped her, tightening the muscles along her jaw and shoulders and down the length of her spine.

Gently, he pushed a stray lock of hair from where it curled across her brow. "Wake up, honey. Dinner's ready."

She stirred, moaning in protest. "Lily?"

He shut his eyes for an instant. He felt like the world's worst bully, forcing her back to the real world. But they needed to talk. He had to get the details of the kidnapping from her. "Come on, sweetheart. Up and at 'em."

Her lashes flickered and her lids struggled to lift. Eyes the color of gold-flecked amber stared at him. He'd always been fascinated by her coloring. Her eyes were such an unusual hue, the brilliant irises surrounded by a ring of darkness. It made a striking contrast to the pale gold of her hair and the creaminess of her skin.

"Ethan?"

"Right here."

She closed her eyes with a sigh. "I thought I'd dreamed you into existence."

"Not a chance." He helped her sit up and handed her the coffee. "Here. See if this doesn't help."

Her chin quivered for an instant before she gained control over it. "Nothing will help except getting Lily back."

"We'll find her. I promise."

"Can you promise you'll find her in time?"

He held her gaze, refusing to back away from the fear and agony that gleamed there. "You know I'll do everything in my power to get her back safe and sound."

She lifted the mug to her mouth, hesitating just as she was about to take a sip. Reaching out with a finger, she touched the ring resting in the hollow of his throat. "Where did you get this?"

"From Lily's room."

"A memento?"

"Not exactly. More of a reminder. A...compass."

Understanding dawned. "It keeps you centered, doesn't it? Focused."

"It helps." He inclined his head toward the dining room table. "Come and eat."

She shied away from the suggestion. "I told you. I'm not hungry."

"We discussed this already. You have to try and keep up your strength. You won't do Lily any good by refusing to eat. You can't think straight without food. And right now our daughter needs us thinking straight."

He'd chosen the right approach. Without a word, she stood and crossed to the table. He sat and ate with her, maintaining his silence until she'd polished off every scrap of food on her plate. The minute she'd finished, he cleared the table and took care of the dishes. Then he returned with another round of coffee.

"You remember how I take it," she said as he resumed his seat.

"You'd be amazed at the things I remember."

"Don't." Her voice was little more than a whisper. "Don't go there. I can't...I just can't."

Her hands tightened around the mug, the knuckles bleached white from the pressure she exerted. He reached across the table and closed his hands over hers. "We're going to have to talk about it at some point. But not yet. This isn't the time. We need to focus on Lily." He allowed a hint of toughness to slide into his voice, an authoritativeness that, in the past, guaranteed him the results he needed. "Tell me what happened. Walk me through your day."

Faith closed her eyes. "I don't want to go over it again. Doing it with the police was horrible enough."

As much as he'd like to leave it alone, he didn't have that option. Neither did she. "I know this is rough, but you have to try. It's important."

Her eyes slowly opened and she nodded. ''Okay. I'll do my best.'' She took a deep breath and began. ''It was a normal day. Well, maybe *normal* is a poor choice of words. We haven't lived here long enough to establish any sort of regular routine.''

''How long have you been in Seattle?''

''Almost four months.'' That confirmed what he'd been told. ''Between the sale of Elizabeth's house and what she left us in her will, Lily and I don't have to worry too much about finances. Don't misunderstand,'' she added quickly. ''We're not rich by any stretch. But we have enough to get by.''

''There's not the sort of cash to make someone think about taking Lily? Even the appearance of wealth?''

''No. Especially not in comparison to some of the other parents whose children attend the day care. If I were to hazard a guess, I'd say that Lily and Emily would have been a kidnapper's last choice.'' Her voice dropped a notch. ''At least, someone after money.''

He didn't give her time to dwell on the other, more frightening reasons someone would take a child. ''Okay. So you moved here a few months ago. Then what?''

''We rented a place until two weeks ago. That's when escrow closed on this house and we moved in.'' She inclined her head toward the stack of boxes grouped against one wall. ''We haven't even finished unpacking.''

''Why did you choose this particular day care? What's the name?''

''Forrester Square. It opened not long before we moved here. I chose the day care because it's close to the paper where I'm hoping to get on staff.'' A small smile touched her mouth. ''I'm a freelance photojournalist now.''

That snagged his attention. ''You did it? You're working at a paper?''

''Well...not full-time. Not yet. But I'm getting there.

There's a spot opening up in a couple of months that they've promised me."

"Good for you," he said, meaning it. She'd accomplished far more with her natural talents than he had. It was just one more difference between them in an endless list of differences. One more reason why they didn't belong together. He frowned, aware that he was allowing himself to become distracted. He focused on Lily once again. "What time did you leave here?"

"About eight-thirty. Normally we leave earlier, but for some reason we couldn't get our act together this morning."

She'd left a few minutes before he'd gotten here. He must have missed her by mere seconds. "You drove straight to the day care?"

"Yes. It's located in the Belltown section of Seattle."

"Belltown." An image of the area clicked into place. "Newly renovated. Upscale businesses. Apartment buildings. Lots of professionals."

"That's it."

"Where's the day care center?"

"On Sandringham, across from Emerald City Jewelry Exchange."

It took him a minute to place it. "Right. Got it. Keep going."

"I parked in the small lot for the day care, and Lily and I walked into the yard. Abby was there with Emily. She was running late, too."

"Abby's a friend? Emily's mother, I presume?"

Faith nodded. "We first met at the day care, and Lily and Emily hit it off right away. We probably arrived a little after nine, and Abby and I sat down to talk for a few minutes. Lily's teacher, Marilyn Albee, came outside and pointed to the girls and waved. I assumed that meant she'd watch them."

"She didn't?" he asked sharply. Too sharply. Not that

he cared. He'd like to have words with the woman about how she performed her job. Then he'd like to rip her limb from limb.

Faith must have known what he was thinking. It was her turn to grip his hands. "Easy, Ethan. She told the police she saw some man hanging around one side of the property, so she went over to confront him. The two girls wandered toward the fenced area by the street."

He nodded calmly enough, but his anger hadn't lessened. "What happened next?"

Faith released his hands and rubbed at a spot between her eyes. She drew inward, as though shrinking from the pain and horror of the moment. "They were out of sight for two or three minutes, tops, when Emily started screaming. We all charged toward the fence, but there was no sign of Lily. I ran out into the street. There were a few cars driving by, but nothing suspicious. No squeal of tires. No one speeding away. Nothing to suggest who had taken her and which direction they'd gone."

"What about this man the teacher went after?"

"He disappeared in the middle of all the confusion."

"A decoy. He was probably there to distract everyone while his partner snatched Lily."

Faith hesitated, then slowly shook her head. "Alexandra—she's one of the owners of the day care—doesn't think so. She says he's a homeless man who's been hanging around for a while. Harmless."

Ethan didn't bother arguing. Time would tell. "What happened next?"

"Marilyn called 911. Abby called Luke."

The name rang a bell. Then Ethan remembered where he'd heard it before. "When I first arrived you thought I was him. Who is he?"

"Abby's fiancé. He's a detective with Homicide and Robbery. He arrived at the same time as the patrol officers. They spoke to Emily. Unfortunately, she was hysterical. All she'd say was that the kidnapper was a woman.''

''Did the police issue an AMBER alert?''

Faith shook her head in confusion. ''I don't know. What's an AMBER alert?''

''It stands for America's Missing: Broadcast Emergency Response. It's an announcement that goes out to all the TV and radio stations immediately after a kidnapping like this. It was named in memory of a little girl who was taken a few years back, Amber Hagerman. It interrupts the regular broadcast so the local community is alerted to the situation and can assist in the search for the child.''

Faith's head dipped forward in thought, silky blond hair framing her face. ''I vaguely remember that being discussed,'' she said at last. ''They couldn't do it because no one caught a glimpse of the car, and Emily wasn't able to give a description of the kidnapper other than to say it was a woman.''

''Why Lily? Why not Emily? Or why not both girls?''

The question brought tears to Faith's eyes. ''I don't know. I wish to God I did. I don't understand how anyone could do something like this.'' She shoved her mug of coffee to one side. ''Oh, Ethan. What's going to happen now?''

''Somehow we're going to get through this.'' He made his voice as positive and reassuring as possible. ''Tomorrow, we'll go in to the day care and talk to them. Go through everything again. Maybe Emily will be able to tell us more. The police will want to speak to me, so I'll get that taken care of, as well.''

''The police?'' She looked puzzled. ''Why would they want to talk to you?''

''They'll think the same thing you did at first. That I was involved. They'll think it's too coincidental that I showed up here the same day Lily was taken. They'll want to know if I have an alibi.''

That shook her. "And do you?"

"Yeah." He offered a humorless smile. "At the time of the kidnapping I was looking at pictures of my daughter. Right here, as a matter of fact. With your neighbor, Mrs. Thorsen."

CHAPTER FIVE

"I DON'T LIKE IT HERE," Lily announced. "I want to go home."

"So do I, kid," Bettina responded.

It was the middle of the night, but she couldn't sleep. Neither, apparently, could the little girl, maybe because the two of them had slept most of the afternoon. Bettina paced from one end of the room to the other. Considering it was little more than a cubbyhole, it only took a half-dozen steps to reach her destination. Did Julian seriously expect them to stay here for the next couple of days? She'd go insane. Hell, she was already going insane. With the exception of a few books and magazines, there was no TV or radio, and nothing to do except measure the floor with her feet.

She glanced at the little girl and shrugged. Well, why not? She didn't have anyone else to talk to. The kid was better than nobody. "So, what's your real name, anyway?" she asked. "I know it's not Emily."

"Lily."

"Nice. Mine's Bettina."

Lily folded her arms across her small chest. "I don't like you," she announced in no uncertain terms.

Bettina nodded, not in the least insulted. "Yeah, well, some days I don't like me much, either. But we're stuck here together. I suggest we make the best of it."

Brilliant blue eyes narrowed in suspicion. "What's the best of it?"

"We have to be nice to each other because otherwise

those bad men will win.'' Bettina threw herself onto the narrow bed opposite Lily's. ''You might as well learn right now that you should never let a man win. It's a bad habit to start.''

Lily took a minute to consider the advice before nodding decisively. ''I want to win.''

Bettina gave her a thumbs-up. ''Good girl. Now we just have to figure out how we're going to do that.''

''Let's go home.''

Practical. Appealing. But impossible, thanks to the dead bolt Julian had installed. ''Can't. The door's locked. Besides, Crock's out there. And he doesn't play nice. We're going to have to come up with another idea.''

''We could 'scape through the window.''

''It's too little.'' Bettina lifted her bare feet so her heels rested on the wall and wiggled her toes. Past time for a pedicure. ''Or I'm too big.''

''Maybe I can fit.''

She couldn't, but Bettina didn't bother arguing. Glancing at Lily, she was amused to discover that the kid had braced her feet against the wall, as well, copying Bettina's pose, right down to the toe-wiggling. ''There's still Crock. He'll see you.''

''If I was a snake, I could get out.'' She thudded her heels against the wall, took a second to consider whether the activity appealed, and must have decided she liked it. The thudding resumed. ''Snakes are very sneaky. A snake could sneak all the way home.''

Bettina thought about it. ''Wouldn't have to,'' she said after a minute. ''If you were a snake, you could just bite the son of a b— Crock.''

''Yeah.'' The kid grinned in pleasure. Bloodthirsty brat. ''Let's bite him.''

Then Bettina remembered the bulge beneath Crock's jacket. A gun sort of bulge. ''On second thought, let's not.''

She brightened. "You want to sing some more? I'm pretty sure that'll drive him nuts. It sure drives me nuts."

"Okay."

With that, Lily launched into a truly peculiar song about a bunny named Foo Foo, bopping field mice on the head, and turning into a goon. She was especially enthusiastic about the bopping parts—no doubt picturing Crock on the receiving end of all that whacking. Even more impressive, she managed to thump her heels in perfect rhythm to the song.

Bettina suppressed a grin, not sure why she was tempted to smile, since she didn't like any part of her current situation. Now that she thought about it, she also wasn't all that wild about her life in general, her future prospects—they were looking particularly grim—or being stuck in a small, confined space with a temperamental four-year-old. Dealing with her had to be the worst part, because Bettina really didn't like kids. Nope. Not even a little. A grin broke free, anyway.

Bloodthirsty brat.

"ARE THE NEWS TRUCKS still out there?" Faith asked, walking toward the nearest window.

Ethan stopped her before she could twitch the drapes to one side. "There weren't many when I snuck in at midnight, maybe a couple diehards huddled in their vans. Let's not give them an excuse to start pounding on the door again."

That made sense. She stepped back from the window and wandered to the back of the house, switching off the lights there. Where before she wanted as much light as she could get, now she preferred to slip into the shadows and hide. Eventually, her trek through the house returned her to Ethan's orbit. His face was set in grim lines. Uh-oh. That didn't look good.

"I'm not leaving," he announced, forestalling any comment from her.

How did he know she'd been about to suggest that? "It's late. I'd like to go to bed."

He inclined his head. "Okay by me. But I'm staying."

Something in his gaze froze her in place, and a torrent of emotions cascaded over her, none of them related to Lily. She was bitterly aware that her reaction to him was wrong, particularly when all of her energies should be focused on her daughter. But that didn't stop what she was experiencing.

A softness swept through her, a gentling, accompanied by a feminine warmth that kicked her thermostat up a notch. She was suddenly, keenly conscious of him—of how desperately she'd loved him all those years ago, and how desperately she'd missed him. The silence thickened, broken only by the harshness of their breathing. He didn't say a word, but he knew what she felt.

A man like Ethan always knew.

She held up her hands, warding him off. "You have to leave." She wouldn't let him suck her back into a situation she couldn't handle. "I told you I'm not prepared to talk about us."

"I wasn't planning on doing any talking." What did that mean? If he didn't plan to talk, that left...action. She sneaked a quick peek, but found him impossible to read. Apparently, she wasn't as unfathomable, because he clarified his comment. "We'll have plenty of time to deal with what's happening between us later on. For now, I want to spend the night here—or what little is left of it—in case we get a phone call."

"The police don't think we'll hear from the kidnappers."

"The kidnappers aren't the only people who might call."

"You mean the police."

"They may find her. I plan to be here if they do."

It took a moment for comprehension to set in. When it did, her eyes widened in horror. ''No,'' she said frantically. ''Don't you dare say that. Don't you even think it. Do you hear me, Ethan? Lily's okay. And we're getting her back. Alive.''

His eyes were like pitch in the darkened room. ''I intend to do everything I can to see that happens. Which means I stay here, where I can remain on the front lines and have access to the latest intel as it comes in. You want me gone, you'll have to physically remove me.''

''If I call Luke...''

An odd response shifted across Ethan's expression, a momentary tensing, as though in anticipation of a blow. He was hurting, too, she realized with something akin to shock. He just hid it better than she could. She stared at him, fighting to see through his mask of indifference. What else was he hiding?

She saw it then. Exhaustion from an endless night allowed emotions to slip from beneath his iron control. She caught the stark loneliness. The feeling of being left out in the cold. The painful stoicism. And, worst of all, helplessness coupled with anger at being caught up in a situation over which he had no control.

He stood before her, tall and unflinching. ''You going to make the call?'' he asked.

She shook her head. She couldn't do it. She couldn't add to his pain. ''No. But starting tomorrow, you have to find somewhere else to stay.''

''We'll discuss it tomorrow.''

There was no point in arguing with him now, not when they were both so tired and on edge. An argument might help relieve the stress, but it would leave untold damage in its wake. ''We only have two bedrooms.''

''Lily's room has twin beds.''

''For when she has friends sleep over,'' Faith confirmed.

"Do you mind if I use the spare bed in her room? Or would you rather I take the couch?"

Strangely, she didn't mind his sleeping in Lily's room. It seemed appropriate, somehow. "It's all yours."

"Thanks." He closed the distance between them, and her awareness of him came surging to the fore, causing her to stumble back a step. "Fair warning, Faith. I am staying. And we will talk about our relationship." With that he disappeared up the steps.

ETHAN HEARD FAITH SLIP into Lily's room two hours later. The light from a three-quarter moon leaked softly through the dormer windows, highlighting her slender figure. She wore something white and diaphanous that swathed her from neck to ankles. She glanced his way with a nervous swivel of her head as she tiptoed toward Lily's bed. Easing back the covers, she checked him with a final, over-the-shoulder look, before inching her way between the sheets. He waited until she was all snug and tucked in before speaking.

"Can't sleep?" he asked.

Her breath escaped in a surprised rush. "You're awake."

"What do you expect after you came stomping through the door? Good Lord, woman. I thought a herd of buffalo was on the rampage."

She laughed, a light, carefree sound cut off with painful abruptness. "I needed to be close to Lily. When I'm in her bed..." She pulled Lily's pillow into her arms, cradling it like an infant. "I can almost feel her."

"Hey, you don't have to justify yourself," he reassured her. "I understand."

"I didn't think you'd hear me come in. Is that part of your training—sleeping with one eye open?"

"Yeah. Tonight's my right eye. Tomorrow the left one gets the job."

"Don't," she whispered. "Don't make me laugh. I don't want to laugh until Lily comes back."

He didn't argue. "Tell me about her," he prompted instead. "Tell me about our daughter."

She fell silent for a moment, then said, "She's so much like you it frightens me."

Like him? "How do you mean?"

"She's charming—"

"You mean...like your father and me."

To her credit, Faith didn't pretend to misunderstand. She'd always considered charm a defect, but maybe that only applied to the men in her life. "Yes. Like you and my father. She's also full of life. Mischievous. Everything's an adventure. She loves people. Has no fear..." Faith burrowed into Lily's pillow, her voice muffled. "Maybe I should have made her more afraid. Maybe—"

"Stop it, Faith."

But she didn't stop. Couldn't, most likely. "I swear to you, I taught her to be cautious around strangers. Not to go with them. Not to speak to them without permission. But she loves talking to people. Sometimes she forgets."

He'd heard other parents do this under similar circumstances. They'd blame themselves, or second-guess every parenting decision they'd ever made. He would try his best to keep Faith from flaying herself alive, but he doubted he'd succeed. He knew from personal experience what guilt did to a person.

"She's too young to understand the importance of your warning," he said.

"I should have found a way to make her understand. In this day and age—"

"Is she smart?"

The distraction worked. "Very. She has every book she owns memorized. And she's creative. She makes up these long, convoluted stories using her favorite fictional characters."

"Huh. I did that, too. I even acted out the stories I read."

"So does Lily. Her latest game is pretending to be different animals. Just last night I was treated to her version of a cat. She even climbed the Christmas tree. It took me forever to find her. I don't think I would have if she hadn't meowed."

He grinned in the darkness. "I wish I could have seen that. You said she looks like my grandmother, Lily?"

"A little. From what I remember of the pictures you showed me, she has the same bird wing eyebrows and aristocratic nose. But her features and dimples are yours. And her eyes are the exact same shade."

"The photos in the hallway made them look darker."

"That was when she was a baby." Faith paused for a minute. "Why didn't you tell me you were alive?"

The question caught him off guard and he reacted badly. Defensively. "Why were you marrying that guy? What's his name?"

"Christopher."

"Christopher the banker."

"You mentioned that before. How did you know he was a banker?" Her voice sharpened, stress replacing the sleepy tones. "Have you been spying on me?"

"I went to Elizabeth's house before coming here and spoke to the people who'd bought the place. They mentioned him."

"Marnie and Bill." When he didn't immediately respond, she added, "The couple who bought my grandmother's house. Their names are Marnie and Bill Robertson."

"I didn't bother to ask. I just know..." He stared at the ceiling. "When I first saw Marnie standing in the doorway, I thought she was you."

"I suppose there's a passing resemblance, if you ignore

the fact that she's..." There was an awkward pause. "She's eight months pregnant."

"So I noticed."

"And you thought I was Marnie."

"Yeah." It was his turn to pause. "I didn't take it well."

"Why not? You believed I was married. Children are a natural progression from there."

"I didn't take it well," he repeated.

She rolled over to face him. "Explain something to me, Ethan." He could hear the hurt in her voice and braced himself for what was coming. "Once you were rescued, why didn't you get in touch with me?"

He'd anticipated the question. It was inevitable. "I did."

"The night before my wedding."

"Right."

"I mean, why didn't you call me immediately afterward? You were held for, what? Six months, you said?"

"Yeah."

"Why wait another six months before getting in touch?"

"I...wasn't well," he hedged.

It didn't take her long to figure out what he meant. She bolted upright in bed. "You were injured?"

"It happens."

"Where were you between the time you were rescued and the time you came for me?" She didn't wait for his response. "You were in a hospital, weren't you?"

There was no point in keeping it from her. "First a hospital. Then rehab."

"Rehab. For what?"

"I was learning to walk again."

She flinched. "Is that why you limp?"

"No. That was a more recent injury."

"You're a fool, Dunn." He registered the anger running through her words. He also registered the fear that drove it.

"It wasn't bad enough that you were hurt once, you had to go back and do it all over again?"

"I'm a slow learner."

"Can the sarcasm. You should have called me when you returned from that mission."

He turned to face her, lifting up onto one elbow. "And say what? Guess what, babe, I'm home? Or how about... come and get me, just don't forget to bring a wheelchair."

"Do you think I would have cared?"

"*I* cared." He fought to lower his voice. "I wasn't going to stick you and Elizabeth with an invalid. How was I supposed to support myself? Better yet, how was I supposed to support you, not to mention a baby I didn't know about?"

"I would have taken care of it." Her voiced hardened. "Actually, I did take care of it."

"You took care of our daughter, and I don't doubt you did an incredible job. But instead of one helpless person, you'd have been responsible for two. No way was I going to let that happen. Believe it or not, there are worse things than having the person you love run off, despite what you may think. Sometimes it's worse when they stay." He didn't give her time to pursue the issue further. "Now I have a question for you. Why didn't you tell me you were pregnant? And don't claim you didn't know. I can add. You got pregnant in early April. I didn't leave until June."

"I knew," she conceded. "And I should have told you."

"You're damn right you should have. Why didn't you?"

"At the time, I convinced myself it was because I didn't want you distracted. If you knew about the baby, you might lose your focus." She wrapped herself up in a tight ball, pulling her knees to her chest and knotting her arms around her legs. "Later I realized that I kept it from you because I was angry. And hurt."

"I wouldn't have gone if you'd told me."

"I wondered about that," she admitted. "But that wouldn't have been fair, either. You shouldn't have stayed just because of the baby."

He knew what she meant. "I should have stayed because I promised you I wouldn't go on any more missions."

"Yes."

It was a choice he'd revisited more times than he could count. "Leaving you meant I was able to save Davis. Saving him should have made everything I've been through worthwhile. It should make a difference."

"And it hasn't?"

He dropped onto his back and stared at the sloping ceiling. Light and shadow played across the surface as the moon flirted with a bank of clouds. "If it had just meant being imprisoned, yeah. That was a fair enough exchange for saving a man's life. But losing you..."

"That wasn't worth saving a life?" She sounded shocked.

"You want the truth?"

"Yes."

"There are nights when I know it wasn't worth it." The confession was ripped from him, the words raw and painful. "And now, discovering I have a daughter, part of me wishes I'd let the man die."

"Ethan?"

He didn't answer, waiting for a condemnation that never came.

Instead, her voice slipped across the room, soft and gentle and infinitely tender. "You may secretly wish you hadn't gone. And you may secretly believe you would exchange his life for a life with us. But if you were given the choice—even knowing what you do now, and the ultimate consequences of your action—you would still have gone after Davis."

It took him a minute to respond. "What makes you say that?" The demand was little more than a hoarse whisper.

"Your honor wouldn't have let you do anything else. You know that." She scrunched down in the bed and pulled the covers up to her chin. "And so do I."

"BETTINA? Are you awake?"

"What is it, kid?"

"I'm scared."

"That's because it's dark. All kids get scared when it's dark. It's a rule or something."

"I want my mommy."

"How about if I turn on a light?"

"No. I want to go home."

"Hey, you're not crying, are you?"

"No." There was a long pause, then Lily whispered, "Just a little bit."

Crud. How did she get stuck playing mommy to a four-year-old? Bettina had made one vow as a child, a vow she'd made a point of keeping. She would never, *ever* have a baby, particularly a daughter. Then had come the other vows. She'd never be poor. She'd never turn into her mother. She'd never let anyone hit her. So far, she'd failed to keep every one of those vows, with the exception of giving birth to a child. That one she'd kept.

In the past twenty years, she'd gone from a defiant thirteen-year-old to a woman with a certain surface polish. Unfortunately, those vows had proved to be a major stumbling block in her progress toward true sophistication. Granted, she hadn't turned into a lush like her old lady, but she had allowed her better judgment to become impaired by Julian's druglike influence. And while she wouldn't classify herself as poor, her bank account wasn't as healthy as she'd like. The generous salary Julian paid her had gone toward classy suits and dresses with designer labels, along with a fancy apartment and a jewelry box brimming with twenty-four-carat gold and good quality gems. Living high cost money.

As for allowing anyone to hit her… She fought back tears. Every once in a while Julian would backhand her. She'd tried telling herself it didn't mean anything. She'd invented a thousand excuses. He'd been upset. She'd run off at the mouth. She'd pushed him to make a commitment. Afterward, he would act totally guilt-stricken, which kept her litany of excuses going, mainly because she'd wanted so desperately to believe him.

But that didn't change the path she'd taken, a path eerily similar to her mother's. And look where it had gotten her.

Bettina threw an arm across her eyes. Damn it. Now, because of her, another little girl would be traumatized, just as she had been—assuming they managed to get themselves out of this. She turned to glance at the bed across from her. A faint light allowed her to make out general shapes and shadows. Lily lay curled in a pitifully small ball. Every once in a while, her breath would shudder softly.

Shoot. She *was* crying.

"Hey, kid?"

"Yeah?" Definitely crying.

Bettina scrunched over to one side. "You want to crawl into bed with me?"

A minute later, a soft, warm body slid in beside her, squirming close. A tiny hand crept into hers, and wisps of hair tickled her chin. Bettina wrapped her arms around the girl and released her breath in a silent sigh. It looked as if she'd be breaking that final vow, too. For the time being, she was going to be a mother. Not much of one, granted. But she'd do whatever she could to protect her temporary daughter.

"Hang in there, Lily," she whispered. "I'll get you home as soon as I can."

"Promise?"

"Cross my heart, kid. Cross my heart."

"ETHAN? Are you awake?"

"What is it, honey?"

"I'm scared."

"I know you are. I am, too."

"I want her back, Ethan. I need her. I—I don't think I can survive if something happens to her."

He swallowed, struggling to keep his voice even. "We'll find her, Faith. I swear we'll find her. Try and sleep."

"I can't. It's so dark."

"How about if I turn on a light?"

"No. No, don't turn it on."

He levered himself upward. "Hey, you're not crying, are you?"

"No." There was a long pause, then she admitted, "Just a little bit."

He turned to glance at the bed across from him. A faint light allowed him to make out general shapes and shadows. Faith lay curled in a pitifully small ball. Every once in a while, her breath would shudder softly.

Hell. She *was* crying.

"Hey, honey?"

"Yes?" Definitely crying.

He scrunched over to one side. "You want to crawl into bed with me?"

A minute later, a soft, warm body slid in beside him, squirming close. A delicate hand crept into his and soft curls tickled his chin. Ethan wrapped his arms around her. She'd come home where she belonged. And soon he'd have his daughter home, as well. Once they were all together, he wouldn't let either of them go. Not ever again. Nor would he walk out on her like he had before—like her father had, as well.

Ethan tightened his hold. Now that he'd found her, he was staying put. No more missions and no more saving the world. Let someone else fill the void. He'd done his part.

''Hang in there, Faith,'' he whispered. ''I'll get our daughter home as soon as I can.''

''Promise?''

''Cross my heart, honey. Cross my heart.''

CHAPTER SIX

BETTINA ATTEMPTED an offhand smile, praying her fear wasn't apparent. "You can go back outside if you want, Crock. You really don't need to entertain us." She kept her voice low so she wouldn't waken Lily. "We're fine on our own."

Crock simply stared at her. The expression on his face sent an involuntary shiver through her, and she covered it by standing and crossing to a small table bolted to the wall. He shifted in his chair and she caught a glimpse of the gun he wore beneath his jacket. She'd seen the gun only once before, and that had been one time too many.

He must have interpreted her glance as interest, because he tugged the pistol from his holster and showed it to her. "Sig Sauer P-228," he said, as though that meant something to her. "Not a huge gun."

No? It looked big enough to her. "Size isn't everything," she attempted to joke. It was a weak attempt at best, one he acknowledged by twisting his mouth into something that passed for a smile.

"You're right. Size isn't everything. Power is. This baby will drop anything it hits."

What was she supposed to say to that? "Nice."

Crock had a surprisingly pleasant voice, the calm, soft tenor as nondescript as his appearance. Every once in a while, she thought she caught the hint of a Southern accent. It wasn't strong, just a slight blurring of some of his words and a rounding of his vowels. But for some reason she found the lyrical hint of the South a stark contrast with the reptilian coldness of his personality.

"German made. Excellent balance." He proved it with a swift flick of his wrist that sent the gun from a prone position in his palm to a deadlier hold, one that brought the muzzle up in her direction. "Nine millimeter. Ten shot magazine."

"Huh." The gruff sound was the best she could manage with a gun pointed at her.

He fixed her with his mud-brown eyes. "You don't want to be on the wrong side of this. There's no coming back once that happens."

Okay, she knew a threat when she heard one. She tried to swallow, but her mouth had gone bone-dry. "How about putting that thing away?" The request was barely audible. "You don't want the kid to wake up and see it. You'll frighten her."

He continued to train the gun on Bettina for another full minute. Then, in a practiced move, he thrust it into its holster and leaned back in his seat. "Mr. Black should be here shortly with breakfast," he said. "You hungry?"

If anything, the ease with which he moved from death threat to the innocuous topic of food frightened her more than anything that had gone before. How did a normal person do that? Simple. They didn't. All he'd done was confirm that he wasn't normal, something she'd figured out long ago.

He was waiting for her answer, and she nodded. "I'm starving," she lied.

The silence stretched between them, broken only by the soft burr of Lily's breathing as she slept. A half hour later, just as Lily stirred, the door to the cabin slammed open. Julian stepped across the threshold. One look told Bettina he wasn't happy.

He had a newspaper tucked under his arm, and dropped a bag of doughnuts and a cardboard tray loaded with coffee and orange juice onto the table. Then he threw the paper at Bettina's feet. "You snatched the wrong kid, you stupid bitch," he announced furiously. "How could you be so incompetent?"

"What are you talking about?" She deliberately injected a hint of irritation in her voice. "Damn it, Julian. I've done everything you've asked and then some. What's wrong now?"

"I'm talking about the kid." He pointed toward the bed where a sleepy Lily sat, rubbing her eyes. "That kid. She's not Abby's daughter. She's someone else."

Bettina picked up the paper and took her time scanning it. "Lily Marshall." She frowned in feigned confusion. "Who's Lily Marshall?"

He jerked his head toward the corner of the room. "Apparently, that is." By *that,* he clearly meant Lily.

"You've got to be joking." Bettina crumpled the newspaper and made a production of flinging it into the corner of the room, swearing as she did so. "I was so sure..."

"Yeah, well, you were wrong, weren't you?"

Time to salvage the situation. She approached Julian, sliding her hands across his chest. She carefully straightened his tie, a pale blue Mila Schon that matched his eyes. "I'm really sorry, Julian. I swear I did my best. Those kids...even you said they looked identical."

Her touch proved soothing. His anger dropped half a notch. "All you had to do was ask them." He glanced at Lily with patent distaste. "They're old enough to talk, aren't they?"

She shot a quick glance over her shoulder at the little girl. The poor thing appeared scared to death. "Look. Why don't we discuss this outside where we can be more private? Crock can feed her some doughnuts and juice. That should keep her quiet while we talk this over. If we argue in here, there might be waterworks, if you catch my drift."

He did, the mere suggestion making him shudder. ''Good idea. Stay here, Crock.'' Grasping Bettina by the elbow, he hustled her through the door and slammed it behind him. They trooped up a flight of steps to a windswept deck. ''You screwed up, Bettina.''

''I know, honey. But it was a natural mistake. I asked them their names, but they wouldn't tell me. I had to act fast.'' She peeked up at him to see how he was taking her explanation. Well enough. At least he hadn't hit her. She worked another angle. ''Besides, I've only seen Abby's daughter a couple of times, and you know how kids are at that age. They all look and act alike, especially those two.''

She'd chosen the perfect tack. Julian nodded in reluctant agreement. His anger continued to ease, but she still had to be careful. It could flare up again at the slightest provocation.

''Damn it, Bettina.'' He paced restlessly. ''How am I supposed to get Abby to keep her mouth shut if we don't have any leverage?''

The complaint held a roiling frustration. She needed to find a way to calm him down, and fast. ''We'll find a way.'' She smiled at him admiringly. ''You're so good at that sort of thing.''

He nodded in absentminded acceptance. ''But we don't have much time. And now we have this other kid to deal with.'' He smoothed a finger across his upper lip, a clear signal of his agitation. ''What are we supposed to do with her?''

He'd given her the perfect opening. ''There's an easy solution to all this, Julian. We can let her go. We can drop her off someplace unpopulated. Someone will eventually find her and return her home. Since she's so young, she won't be able to tell the cops anything that could implicate us. Then we regroup and figure out a different way to get at Abby.''

She almost won. She could see it in his eyes. He opened his mouth to agree, and then hesitated at the last instant. Finally, he shook his head. "Too risky, darling. She's seen us. She's heard our names. I have a much better solution."

She didn't like his expression. It reminded her of Crock's when he'd pointed his gun in her direction. "What?" Bettina reluctantly asked.

"We'll take her to that unpopulated place you mentioned and we'll kill her. It's our safest option."

JUST BEFORE DAYBREAK, Faith experienced a few blissful hours of oblivion, held safe in Ethan's arms. From the minute she'd crawled into bed with him, her fears had faded. She couldn't explain it, but there was something about him that calmed and reassured her. That filled her with a certainty that he, above all others, could bring about a Christmas miracle and return Lily home.

But even as she sank into his embrace, another more traitorous part of her reacted on a purely sexual level. It had been such a long time since she'd been with a man. She reveled in the strength inherent in the sculpted masculine lines, as well as the sheer uniqueness. There was something about the slide of soft feminine skin against its rougher male counterpart that was as distinctive as it was unforgettable. The abrasive sensation ignited a wildfire in her blood, setting off a burning need that shot from breast to belly to womb.

She wiggled against him, relaxing only when he held her close. She still couldn't quite get over the fact that he was alive. She needed to touch him, flesh against flesh, just to reassure herself that he wasn't a figment of her imagination, or that the events of the past twenty-four hours weren't some bizarre fantasy, part nightmare, part dream come true.

As though sensing how she felt, he wrapped his arms around her as he had countless times in the past. One hand settled low on her abdomen, the other just beneath the jut of her breasts. The minute the familiarity of his hold registered, she fell into a deep, peaceful sleep.

It didn't last long. The pounding at the front door started promptly at seven in the morning. Ethan dealt with the first three callers while she was in the bathroom, struggling to wake up beneath a hot shower. The fourth time someone came to the door, she heard him swear harshly and then disappear outside.

She didn't know what he said to the media gathered in front of the house, but by the time she'd finished dressing, silence reigned and the news people had regrouped on the street, maintaining a cautious distance.

"Breakfast is ready," Ethan announced as she entered the kitchen.

He said it so matter-of-factly that she didn't feel the least self-conscious about the time they'd spent in bed together. "What did you fix?" His response was to slap a man-size steak onto a plate, along with three fried eggs. She stared at the food in disbelief. "You don't really expect me to eat that, do you?"

"Yup."

"I can't, Ethan. I'm not—"

"Hungry. Yes, I know." He dropped the plate onto the table. "Try and eat, anyway."

She was too tired to argue. Taking her place across from him, she picked up a knife and fork and dug in. To her amazement, she discovered that she managed to polish off most of what he'd given her.

"I guess I was hungry, after all," she said, offering a weak grin.

"I thought you might be." He shoved a coffee mug in her direction. "Drink up. Trust me, it'll help."

She didn't need any further encouragement on that front.

''What do you have planned for us?'' she asked, before inhaling the coffee in a few quick gulps.

''Your police detective, Sloan, checked in while you were showering.''

''Luke called?'' Faith looked up eagerly. ''And?''

''Apparently, Emily had a nightmare about the kidnapping last night. She was able to give Sloan and her mother a few more details to go on.''

''Is she okay?'' Concern for Emily vied with excitement at learning about the new information. ''What does she remember?''

''Emily's fine, but Sloan didn't tell me what they'd discovered. He seemed more concerned about who I was, the details of my return from the dead, and why I was with you. I arranged a meeting at the day care so we can get the latest update. At the same time, we'll talk to the owners and hear what they have to say. I also need to give Sloan a statement.''

Alarm crept into Faith's voice. ''Do you really think he'll suspect you're involved in Lily's kidnapping?''

''Yes.''

''Because you showed up on the same day Lily was taken.'' It wasn't a question.

''That'll play a big part.'' He shoved a hand through his hair, and she realized that it was the longest she'd ever seen it. In the past, he'd preferred a military cut. Now it had grown to a general white-collar-tidy length. Add dimples, striking blue eyes, a sleepy, come-to-bed grin and a sexy limp, and he was seriously irresistible. ''Fortunately, Mrs. Thorsen can vouch for me. But they might think I have an accomplice.''

''The woman who took Lily.''

''That's the one.'' He nodded toward Faith's plate. ''You through?''

"Yes." She jumped to her feet. "Since you fed us, let me get the dishes. Then we can go."

As soon as she'd finished in the kitchen, they collected their coats and headed out the back door. Sunshine had given way to a sullen sky. Heavy clouds raced overhead, dropping a smattering of icy rain as they scurried eastward, eager to close down the passes over the Cascades with winter's first blizzard.

"We'll take my car," Ethan said. "I parked it on the next street over."

Interesting. "Luke did the same thing when he drove me home."

"Smart move, so long as the media doesn't catch on."

Ethan led her through her neighbor's yard and down a couple of doors to a bright red Trans Am. Unlocking the passenger door, he held it open for her. When she didn't make an immediate move toward the car, he shot her a questioning glance. "What?"

"I don't believe it," she said.

He appeared vaguely insulted. "You don't like Lil?"

"No, no. It's not that." She circled the Trans Am. "I've seen this car before. Yesterday, as a matter of fact. Lily and I were on our way to the day care center. You were driving in as I was leaving. I remember thinking—" She broke off, blushing.

He took in the blush and lifted a questioning eyebrow. "You remember thinking what?"

"That the driver looked familiar," she finished lamely.

Actually, she'd told herself that she had to stop mistaking every man she came across for Ethan. Five years was a long time to obsess over someone. Of course, when that someone was Ethan, it was understandable. He wasn't like other men. He wasn't someone you simply "got over." When she'd fallen in love with him she'd known, down to the very bone, that it was a forever-after love. Five years hadn't changed her opinion any. She doubted fifty years could have.

She frowned, something he'd said finally sinking in. "Did you call your car...Lil?"

It was his turn to look uncomfortable. "What about it?" he asked, a defensive note in his voice.

She planted her hands on her hips. "Let me get this straight. I named your daughter in honor of your grandmother and you named a *car* after her?"

"Honey, it's a Trans Am," he said, as though that explained everything.

Faith buried a smile. No doubt in his mind, it did.

They arrived at the day care center a half hour later. When they walked into the office, the three owners—Alexandra Webber, Hannah Richards and Katherine Kinard—were there, along with Lily's teacher, Marilyn Albee.

"You can't quit, Marilyn," Katherine was saying. She flipped a piece of paper back across her desk. "I won't accept it."

Faith hovered in the doorway. "You're quitting?" she asked, stepping into the room. "Why?"

Marilyn turned, anguish filling her dark eyes. "Ms. Marshall. Faith. I'm so sorry. This is all my fault. I was supposed to be watching the girls and I allowed myself to be distracted. How can I stay after that?"

"Good question," Ethan said. "Why don't you explain it to me."

Katherine stood. "And you are?"

"Ethan Dunn. Lily's my daughter."

Katherine's confused gaze switched from Ethan to Faith and back again. "My understanding was that her father died before she was born."

"Your *mis*understanding was that I'd died." He returned his attention to the teacher. "You were going to explain to me what happened."

''Ethan...'' Faith began.

He spared her a brief glance. It was enough of a warning. He was owed an explanation and he intended to have one. She fell silent. ''Go ahead, Ms. Albee.''

In a halting voice, she took him through the few minutes preceding the kidnapping. ''I shouldn't have left the girls unattended, but the front yard is fenced and they were only a few feet away. And I assumed the threat came from this homeless man. I thought I knew best. I thought it was so simple and clear-cut. Run him off and the girls would be safe.'' She bowed her head. ''I was wrong.''

''And as a result of your mistake, my daughter was taken.''

Her mouth worked for a moment before she nodded. ''Yes.'' She gathered herself. ''Mr. Dunn, I just want you to know how sorry I am. I adore your daughter. I'd have done anything to protect her.''

Ethan's anger still raged, but he couldn't mistake her sincerity. He blew out his breath and faced facts. Blaming Marilyn Albee wouldn't change what had occurred. It would only add one more victim to an overcrowded list. ''Okay, look. If something like this happened again, what would you do differently?''

Answering didn't take her any thought at all. No doubt she'd run it through her mind a thousand times over the past twenty-four hours. ''I'd take the girls to their mothers.''

''And then you'd have approached the man?''

Again she didn't hesitate. Her chin squared with a hint of defiance, and she nodded. ''Yes, I would. Because I'd still consider him a danger to my students.''

Ethan was reluctantly impressed. ''One last question. How many of your children have been kidnapped during your tenure here?''

He'd caught her by surprise. ''None—never,'' she stammered. ‘‘This is the first time anything like this has happened. I swear it is.’’

‘‘I get the feeling nothing like this will happen again. At least not on your watch.’’

‘‘No!’’

‘‘Then why are you quitting?’’ he asked mildly. ‘‘If anything, you’ll be even more vigilant than you were before. That means the children in your care will be some of the safest in the city.’’

Katherine Kinard approached, wrapping an arm around Marilyn’s shoulders. ‘‘It’s a good question, Marilyn. Why are you quitting?’’ She glanced at Ethan. ‘‘Do you have any more questions? I’d like to discuss this with her, if you don’t object.’’

‘‘I’m done.’’

Katherine and Marilyn left the room just as Abby and Luke entered. Abby slipped to Faith’s side and gave her a quick hug. ‘‘Luke gave me the news about Ethan,’’ she whispered. ‘‘I couldn’t believe it! I thought you told me Lily’s father was dead.’’

‘‘Until a few hours ago, that’s what I thought, too. I got the shock of my life when I opened the door last night and found him standing there.’’ Faith’s gaze strayed to Ethan and Luke. The two men were faced off, giving an uncanny imitation of a pair of ornery bulls determined to lay claim to the same pen. She stifled a groan. ‘‘This doesn’t look good.’’

Abby offered a reassuring smile. ‘‘Don’t worry. Once Luke determines what sort of man Ethan is, he’ll back off.’’

Introductions were made all around and Luke gave Ethan a searching look. ‘‘You’re Lily’s father?’’

‘‘Yes.’’ His reply was honest, if abrupt.

‘‘I’m always suspicious when it comes to miraculous resurrections, especially ones with such impeccable timing.’’

Ethan folded his arms across his chest. ''You mean my arrival coming on the heels of Lily's abduction.''

''Exactly. I assume you have identification proving who you are?''

''I do.''

Luke's eyes narrowed. ''Mind telling me why you showed up now instead of, say…last week?''

''Last week Faith didn't need me complicating her life. This week she does. So does Lily.'' Ethan fought for patience. ''Look, could you give us an update? I'll provide you with any information you need after that. But Lily's our primary concern right now.''

''Fair enough,'' Luke conceded. His manner turned businesslike. ''We've learned a bit more since yesterday, thanks to Emily. Basically, we know that a woman wearing sunglasses and what we presume was a bluish-purple wig grabbed your daughter. We believe it was a wig because Emily said the woman's hair started to fall off while she was carrying Lily to the car. Unfortunately, it didn't come off enough for Emily to see the true color of her hair. There's one more thing.… And this is where it gets strange.''

Ethan didn't like the sound of that. ''Strange, how?''

''The kidnapper gave Emily a message.''

''A ransom demand?''

Luke shook his head. ''That's what was so peculiar. It was a message for Abby.''

Ethan fixed his gaze on Faith's friend. ''The kidnapper mentioned Abby by name?''

A telling frown darkened Luke's face. At a guess, that particular detail bothered him, as well. ''She wanted Emily to give Abby a message. And yes, Abby was mentioned by name.''

''There's got to be a reason for that. Obviously, she knew Abby, if she wanted a message passed on.''

"Could we get to the point?" Faith interrupted. "What did the woman say?"

Ethan could hear the stress rippling through her voice, and he crossed to her side, dropping a reassuring arm around her shoulders. "Easy, honey," he murmured.

"Something about them playing hide and seek," Luke replied. "It's not much to go on, but Emily may come up with more details, given time."

Ethan's mouth compressed. "Time isn't something we have in abundance right now." After forty-eight hours, the chances of finding Lily alive dropped significantly. Not that he'd mention that detail to Faith. But Luke knew precisely how short their window of opportunity was. Ethan could see it in the detective's eyes and the grim set of his jaw.

"I promise you, we're doing everything we can," Luke stated.

Ethan moved on to the next item of concern. "What about this homeless man? Faith said he's been hanging around for a while. What's being done to locate him?"

Luke tensed. "What do you mean, hanging around? Yesterday wasn't the first time he was here?"

Alexandra reluctantly spoke up. "He's shown up on and off for the past few months. I truly don't believe he has anything to do with the kidnapping, or I would have said something earlier."

Luke didn't look pleased. "Ms. Webber, you shouldn't have kept that information from us. It could seriously impede our investigation." The furrows lining his brow deepened. "I'm going to take a quick look around the perimeter and see if there's any indication he's been back since the kidnapping."

"Mind if I join you?" Ethan asked.

Luke inclined his head. "Might as well. I have a few additional questions I need to put to you, as well."

"Thought you might." Once they were outside the day care center, Ethan spoke up. "So what do you really think?"

"I think we're in trouble," Luke answered promptly. "We're canvassing the area, but unless we find someone who actually witnessed the kidnapping and can give us more information, we're dead in the water. A woman wearing a blue wig isn't much to go on."

"Have you called in the Feds?"

"They've been alerted. We'll probably use them for some of the legwork. Other than that, they're of limited help. We know the area better than they do."

Ethan buried a smile. He'd never yet met a cop who thought the Feds were worth jack. Asking them for help was akin to admitting failure, something they'd avoid at all costs. He and Luke paused in the area where Marilyn had indicated she'd been talking to the homeless man. A couple of cigarette butts lay near the fence.

"It's something," Luke offered.

"Only if he's in on the kidnapping."

"If he's not, he still might have seen something. The cigarettes suggest he was standing here for a while."

Ethan nodded. He examined Luke's face for a minute, then said, "You Makah?" He referred to a tribe of Native Americans located on the northeastern tip of the Olympic Peninsula.

"Yeah."

"Thought you might be. You know Joe Copper?"

"Sure. Everyone knows old Joe."

Ethan grinned. "Is he still fishing?"

"Hell, he'll never give it up." Luke matched Ethan's grin. "One of these days I expect him to take that old tub out and keep sailing until he falls off the edge of the world."

"Fishing every inch of the way."

Luke chuckled. "That's our Joe."

They continued around the perimeter of the day care center, but didn't find any more evidence of the homeless man. ''Once all the police cars showed up, he probably took off,'' Luke commented. ''He's long gone now.''

''That's what I was thinking.'' Ethan paused in the front yard and squared off against the detective. ''Come on, Sloan. Let's get this next part over with. Ask your questions.''

Luke took him at his word. ''Fine. First question. Did you take your daughter?''

''That's blunt.''

''How about an equally blunt answer. Did you?''

''No.'' Ethan reached inside his jacket pocket and handed Luke a folded piece of paper. ''References. My movements for the past twenty-four hours. I can also give you credit card receipts that prove I was where I say, when I say. I've also jotted down the phone number of Faith's neighbor. I was with her at the time of the kidnapping.''

''That's a lot of proof.'' Luke dissected him with cold green eyes. ''Maybe a little too much proof for someone who didn't know he'd be needing an alibi.''

''Maybe. If I were the sort to play those kind of games.''

''But you're not.''

''No.'' He gave Luke a few minutes to size him up. When he nodded in satisfaction, Ethan dropped the next bombshell. ''Just so you know...I'm going to be looking for my daughter on my own.''

Luke's face froze up. ''I don't recommend that.''

''I'm sure you don't. I'm still going to do it.''

Luke crowded closer. ''You interfere with a police investigation and I'll have your ass locked up so fast you won't know what hit you.'' His tough-cop shtick was the best Ethan had ever seen, possibly because it was a true reflection of the man's personality. ''I'm not going to have some crazed father mucking around in my case.''

''Don't let this pretty-boy mug fool you, Sloan.'' Ethan

did some crowding of his own. "I know how to get things done. I also have contacts in the area." Jack, for one. He'd left the unit the year before Ethan. After that, Jack had returned to the old neighborhood and, no doubt, had a whole network set up by now, a network Ethan could tap into.

"Contacts." The detective tried out the word and apparently decided he didn't like it. "What does that mean?"

"Contacts who also know how to get things done."

That stopped him. "What did you say you did for a living?"

"I'm currently unemployed."

"And before that?"

"I got around."

"Uh-huh. Ex-military?"

Ethan shook his head. "Freelance." He didn't wait for the reaction he typically received—scorn, derision, distaste. "One way or another, I'm going to find Lily—and I'm going to do it my way."

To his surprise, Luke didn't react the way most cops did. Not that it kept him from issuing a warning. "You better make sure your way doesn't get in my way."

"And if it does?" Ethan was genuinely curious.

"You're going to have two knees out of commission, instead of just one."

"Damn. You guys still do that?"

"No. But it sounds good."

There wasn't much more to say after that. The two returned to the front of the day care, where Faith and Abby were waiting. Just as they were preparing to leave, the front door burst open and Emily raced down the steps. Marilyn Albee came tearing through the door after her, her breathing frantic. The minute she saw Luke and Abby, she leaned against the brick edifice and closed her eyes, gulping air.

"Wait, wait!" Emily shouted. "I remember! I remember the names!"

Luke crouched in front of Emily and caught her by the shoulders. ''Easy there, princess. Take it slow and easy. What names do you remember?''

''The names the bad lady said.'' The words tumbled out. ''She said her name was Betty, and she'd be playing hide and seek at Mary Lou's. I remembered when Danny asked if we could play hide and seek. The lady wanted to play, too, and those were the names. Betty and Mary Lou. You said to tell you right away if I remembered more, so I ran to find you.''

''Good girl.'' Luke ruffled the top of her head. ''But next time, tell your teacher before leaving the classroom. After what happened to Lily, she doesn't want you to go anywhere by yourself, okay?''

''Oh.'' Emily shot Marilyn a guilty look. ''Sorry. I forgot to wait.''

Marilyn offered a weak smile. ''Just promise you won't forget next time.''

''I promise. Cross my heart.''

Ethan addressed Abby. ''The message from the kidnapper was meant for you, right? Isn't that what Emily told you last night?'' At her nod, he asked, ''Those names your daughter mentioned—Mary Lou and Betty. Do they mean anything to you? Do you know anyone by those names?''

Abby shook her head in bewilderment. ''I'm sorry. I don't. I don't know a Mary Lou at all, but—'' She stopped abruptly and her face whitened. ''Oh God, Luke. Could she mean Bettina?''

CHAPTER SEVEN

ABBY KNELT BESIDE her daughter. ''Honey, did the woman say her name was Betty or Bettina?''

Emily looked uncertain. ''I don't know. But I'm *sure* it was Mary Lou. 'Cuz that's what I named one of my dolls that lives in the dollhouse I built with Lily.''

Abby turned to Luke. ''Didn't you tell me that Bettina had been released from jail?''

''Who's Bettina?'' Ethan demanded. ''And why would she take my daughter?''

Luke gestured across the street toward the Emerald City Jewelry Exchange. ''Bettina Carlton was operating a fencing operation out of the exchange. I was conducting surveillance at the day care because it's situated directly across from there and we could watch the comings and goings of all the employees. With Abby's help, we nailed Bettina for masterminding the operation and arrested her. She was arraigned and released on bail just yesterday.''

''Yesterday. The day of the kidnapping.'' Ethan fought to organize a mental time line. ''The kidnapping occurred around nine. Was she released before or after then?''

''Good question. Unfortunately, I don't have an answer. Yet.''

''Then here's another question. Why the hell would she take my daughter?''

Luke gave a quick shake of his head. ''Take it easy, Dunn. Let's not leap to conclusions. We don't know anything for certain yet. Bettina might not have anything to do with this.'' He shot Abby a pointed look. ''Honey, isn't it time for Emily and Ms. Albee to get back to class?''

Abby gave a quick nod of understanding and wrapped her daughter in a tight hug. ''Thank you, sweetheart. You've helped a lot. Go back inside with Ms. Albee, and Luke and I will pick you up after work. Okay?''

''Will you find Lily now?'' Emily's gaze shifted from her mother to Faith. ''Will Lily come to school today?''

Faith blinked away tears. ''I'm sorry, Emily,'' she managed to say. ''Not today.''

''But soon,'' Ethan interjected. ''I promise we'll have her back real soon.''

A brilliant smile lit the little girl's face. ''When you find her, tell her we miss her a whole lot, and she can come stay at my house and we can even have pizza in front of the TV. Mommy said we could.''

Ethan could hear Faith's breath catch and knew a response was beyond her. ''I'll tell Lily first thing,'' he assured the little girl.

Apparently satisfied, Emily turned and pelted up the steps, her braids bouncing against her shoulders. Marilyn opened the door and followed her charge inside. The minute they'd disappeared from view, Ethan resumed his questioning of Luke.

''Tell me about this Bettina Carlton. You said you arrested her with Abby's help. From what Faith's told me, you and Abby are getting married soon. Is it possible that this kidnapping is some sort of payback? Carlton is released from jail and the first thing she does is hit the day care center to get even with everyone involved—you for arresting her, Abby for assisting the police, and Forrester Square for allowing the police to conduct their surveillance here?''

Luke gave it a moment's thought. ''If she'd taken Emily instead of Lily, I'd suspect precisely that.''

''Unless she couldn't tell the two girls apart,'' Faith offered, tension underscoring her words. "They were dressed alike yesterday. And the two could pass for sisters. How well does Bettina Carlton know Emily? Maybe she took the wrong girl, thinking Lily was Abby's daughter. That might explain the message she wanted delivered to Abby."

"That they were going to play hide and seek?" Abby asked. "How..." Her eyes widened. "What if this is Bettina's idea of a game? 'You and Luke are responsible for my arrest, now try and find your daughter.'"

Luke held up his hands. "Whoa. Slow down, people. Let's take this one step at a time. We're getting way ahead of ourselves. We're assuming Bettina took Lily when we don't even know if she was out of jail at that point. That's a big jump based on scant evidence given by a four-year-old."

"But it's a possibility," Ethan said. "A strong possibility."

Luke hesitated. "Two serious crimes in such close proximity, within a few weeks of each other?" He nodded. "Yeah, I think it's a distinct possibility. Assuming the timing fits, it feels...right. At the very least, it calls for a closer look, especially since it was a woman calling herself Betty—or possibly Bettina—who snatched Lily."

Abby spoke up abruptly. "What if we're right and it was Bettina? What if Lily was taken by mistake and the real target was—" She broke off abruptly and her gaze shot to the day care center. "*Emily!* Emily could be in danger. Luke, we have to get her out of here!" Without another word, she raced up the steps and through the front door.

Luke swore beneath his breath, then gestured toward the Trans Am. "Look, you and Faith head home while I check into all this. I should have some information for you soon. The minute I do, I'll call."

"In other words, shut up, sit tight and wait."

"Yeah. In other words." Luke tossed the comment over

his shoulder as he took the front steps two at a time and followed Abby inside.

Faith walked into Ethan's arms. ''I keep thinking this can't get any worse, and each time I'm proved wrong. First Lily, and now Emily.'' She tipped her head back to look at him. ''Do you think she's in danger, too?''

''Not with Luke looking after her.'' Ethan ran his thumb along Faith's cheek in a reassuring gesture, then jerked his head in Lil's direction. ''Come on. Let's get out of here.''

''And do what?''

''The toughest job of all.'' He crossed to the car and opened the passenger door. ''For the rest of the day, we wait. Hope someone calls. Hope the police find a witness. Hope someone sees our daughter and reports it.''

Faith slid into the bucket seat and he closed the car door before circling around to the driver's side. ''I meant to ask you earlier and got sidetracked,'' she said as he climbed behind the steering wheel. ''What did you and Luke talk about while you were wandering around outside?''

The change in topic caught him off guard. ''This and that,'' he answered evasively.

For some reason his response roused her suspicions. ''Yeah? Which part made him so unhappy? The 'this' part or the 'that'?''

''The part where I told him I was going to look for Lily my way.''

''What's your way?''

''I have...contacts.''

The glance Faith gave him warned she didn't like his answer any more than Sloan had. Her hands started revving up for action, which made driving a bit of a challenge. He could always point out the small foible. But he was afraid it would hurt her feelings or make her self-conscious. Besides, it was kind of cute. And he hadn't had cute for a lot of years.

"Contacts," she repeated. "You mean other mercenaries, don't you?"

"Some are—were. Like Jack."

"He lives in Seattle?" she asked in surprise.

"Yup. The rest are people I know from when I lived here. Or people I've met between now and then."

"How will they be able to help?"

"I'll have them put out feelers, see if they've heard anything about the kidnapping, especially now that we have a few names to go on. There's also Marilyn's homeless man. He either witnessed the abduction or participated. Maybe he saw something that'll help. My contacts are in a position to track him down, and maybe when they do, he'll be more willing to talk to them than to the cops."

"And if none of that happens?"

Ethan set his jaw. "Then I'll make something happen."

"Huh." She took a moment to digest his comment, before saying, "Wonder what Luke will have to say about that."

"I'll let you know when I tell him. At least, the parts without the four-letter words."

"Spoilsport."

LUKE CALLED SHORTLY after noon to update them on the progress of the investigation. "I picked up another warrant to search Bettina Carlton's apartment."

"I assume you searched it after she was arrested for fencing?" Ethan asked.

"Yes. Now we're going through it again, this time looking for anything that might connect her to the kidnapping."

"What have you found?"

"So far, nothing. But she was on the streets when your daughter was taken. And we haven't been able to find her, which puts her in violation of her release."

"Do you think she took Lily?"

There was a long pause, then Luke said, "I think it's a distinct possibility. I can't point to anything concrete, other than a gut-level suspicion. But all the little pieces add up in a way that tells me we should be looking at her long and hard."

"In that case, I want into her apartment after you've searched it."

"Not a chance in hell."

Ethan attempted to control his impatience with only limited success. "Look, Sloan, either you can let me in for a quick peek or I'll talk my way in. If I have to, I'll break down the damn door. But I'm going to check out this Carlton woman's apartment with your help or without it."

"What do you think you'll see that we've overlooked? We're not idiots, Dunn. We've tossed an apartment a time or two before."

"I want to get a sense of the woman. Pigeonhole her. There are a lot of pieces to this abduction that don't fit. I'm hoping if I see where she lives, I can figure out where some of those missing pieces belong." He added just a touch of pressure. "If you won't do it for me, do it for Faith. How can it hurt to have an extra pair of eyes checking out the place?"

Luke hesitated for a minute before releasing a gusty sigh. "Since we haven't sealed the apartment, I'll let you take a fast look around. But only as a favor to Faith. Abby and I would do almost anything for her."

"So would I." At least they were in agreement on that front. "What's the address?"

Luke gave it to him. "Meet me here in half an hour. We should be done by then."

Ethan and Faith arrived just as Luke's team was leaving. A very unhappy building manager hovered nearby. "More of you?" he complained. "You have no idea how upsetting this is. We've never had a police problem arise with any of our tenants until now."

"First time for everything," Ethan offered.

"No, no. You don't understand," the manager protested. He gave up on a clearly unsympathetic Ethan and trailed after the departing detectives. "We can't have this sort of thing going on. We're exclusive."

"Nice place," Ethan commented as he entered the apartment.

"I'll say." Faith followed him in and turned in a slow circle. "This is serious money." She paused by a series of delicate watercolors and whistled. "Tillis. I'm impressed. Those will run you somewhere in the neighborhood of ten to twenty grand apiece."

Luke's mouth drew into a tight line. "The by-product of a very lucrative fencing operation, I'd say."

Ethan decided to give him a hard time, just for the hell of it. "Or maybe they pay her well at the jewelry exchange."

The potshot hit its mark. "They'd have to be paying her a damn sight more than the other employees," Luke growled. "No way can Abby afford to stick pricey paintings on her walls."

Faith's voice came from the direction of the bedroom. "You can add another minor fortune for the cost of her clothes. We're talking serious designer labels here." She reappeared in the living room. "So how do we do this? I've never searched an apartment before."

"I have gloves for you to wear," Luke said. "Then you have fifteen minutes to look around."

Ethan thought fast. "Okay, here's how we work it. Honey, I want you to go from room to room. Pretend you're going to photograph the place."

The request intrigued her. "What for?"

"See if you notice anything odd. Something missing.

Something there that shouldn't be. Anything that looks...I don't know. Wrong."

The challenge appealed. "Okay. I can do that."

She took her time. As she entered a particular room, she first stood in each of the four corners and studied the layout. Next, she closed her eyes and visualized it from a photographer's standpoint. Finally, she created camera frames with her index fingers and thumbs and pretended to snap off a few shots. A flurry of details sprang out at her, none of them vital until she returned to her starting point.

She paused in the living room, where Ethan and Luke were inspecting an entertainment center, just to be certain. "I know what's wrong," she announced.

"I haven't seen anything," Ethan admitted. "What do you have?"

"There are only three photos."

"Come again?"

She smiled, pleased with herself. "There are only three personal photos in the entire apartment." She gestured toward a trio of sterling silver frames prominently displayed on an ornate glass-and-chrome table. "That's it. No photo albums. No pictures of her family. No boyfriend on the nightstand table. Nothing."

Luke confirmed her observation with a nod. "I noticed that earlier. But I think I can explain the reason."

"Which is?"

"When we first began our investigation into the jewelry exchange, we ran checks on all the employees. Bettina came up with a couple of petty priors. According to the profile we put together, she's a self-made woman. She grew up on the wrong side of town, had an abusive, alcoholic mother, and spent the past ten years gaining a surface polish while shaking the muck of her former life off her heels. I doubt we'd find any family photos or other memorabilia. Why would she want to keep any memories of a life she's trying to forget?''

Faith's brow furrowed in consideration and she crossed to the table to get a closer look at the photos. Bettina was the centerpiece in each one. Faith studied them carefully, struggling to gain an impression of the woman who might have taken Lily. ''If what you say about Bettina's background is accurate,'' she said slowly, ''then I think this apartment epitomizes the lifestyle she's always wanted and has worked so hard to attain. She's built all this, and I'm betting that a woman with Bettina's drive and determination would want a visual record detailing her current success. I mean…look at these pictures.''

The first photo was formal. It was a head and shoulders shot of Bettina. A white fur slid off her bare shoulders and she pouted at the camera in mock-Hollywood style. Masses of dark hair were piled on her head and fell in studied abandonment around her face and neck. Dark eyes stared directly at the camera, the expression too knowing. Jaded. She was clearly someone who'd seen too much at too young an age.

The next photo was informal. Bettina, wearing low-slung jeans and a cropped shirt, lay on a couch, sleeping. Or pretending to sleep. There was something a shade too posed about the way she sprawled across the cushions. She'd gracefully extended one arm above her head, bending it to frame her face. The other she'd draped between the provocative thrust of her breasts and her bared midriff.

Faith picked up the final photo. Bettina, Sports Girl, was featured. She stood on the deck of a boat, wearing a jaunty sailor's cap, a crisp white shirt and a pair of red shorts that barely covered her assets. She'd planted one foot on the railing and held a line that trailed off camera. The wind blew her hair into a sexy tangle and she was staring intently out to sea, though it was clear the boat was still tied to the dock. A blurry row of yachts could be seen lined up behind her.

"This is a woman with a healthy ego," Faith said, returning the photo to the table. "There should be other pictures to show off how far she's come. There are plenty of empty spaces where they might have been. I mean, check out the entertainment center. The arrangement's off. There should be a couple of picture frames where those gaps are. Same with the nightstand beside her bed and the hallway wall leading to her bedroom. I think someone's taken some of her things."

"That begs an interesting question," Ethan murmured. "Why remove some photos, while leaving others?"

"I have an even more interesting question," Luke stated. "Assuming there are photos and other personal items missing, then who took them?"

"What do you mean?"

"The apartment is in the same condition now as it was when we searched it the first time. According to the security desk, Bettina hasn't been back here since her arrest. That suggests the items—assuming any items were actually taken—disappeared before we searched this place the first time."

"Well, someone's been here since Bettina's last visit," Faith commented. "Her toiletries are missing."

Luke shook his head. "I checked that. Comb, brush, toothpaste, toothbrush. All there."

"All new," Faith corrected. "And all generic products. Not Bettina's style. Also, her makeup's gone. So's her perfume. I can't tell if any of her clothes are missing, but I'll bet someone's been here, packed a few things for her and taken a number of personal mementos that they hoped the police wouldn't notice were missing. The question is...why?"

"Okay, let me get this straight," Ethan interrupted. He ticked off the items on his fingers. "Assuming Bettina's our girl, she was released from jail in time to commit the kidnapping and had a motive for taking Emily, but grabbed Lily instead, possibly due to mistaken identity. Between the time of Bettina's arrest and the time the police searched the apartment the first time, someone—not Bettina—stopped by the apartment and packed up toiletries, maybe a few items of clothing, and a bunch of photos and albums. That leaves us with a couple of questions. First, who took the stuff? Second, why those particular items? Third, if this person was going to take a bunch of photos, why leave the three on the living room table?''

''There's only one reason I can think of,'' Faith replied. ''There was something incriminating in the ones that were taken, but not in the ones left behind. A place. A person. Something that would provide the police with a clue to where Bettina was going or who'd she be with.''

''Sorry, Faith. But the time line's wrong,'' Luke argued. ''You're forgetting that she hasn't been here since her release from jail. She—or someone acting on her behalf—would have had to remove the pictures *before* she was arrested and *before* we searched the apartment the first time. Since she didn't know an arrest was imminent, there'd be no reason to remove anything. At this point, we can't even say that Bettina's involved in the kidnapping, let alone the rest of this scenario you've dreamed up.''

''But it's possible.'' A hint of desperation crept into Faith's voice. ''There are items missing, Luke. I'm positive. If I'm right, then someone took them. And they took them for an important reason.''

Ethan leaped to Faith's support. ''Let's say we have a phantom visitor who arrived shortly before the police. They know Bettina's been arrested and it's open season. They can grab anything their little hearts desire. What did they take? Her jewelry?''

Luke shook his head. ''No, we found a small fortune in

gems when we searched the place. We booked it as possible evidence.''

''Were any other expensive items taken?'' He locked gazes with Luke, not waiting for an answer. ''Nope. Sixty grand in watercolors are still on her walls and a fortune in designer clothing is hanging in her closet. All our visitor lifted were photos and maybe an overnight bag. Even more interesting, they left the apartment neat, so the cops wouldn't suspect anyone had been here ahead of them. That suggests that their main objective was the photographs.''

''You're saying that in the few hours between her arrest and the time my team pulled up the first time we searched the apartment, someone came in and swiped a bunch of pictures? Do you realize what a stretch that is?''

''So it's a stretch. Take two minutes to play along. What do you have to lose?'' Ethan pressed. ''Everything we've discussed so far leads us to a simple question. Knowing what you do now—that Bettina's probably involved in a kidnapping, in addition to a fencing ring—who or what would you have recognized in those missing pictures? What would have put a whole new twist on your case?''

Luke started to shake his head, then hesitated. ''Son of a—Julian Black.''

''Who's Julian Black?'' Ethan asked.

''The owner of the jewelry exchange,'' Luke explained. ''Bettina's boss. We considered Black as a possible suspect in the fencing operation, but the logistics didn't work. Abby even wondered if he wasn't romantically involved with Bettina. Unfortunately, no one could say for certain that their relationship was anything other than professional. It also bothered me that Bettina was able to pull off her operation right under his nose. Black's a bright boy. She shouldn't have been able to put anything past him.''

Ethan looked intrigued. ''Do you think he might be the actual mastermind behind it all?''

Luke shrugged. ''There was nothing to link him to the operation. Nor did Bettina point any fingers in his direction, which I would have thought she'd have done in exchange for a reduced sentence. In fact, when Black found out about our investigation, he was Mr. Helpful himself. He's also a veritable pillar of the community.''

''Was Julian Black at the exchange when Bettina was arrested?''

''Yes.'' Luke thought it through. ''If what you suspect is true, he'd have had just enough time to arrange a visit to Bettina's apartment, grab some items and get out before we arrived. But you realize this is all speculation. *If* it was Bettina who took Lily. *If* Bettina and Julian were romantically involved. *If* Julian was the actual mastermind behind the fencing operation. That's a hell of a lot of *ifs*.''

Ethan inclined his head. ''I understand we need proof. But let's play this out just for the hell of it. Let's say, again for the sake of argument, that Julian Black was the mastermind behind your fencing operation. The cops don't know he's in on it.''

''But Bettina does,'' Luke interjected. ''Because she's his lover, she remains silent—for the time being.''

''Julian knows that if Bettina strikes a deal with the cops, he'll go down.''

Faith picked up the sequence of events from there. ''So Julian, sensing imminent disaster, bails her out. And he has her kidnap Emily to silence the main witnesses against him—Abby and Luke. He's not worried about Bettina as a potential witness, because he already has her.''

Luke nodded. ''Now, our girl Carlton, she's a clever woman. Going down for fencing, she'd be out in a few years. But kidnapping a child... We're talking serious time.''

It was Ethan's turn. ''Time she's reluctant to serve. So how does she wiggle free of her predicament? As you say, she's a sharp number. She knows she could go to the police and sell out Julian, and probably get off with little or no jail time on the fencing charge."

"But she didn't go to the police when Julian suggested the kidnapping," Faith argued. "She's the one who took Lily."

"Maybe she's too in love with Julian to turn on him," Ethan surmised. "She'll do anything he asks, no matter how wrong. After all, he's her ticket out of town."

Luke cut him off. "That doesn't explain the message she left with Emily."

Ethan thought fast. "Okay. Maybe Julian is dangerous. Maybe he's threatening her. She starts thinking…if Julian's willing to kidnap a poor, helpless kid in order to silence Luke and Abby…hey, she's a witness, too. A risk, and therefore expendable. So she snatches one kid, and leaves as simple a message as possible with the other, hoping to clue in the cops."

Luke was still playing along, which meant the idea held merit. "Only the message gets a little garbled in the excitement of the moment. Betty, instead of Bettina."

Faith exploded into motion, pacing the length of the living room. "We still don't know who Mary Lou is. It could be anyone."

"Not anyone," Ethan assured her. He crossed to her side, catching her midstep and wrapping her in his arms. "I think Bettina took Lily deliberately because she wanted to get a message to Abby. If she'd given Lily the message, it would have been relayed to you. It wouldn't have made any sense. But if Abby heard 'Bettina is playing hide and seek at Mary Lou's,' she would have made at least part of the connection."

"I think we're on the right track," Luke said. "And if we are, then Bettina had to believe that Abby would understand the message."

"But she doesn't." Faith's words were muffled against Ethan's shirt.

"At least now we have a place to look," Luke told her. "There's a Mary Lou somewhere in Bettina's background, and I intend to find her. I'll also drop by the exchange and have a conversation with Julian Black. At the same time, we'll see if we can't link him romantically to Bettina. Maybe the building security has seen him visit here, or we can find a paper trail indicating they've vacationed together, or one of the other employees at the exchange can tie them together. I'll push to find out who put up the money to bail Bettina out of jail. Maybe it'll lead back to Black. Something. If there's any connection between them, I'll find it."

A quick, hard glance passed between the two men, one of complete accord. They'd accomplished all they could for the moment, and the three of them filed out of Bettina's apartment. As they left the building, Ethan gave the high-rise a final glance over his shoulder. He hesitated, a stray thought intruding, one that filled him with unease.

There were details missing.

CHAPTER EIGHT

GETTING THROUGH the rest of the day without a phone call from Luke was one of the toughest experiences of Faith's life. The seconds dragged into minutes. The minutes crawled into hours. And the hours inched past so slowly that by early evening she was ready to scream. Ethan, much to her frustration, seemed totally unaffected by the wait. No doubt it was an attitude he'd adopted to keep her calm. Instead of finding it calming, she found it irritating. Their daughter had been stolen from them and all they could do was sit and wait. Who could remain calm under those conditions?

As though sensing her annoyance, Ethan stood and stretched. "I'm going to shower before bed. Is there anything I can do for you before I go up?"

A thousand retorts leaped to mind, not one of them an appropriate, let alone civil, response. "Not a thing," she replied in a reasonably polite tone of voice.

His expression turned sympathetic. "I know it's tough, but hang in there, honey. This is the calm before the storm, so try and rest while you can. Once this thing breaks open, we'll be going nonstop."

"Rest. Got it. I'll hop right on that. Don't know why it didn't occur to me sooner." She clamped her mouth shut before anything else could escape. Probably a good idea, based on the hard glitter that turned Ethan's eyes a steely blue. She blew out her breath in a sigh. "Sorry. Nerves."

"Forget about it. We're both hanging on by a thread. It's surprising we haven't snapped long ago."

She couldn't hide her surprise. "Really? You're hanging on by a thread, too?"

"Really." He cocked his head to one side. "You can't honestly believe I'm not feeling the strain?"

"You don't show it."

"Years of practice. If there's one thing I've learned as a—in my former line of work, it's patience and containing my emotions."

"Wish I'd learned to do that."

He shook his head, a frightening darkness slipping across his expression. "No, you don't. At least, not the way I was forced to learn."

Time to change the subject. "I'm going to fix a cup of tea and then turn in, too. Would you like some?"

"No, thanks. Just a shower." He started to say something more, then changed his mind. Without another word, he disappeared upstairs.

She was in the middle of pouring hot water over her tea bag when the phone rang. It was Luke. The minute she hung up, she raced up the steps and pounded on the bathroom door. "Ethan? Ethan, open up! Luke just called."

An instant later the door opened and a cloud of steam escaped into the hallway. Ethan's wide shoulders filled the doorway. It was clear he'd been in the middle of his shower. He'd wrapped a towel haphazardly around his waist, and a streak of foam formed a finger of white from his temple to his jaw. Water gleamed like diamond shards across his chest and shoulders, drawing attention to his near nudity.

"What's happened?"

She balled her hands and fought against the irresistible. She needed to stay focused. "Luke just called," she repeated.

"And?"

"According to the new manager at the jewelry exchange, Julian Black is on an extended vacation. Luke's also spoken to all the security personnel at Bettina's apartment complex and one of the night guards remembers seeing a man who fits Julian's description entering the building on a fairly regular basis. Apparently, the man in question works hard to be discreet about his visits. The guard had him pegged as a married man conducting an affair on the sly."

Ethan punched the air with his fist, causing his towel to slide to a new low. "Sounds like we have our first romantic link between Bettina and Julian."

"Luke also had a message for you." Perhaps she should paraphrase what Luke had actually said. "He wanted you to know that he has everything under control and to...sit tight."

A hint of amusement drifted across Ethan's face. "You mean, he said keep the hell out of his way, or else."

She dug her toe into the carpet and reluctantly confessed. "Okay, yes. He might have used words along those lines. He also might have mentioned what he'd do if you interfered in the investigation."

Ethan snorted. "I'm betting the words *jail* and *throw away the key* figured prominently."

"Boy, you're good at this," she said, impressed. "I gather you're not staying out of it, are you?"

He grinned. "Not a chance."

The grin dazzled her and she couldn't help but stare. Sheer beauty extended from damp, rumpled hair to widespread feet, despite the various scars that marred him in between. Most of them she remembered examining in great detail during the months they'd been a couple. But there were several on his arms and legs she'd never seen before. His left knee, in particular, had a network of new pink ridges. Most incongruous of all, Lily's dainty ring nestled against his throat, suspended by a blue ribbon the exact shade of his eyes. The combination of intensely masculine and delicately feminine made him downright breathtaking.

Faith couldn't help it. Her gaze skittered down a broad path of crisp hair. White terry cloth brought her journey to an abrupt halt. One more inch and she'd have been in sight of the promised land. She took her time making the return trip, eventually arriving at smoldering blue eyes.

His hands reached for the towel. "Just say the word and I'll drop it."

What the hell was wrong with her? It must be stress. People did strange things when they were emotionally unbalanced, like having sex at funerals or crawling into bed with the first black-haired, blue-eyed, drop-dead-gorgeous male named Ethan they came across.

She cleared her throat. "This isn't a good time."

Did he notice she hadn't said no? She punctuated her comment by shoving him back into the bathroom, hoping the old adage "out of sight, out of mind" might have some basis in fact. It was like pushing against a rock wall. He let her work at it for a moment, then gave way and stepped back.

"You were the one who said we had to rest before the storm breaks," she scolded. "Well, that phone call was our first clap of thunder."

"Storm. Right." He started to close the door, pausing at the last moment. "But, just so you know…you can't pretend last night didn't happen."

"Stress sex doesn't count in situations like this," she kindly explained. "Everyone says so."

An eyebrow winged upward. "All we did last night was sleep together. We didn't have sex, stressed or otherwise. But if it doesn't count, how about we make it not count tonight?"

"Not a chance. You aren't even supposed to be staying here, remember? One night. That was our agreement."

"First of all, I didn't agree to that. And second...do you really want me to leave?"

It didn't take any thought at all. She couldn't bear the idea of him leaving. He'd been an anchor when she'd badly needed one. No way could she handle being cut adrift from that anchor now. She met his gaze with unabashed frankness. "No. I don't want you to leave. I just can't deal with our relationship issues right now." And she couldn't. Not while Lily was out there somewhere instead of home, where she belonged. "That means I won't be sleeping with you tonight or any other night. Are we clear?"

She wasn't quite sure who she was putting on notice—Ethan or herself. She could only hope one of them was listening. Spinning around, she escaped back downstairs and buried her nose in her lukewarm cup of tea. Somehow, tea made a very poor substitute for what she really wanted. *Wanted?* She closed her eyes and groaned. *Or needed?*

ETHAN WAITED two full hours, until the clock had crawled well past midnight, before slipping from his bed. Faith hadn't slept in Lily's bed, or joined him in his, but had kept to her own room. At the time he'd thought it unfortunate. Now, considering what he had planned, he was relieved. He dressed as quietly as possible and then crept down the stairs. The third riser from the bottom squeaked in protest when he stepped on it, and he paused, listening carefully. Faith shifted in her bed, but didn't call out. Still, he didn't move, allowing endless minutes to tick by. When he didn't hear any further sounds from her bedroom, he continued down the steps.

He left through the kitchen, locking the door behind him. Rain drizzled with the sort of slow persistence that suggested it wouldn't clear anytime soon. It blotted out the moon, making the night darker and more foreboding. Lifting the collar of his jacket against the raw chill, he crossed to where he'd parked Lil. He'd left the car door unlocked—a rare mistake and one that spoke directly to his state of mind since he'd reentered Faith's life. Babying his knee, he eased behind the steering wheel. Rain always intensified the ache and made him feel years older than the thirty-four his birth certificate laid claim to.

He turned over the engine with a quick flick of his wrist, wincing when the Trans Am started with a throaty roar, the sound unexpectedly loud in the peaceful neighborhood. To hell with it. A little noise couldn't be helped. With luck, Faith wouldn't have heard. Switching on the lights and wipers, he pulled away from the curb and headed downtown.

The streets were slick and empty of traffic. He didn't push his speed. There was no point. He drove through the downtown area and continued south toward a section that combined a tired jumble of warehouses, bars and pawnshops with an even more exhausted jumble of homeless shelters, motels and flophouses.

Doing a tight U-turn, Ethan pulled up in front of one of the bars. It was a rundown place, the brick facade spray-painted over with gang logos. Above the doorway hung a peeling sign with the name End of the Road written in faded, uneven letters. The bar boasted a single dingy window and he parked in front of it, where—assuming he could see through the glass—he could keep an eye on his Trans Am.

Hunching his shoulders against the rain, he pushed open the door and entered the bar. Cigarette smoke created a cloud layer dense enough to hide most of the patrons—if the place actually had any. With the exception of an old-timer passed out at one of the tables in the back, the room appeared empty. Behind the bar sat the owner, his backside spilling over the sides of his stool. He held a book in his hands, one of Robert Jordan's *Wheel* series. Taking a long drag on his cigarette, he exhaled a stream of Marlboro into the cloud layer overhead.

"You losing weight, Dinky?" Ethan said in greeting.

The owner looked up, his ugly mug cracking into a broad grin. "Dunn. You dirty dog. Last I heard you were down Portland way. What the hell are you doing up in my neck of the woods?"

"Slumming."

Dinky wheezed out a laugh. "Bull. After some of the places you been, this must seem like the Waldorf to you."

"Sure, Dink. This is just like the Waldorf." He climbed onto a bar stool. "Give me a whiskey."

Dinky reached under the counter for his private stash of single malt. He splashed a finger into a glass and dropped it onto the bar in front of Ethan, along with a bowl of peanuts. "So what's brought you into the neighborhood? You looking to sign up some men?"

"No, nothing like that." The whiskey went down smooth as silk. Ethan eyed the bowl, but decided it'd be a shame to pollute the taste of the whiskey with peanuts that were probably older than he was. "I'm after information."

Dinky tucked his book under the bar and pulled out a damp rag. He shoved it along the countertop, nodding as he wiped. "Came to the right place. What can I sell you?"

"There was a kidnapping yesterday. You hear about it?"

"Hell, it's been all over the news, boy." Dinky's hound-dog face quivered into a frown. "You involved in that?"

"It was my daughter who was taken."

Shock held the man still for a moment. "Aw, hell. Damn, Ethan. I'm sorry. I had no idea."

"I didn't, either, until she was snatched."

"Like that, was it?"

"Like that." He crooked his finger at his glass and Dinky freshened it. "A homeless man may have witnessed the kidnapping. He's been hanging around Forrester Square Day Care. I need to get hold of him. Soon.''

Dinky nodded, lobbing his rag toward a bucket of dirty water. ''I'll put someone on it.''

''Thanks.'' Headlights flickered against the window and Ethan squinted in that direction. Lil hadn't moved. ''Also, the woman who snatched my kid said her name was Betty, and she'd be at Mary Lou's. We believe her name is actually Bettina Carlton. Ever hear of her?''

''Whoa. Rewind.'' Dinky's brow knitted into an impressive knot. ''The kidnapper told someone her name and where she was heading?''

''Yeah, that bothered me, too.'' Unable to resist the lure of the peanuts, he shelled a couple and popped them in his mouth. They were every bit as bad as he'd anticipated. ''There were two little girls playing in the yard at the day care. The woman approached them, took Lily, and then she gave the other kid her name and left a message.''

''Huh. Go figure. I seem to recall reading something about giving out your name in the official kidnappers manual.'' The stool squeaked beneath Dinky's weight. ''Pretty sure it says not to. Ever.''

''Yeah, it's not the smartest move, I agree. Can't imagine why she'd do it.'' A peanut escaped the bowl and Ethan chased it around the counter with his fingertip. ''Can you see if there are any rumblings on the street? Or if you can find anyone named Mary Lou who might have some connection with all this?''

''I'll do what I can.''

''Thanks, Dink. I'll owe you. Big.''

''Hell, Dunn. You already owe me big.''

Behind him, the door to the bar banged open and a huge black man overflowed the threshold. ''Dunn...Dinky,'' Jack growled. He walked in, dragging a woman behind him. ''Looky what I found.''

The woman smiled weakly. "Hey there, Ethan."

Ethan closed his eyes, anger vying with— Well, no. Actually, it wasn't vying with anything. He just felt angry. "Damn it, Faith!"

Jack shook his head in disgust. "You're gettin' slack, Dunn. She followed you all the way from Ballard and was sitting outside the bar debating whether or not to go in after you. She musta opened and closed her door a half-dozen times trying to make up her mind. Her interior lights might as well have been flashing a neon sign that said 'Dumb Mother Here. Come and Rape Me.'"

Ethan was afraid to get too close to Faith in case he did something totally un-PC, like upend her over his knee. He settled for trying to shove words through gritted teeth. "Why am I not surprised? *Why am I not surprised?* And you give *me* hell for leading a dangerous life? What do you call this?" Unable to help himself, he went nose-to-nose with her. "I thought you wanted safe. I thought you wanted boring. Do you have any idea how dangerous this neighborhood is?"

"I don't care." Faith lifted her chin in open defiance and swept an arm through the air to encompass Ethan, Jack and Dinky. "If this little gathering has anything to do with Lily, then you should have brought me along, instead of sneaking out of the house without me."

"If I thought you could help, I would have. But you can't."

"Well, as long as I'm here…" She glanced around uneasily. Her hands started to buzz through the air like a pair of crazed bumblebees. They picked up speed as they warmed to their task, until they were motoring along at a cool mile a minute—which was just a tad slower than her mouth usually moved. "There must be something I can do."

"You're right. You can go back home."

"Not a chance." Giving Ethan a wide berth, she crossed

to the bar and struggled onto a stool. Then she had the temerity to smile at Dinky. She jerked her head in Ethan's direction, along with various fingers, hands and arms. ''I'll have what he's drinking. He can pick up the tab.''

''You that little girl's momma? The one who got kidnapped?''

Her mouth quivered for just an instant before she firmed it. This was obviously the wrong part of town to show any vulnerability. She forced down every emotion except a healthy dose of defiance. ''Yes, I am.''

''Sorry to hear about your problems, ma'am.'' He slid a glass in front of her. ''This one's on the house. Hope she's home soon.''

''Thank you.'' She took a generous swallow of the liquor, choked and cautiously returned the glass to the counter. ''Nice,'' she squeaked.

Ethan took the stool next to her and nodded toward her glass. ''First time drinking whiskey?''

''Is that what this is?'' She cleared her throat. ''Heck, no. I drink whiskey all the time. In fact, my grandmother and I used to have a—a...''

''Shot?''

''Right. My grandmother and I used to shoot a couple every Sunday night.''

Ethan shook his head. ''Stand clear, Jack,'' he warned grimly. ''Lightning is about to strike. If Elizabeth ever had anything stronger than tonic water, I'd be shocked. And on a Sunday night? Not a chance.''

''Maybe it wasn't whiskey,'' Faith conceded.

''Right. Maybe not. Maybe it was iced tea and you just pretended it was whiskey.''

Her chin jerked upward. ''Okay, fine. So it was tea. But it was really strong tea.'' She emphasized the ''really.'' ''The kind that grows hair on your chest.''

''Yeah? Prove it.''

Jack joined them at the bar and cleared his throat. "You tell Dinky what we want?" he asked, pointedly changing the subject.

"He's going to check into it."

"Check into what?" Faith demanded. "And who's Dinky?"

The owner spoke up. "I am. We're looking into the kidnapping of your daughter."

Faith snatched up the glass and took another gulp. "And can you?" she asked with a desperate edge in her voice. "Can you help?"

"I'll do my best," Dinky said gently.

"Gimme whatever you got on tap, Dink," Jack requested, before addressing Ethan again. "You said you needed me. What can I do?"

"Answer a question first."

"Hit me."

Ethan stared into the dregs of his drink. "Did you know I had a daughter?"

"Aw, hell."

He pinned his friend with a cold, hard gaze. *"Did you?"*

"Four years ago when we went to the church? No. After that..." His massive shoulders shifted beneath his shirt. "I heard rumors," he admitted.

"You never mentioned any of those rumors to me."

Jack became fascinated with the contents of his mug. "No point in opening that can of worms. Thought she'd married her banker man. Figured by then the kid would think of him as her daddy."

Ethan flinched. "You should have told me."

"Yeah, well—"

Ethan moved so fast that it took Faith an instant to realize what was happening. One second Jack was sitting on the bar stool next to her, and the next he was spread across the floor, cupping his jaw, a trickle of blood tracing a path from the corner of his mouth to his chin. Ethan stood over him. "You should have told me."

To Faith's amazement, Jack didn't immediately rip Ethan's head from his shoulders. Instead he nodded morosely. "You're right. I should have. I'm sorry, man."

Ethan held out his hand and Jack took it, regaining his feet. He gingerly probed the corner of his mouth, before anesthetizing it with a swig of beer. The next minute the two were seated at the bar as though nothing had happened. Amazing.

"That's it?" she couldn't help but ask. "That's the end of it?"

The two men regarded her with identical looks of bewilderment. "You want me to hit him back?" Jack finally asked. "Not sure he'd let me. Not now that he knows I might."

"No, I don't want you to hit him! I just wondered..." She shook her head in confusion.

"Ah." He nodded sagely. "You're wondering why I didn't."

"Something like that."

"Because he had the right of it." Jack blew the top off his beer. "I should have told him I'd heard he might have a little girl. I decided not to."

"Why?"

Jack buried his nose deeper in his mug. When he came up for air, he said, "Because we still needed him. And if he knew he had a kid out there, nothing else would have mattered to him except getting to you and Lily."

"You're tempting me to pound on your face again," Ethan announced.

"Afraid you might say that." Jack's expression grew somber. "You know I'll do whatever I can to help you find her."

Ethan sighed. "I do know." He finished his drink and

faced his friend. ''I want you to take the south end. Get up with your contacts and see if there's been any talk about the kidnapping. See if anybody's expecting to come into money soon. Or if the names Bettina Carlton, Julian Black or Mary Lou ring any bells. Ask about the homeless man. Get me something to work with. Anything. Anything at all.''

''I'm on it.''

''I'll cover from Frankie's north. Put out the word that there's a reward in the offing. At the very least that should pull in our homeless man.''

''You'll have him within twenty-four hours,'' Jack promised.

''What about me?'' Faith asked. ''What can I do?''

''Go home,'' Ethan and Jack said in unison.

Not a chance. ''This is my daughter. I don't care where you go or who you talk to, I'm going, too. I'll do whatever it takes to get Lily back.'' She stepped closer to Ethan, emphasizing the seriousness of her statement by bruising the tip of her index finger against his chest. ''And if that means sticking with you, then consider us glued at the hip.''

''You can't do that, Faith. Something could go wrong.''

''Don't you dare tell me that.'' She cut him off with a swipe of her hand. For some reason he danced backward, as though afraid she actually planned to hit him. It was a tempting thought, but not one she'd seriously entertain. ''Something's already gone wrong, in case you hadn't noticed. Sitting at home waiting for a phone call that never comes is wrong. Having you sneak out of the house is wrong. Not having Lily asleep in her bed is wrong.'' Stark pain rippled through her voice. ''Having my daughter stolen is wrong.''

''*Our* daughter,'' Ethan corrected. ''I've had a daughter for five years and never knew she even existed.''

''And whose fault is that?'' Faith retorted. ''I thought you were dead. And you didn't bother telling me any different.''

"Just as you didn't bother to tell me you were pregnant before I went—"

Jack shifted forward, invading their space. "You two don't want to be doin' this," he insisted quietly. "You need to be working together, focusing on that little girl. Tearing each other apart isn't going to help find her."

There was a long moment of silence. Then Ethan inclined his head. "I hear you."

"You damn well better be hearing me." Jack told him. "And you better be hearing one more thing. I've changed my mind." He jerked his head in Faith's direction. "You should take her with you. Maybe she's got the right of it. Maybe she can help."

"Gotta agree," Dinky offered.

Ethan released his breath in a gusty sigh. "Okay. Fine. I'll take her."

Faith gripped his arm. "I won't get in your way, Ethan. I'll just listen, see if I pick up on anything useful."

"It isn't that." He leaned close to her and cupped her face. His touch reignited the wildfire from the previous night, fanning embers smoldering just beneath the surface. His thumbs slid along her cheekbones, while his fingers forked deep into her hair. He rested his forehead against hers, speaking in a low voice meant for her ears alone. "I don't want you hurt. I don't want anything happening to you, not on top of what's already happened to Lily. What if I fail to protect you? It would kill me. Or you."

"Nothing's going to happen to me." She gave him a crooked smile. "Not as long as I'm with you."

"You say that like..." He shook his head. "I don't know."

"Like I trust you? Like I believe in you?" Her gaze locked with his. "I do."

"Aw, hell." He released her and caught her hand in his. "Okay, sweetheart. You want to help? Then let's go."

"Where?"

"A small dive I know." He shot her a warning look. "Prepare yourself. It's not pretty."

She'd thought this place qualified as a dive. If she had to prepare herself for their next stop, it didn't sound too encouraging. "I'm ready," she lied, following him outside.

The rain had eased, reduced to a fitful sputter. Despite getting peppered with an occasional gust of raw, drizzle-laden wind, being outside was preferable to the smoky interior. At least she could breathe out here.

"What about my car?" She'd parked it down the street from Ethan's and it sat in lonely splendor, a beacon for anyone in the mood for theft or some playful mayhem. "It might not have a name, but I'd just as soon not lose it."

"Park it behind mine. I'll have Dinky keep an eye on both of them."

It took only a moment to arrange. Then she rejoined Ethan, and they walked up the rain-slick sidewalk, their footsteps echoing eerily against the brick buildings. Traffic was light, with only the occasional car or truck rumbling by. The streetlights made her uncomfortable, casting everything in a harsh monochromatic glow. They cut through the gloom with an acidic bleakness that polluted everything within its sphere with the same sick yellow-orange hue. Even the rain cried orange. The world outside the puddles of light descended into darkness. Every so often she'd catch a glimpse of a shadow stumbling from a murky alleyway, before it scurried, ratlike, back into its hole.

She couldn't help it; she shrank closer to Ethan.

He welcomed her by throwing an arm around her shoulders and pulling her close. She gave up on subtlety and burrowed into his warmth. He smelled of damp leather and another, more elusive scent that she'd long associated with Ethan. It combined an earthy base with the sparkle of citrus. After he'd taken off for South America, she'd found a bottle of his cologne among the possessions he'd left behind. Whenever she needed to feel close to him, she'd shut her eyes and pull the stopper from the bottle. The distinctive scent would fill the air and, for just a moment, she could pretend he was home again, safe and sound.

Even under these circumstances, the reality was far superior to the pretense.

He glanced down at her. "Scared?"

"A little."

"I did warn you."

The dampness had turned her shoulder-length hair into a mass of blond ringlets that clung to her forehead and cheeks. She shoved the curls from her eyes, only to have them flutter back into place. She blew out her breath in an exasperated sigh. "Fine. You warned me. But what choice did I have?"

"You know the answer to that."

"If you'd been in my predicament, which would you have chosen, Ethan? Somehow I can't see you sitting at home, waiting."

"Not my style," he concurred.

"But it's okay for me? Is that what you're saying?"

"Hey, you're the one with the white picket fence."

She knew she'd been insulted. She just didn't know how. Her eyes narrowed in suspicion. "What's that supposed to mean?"

"What did you tell me you wanted in a man? Someone safe. Someone boring. A Christopher, no doubt." The name flicked from his tongue like a bad taste.

She recalled the conversation. The argument had occurred the day she'd found out that Ethan's definition of a businessman differed vastly from her own. "Yeah, so? What's wrong with that?"

"Not a thing." His words said one thing, his tone something far different. "That's a fine white-picket-fence lifestyle you've got going for yourself, sweetheart. You even have the house to match."

Her mouth dropped open. "Why, you... It's the same sort of house you claimed to want, in case you've forgotten. Or was that a lie, too?"

"It wasn't a lie."

Her fear faded beneath a growing anger. "Then what's your problem? You wanted white-picket. I wanted white-picket. I just had one more small addendum to my list." She poked him in the ribs with her elbow. "I also wanted a man I could count on."

"Not some crazy Rambo."

"Right. And what did I get instead?"

"Some crazy Rambo."

"Exactly."

"Well, here's a news flash for you, honey. Safe and boring isn't going to find our daughter. Nor is Christopher the banker." Ethan yanked open the door to Frankie's. "I am. Think about that next time you're hiding inside that nice, safe, white picket fence."

She paused on the threshold for a moment. "You still don't get it, Dunn. I wasn't afraid to climb over that fence into the real world. I wanted someone safe and boring because I was afraid Rambo would be too antsy to stick around for long. And he was, wasn't he?" With that, she stalked through the doorway and stumbled to a halt. "Oh, crud."

CHAPTER NINE

ETHAN WAS RIGHT. Compared with this place, the End of the Road was a palace. Once again, cigarette fumes created an atmospheric layer. But that's where the resemblance ended. Frankie's boasted a regular clientele. All the chairs that hadn't been broken into kindling were occupied by the roughest bunch of men she'd ever encountered.

The hitch in her breath must have alerted Ethan to her reaction, because he hooked the collar of her jacket and dragged her forward. "Relax." He nuzzled the side of her face, his mouth close to her ear. "Try and act like you belong."

"No one's going to buy that. It's like Shirley Temple meets the Hells Angels."

He chuckled, his breath a warm caress against her temple. "True. But try not to look too much like the bunny who just bolted into the fox's den."

She winced. "Great analogy. I can already feel the foxes snapping at my fluffy white tail."

"I wouldn't worry so much about those foxes, sweetheart." His hand drifted down her spine to cup the part of her anatomy that tended to waggle when she walked. "Not when you've got a big bad wolf panting back there."

She fought to smother a laugh with a lamentable lack of success. "You're doing that on purpose."

"Got that right. It's called staking a claim. Let's hope it works." Ethan paused by one of the battered tables, where a man nursed a beer with one hand while flicking an old-fashioned gold cigarette lighter with the other. Clearly, not a Bic man. The top snapped open and closed with hypnotic regularity. ''Hey, Benny. Is that you?''

The man at the table dragged his gaze from his half-empty beer mug. He continued to flick his lighter as he stared at Ethan. Recognition slowly filtered through the alcohol-soaked pathways leading from eyes to brain, and he groaned. ''Aw, hell. Dunn, you sorry piece of—''

''Watch your language, Benny. There's a lady present.''

''If she's with you, she can't be much of a...'' He caught a glimpse of Faith and swallowed the balance of his comment. His cigarette lighter clattered to the scarred tabletop and he cleared his throat. ''Lady,'' he muttered, lifting a finger to the brim of his New York Yankees cap.

''Mind if we join you?'' she asked.

''Uh...'' He eyeballed his two companions and jerked his head. Without a word they left the table. ''Looks like a couple of chairs just came available. Have a seat.''

''Thanks.'' Ethan made a production of seeing Faith comfortably seated, then hooked one of the chairs with his foot and spun it around. He sat down, folding his arms along the back of it. ''So, how've you been, Benny?''

''Better than you, I'm guessing.'' He recovered his lighter and started working the top. Open. Closed. Open. Closed. ''Heard you was dead.''

''I was.''

The Yankees brim jerked upward and he lost the rhythm of his flicking. ''So, what happened?''

''I recovered.''

Faith watched as an angry frown settled along Benny's brow. His eyebrows plowed together as he struggled to determine whether Ethan was poking fun at him. Being forced to think must have irritated Benny. But there was also an underlying wariness. He might be annoyed, but he clearly wasn't willing to start anything.

''A miracle, huh?'' he finally asked.

''You could call it that. Ever since then I've had a whole new mind-set.''

''Not so mean no more?'' Faith caught a hint of hopefulness underlying the sarcasm.

''Nah.'' Ethan bared his teeth in a grin. ''I'm a pussycat. If I want mean, I hire it. Saves time. Saves energy. Keeps my blood pressure down.''

Benny shot a quick glance over his shoulder and relaxed slightly. ''I don't see no hired guns. You must not be feeling too mean, huh?''

''Actually, Benny, I thought about hiring some guns. But I decided to handle this problem personally. Now that I think about it, I guess I found a whole new level that goes right past mean. Maybe because it's my daughter who's involved.''

The color bleached from Benny's cheeks. ''Daughter?'' he rasped. ''You've got a daughter?''

''Sure do. And someone kidnapped her.''

''Wasn't me.'' He half rose in his chair. ''On the head of my sainted mother, I swear I had nothing to do with it.''

Ethan settled a hand on the man's shoulder and shoved him back into his chair. ''Your sainted mother's doing time for grand theft auto. Even so, I believe you, Benny. I believe you. Relax. All I'm after is information.''

''You're frightening him,'' Faith interrupted. She offered Benny a wide, friendly smile. Ethan had once called it her cheerleader smile. ''Don't let Ethan worry you. He's retired.''

Benny rewarded her with a sour look. ''Just a regular Joe now, huh?''

''Exactly,'' Ethan agreed. He didn't waste further time on preliminaries, but gave a brief overview of the past forty hours. ''We're particularly interested in this homeless man who was seen hanging around Forrester Square Day Care. We think he's a regular."

"I don't have nothing to do with the crazies." He shook his head as rapidly as he flicked his lighter. "No, sirree. Not me."

"Hadn't heard he was crazy."

Benny shrugged, his gaze sliding away. "Far as I'm concerned, they're all crazy."

Ethan persisted. "This guy's in his sixties. Six foot. Thin. Gray hair and beard, both long. Maybe has blue eyes."

"Hell, man. That could be half the bums in the city."

"Could be. But it's not. This guy has a thing for the day care center."

Benny's chin jerked up and he focused in on Ethan, his lighter held tight in his grasp. "Sorry. Don't sound familiar."

"Put out some feelers."

"Yeah, sure. Whatever."

"That's all I'm asking. There's a few bucks in it for you, if you can help us out."

Benny showed momentary interest. "How much?"

Ethan mentioned a figure that left Faith blinking. Apparently Benny didn't agree with her assessment. The interested light faded from his eyes and the conversation dried up after that. As they rose to leave, Benny addressed Faith.

"Don't know why you're with him, baby cakes, but take my advice. Get rid of him, soon as you can. He's trouble."

"I know he is." She released a sigh. "But I'm afraid I can't get rid of him."

"Why not?"

She planted her hands on the table and leaned in, fighting not to choke on the alcohol fumes billowing off the man. "Because I'm the hired gun. And compared to me, he really is a pussycat." She reached out and locked her hands around the lighter Benny held. "You see, that little girl who was taken is my daughter, too. And when I find whoever took her, he's going down. Hard."

"She'd do it, too," Ethan stated cheerfully. "She may look like a bimbo cheerleader, but the woman's a total psycho."

Yeah. Right. Like anyone would believe that. Still, she could try and pull it off. She nodded in confirmation. "Total...psycho."

She snapped the lid of the lighter closed, accidentally catching the vulnerable web of skin between Benny's thumb and index finger. He yanked his hand away and the lighter clattered to the table. "I don't know nothin'," he yelped.

Faith opened her mouth to apologize. Before she could, Ethan swept her away from the table. "You've done enough damage, sweetheart. Time to go."

She could only hope she didn't look as relieved as she felt. "Good idea."

Ethan turned to face her as soon as they exited the bar. "FYI. Never apologize when you're trying to come across as a total psycho."

"Sort of blows my cover, huh?"

He grinned. "Just a little." He jerked his head toward the bar. "So what do you think about Benny?"

"I think he's lying."

Ethan lifted his collar against a sudden hiccup of rain. "Why?"

She could picture it in her mind's eye, as though through the lens of a camera. A whole series of snapshots flashed past in swift succession. "Most of the time you two were talking, he played with that stupid cigarette lighter. He kept flipping it open and closed. Regular rhythm."

"So?"

"Well, when you started asking him about the homeless man, he stopped flipping it altogether. And he stared you straight in the eye, remember? Like he was willing you to believe him.''

''Okay. Assuming he knows something, why would he want to keep the information to himself?''

She shrugged. ''I'm not sure. Let me think about it for a while.'' Her gaze drifted up and down the street. ''Where next?''

''A few more places.'' Ethan slanted her a quick look out of the corner of his eye. ''You, uh, did okay in there.''

''For a white-picket cheerleading bimbo?'' She turned up the collar of her jacket the same way he had and put a hint of a tough chick swagger in her step. With luck she wouldn't throw her hips out of joint. ''Lead on.''

The next several stops were eerily similar to Frankie's. At two of the establishments, Ethan found contacts he knew from years before. He went through the same routine as with Benny, and Faith teamed him with equal success.

Once again, she picked up on something peculiar in their attitude. It wasn't quite as apparent as the incident with the lighter. It was more subtle than that—an odd shutting down. Ethan caught it as well, and she could tell it bothered him. His mood grew darker with each subsequent incident. By the time they arrived at their final stop, a run-down motel, he was deep in thought.

A woman sat behind the registration desk, and if Lily didn't know better, she'd have sworn it was Dinky in drag. The woman growled a greeting around the stub of a cigar. As soon as she opened her mouth, Faith realized it couldn't be Dinky. This woman's voice was a full octave lower. Harvey Fierstein, without the accent. ''Well, if it ain't Mr. Gorgeous. As I live and breathe. How's it hangin', and when are you gonna show me?''

''Any day, any time, any place.'' He leaned across the counter and gave her a smacking kiss on her cheek. ''How are you, Maudie?''

To Faith's astonishment, the woman blushed like a schoolgirl. "Same old, same old. How 'bout yourself? Heard you racked up that knee of yours on your last mission."

He studiously avoided looking in Faith's direction. "'Fraid so."

"Also heard that's put you out of the business for good."

"You hear a lot."

She shrugged her massive shoulders. "In my line of work, it's smart to keep your ears open. Never know what information might give a boost to my retirement fund."

"In that case, I have something that might help you out."

"Well, don't keep it to yourself, handsome. Lay it on me."

"I'm looking for a woman by the name of Bettina Carlton. There might also be a woman named Mary Lou involved. Neither of them would be opposed to snatching a kid."

"The Lily Marshall kidnapping." Maudie looked at Faith. "You the mother?"

"Yes."

"And I'm the father," Ethan added.

Maudie's jaw hit the floor. Her cigar would have, too, if her bright orange lipstick hadn't kept it glued to her mouth. "Damn, boy. I didn't know."

"Came as news to me, too."

She slanted Faith a swift, searching look. Faith withstood the scrutiny with a pretense of calm, though she found she couldn't quite control her hands. Strangely, they seemed to have a mind of their own, fluttering to her hair, to the collar of her jacket, to the seat of her jeans, before plunging into her pockets. If she thought she could have gotten away with her total-psycho routine, she would have. But somehow she figured Maudie would see right through it and be less than impressed. After an endless moment, the huge woman nodded in satisfaction, and Faith relaxed. Apparently, she'd passed whatever test Maudie had set, though she had no idea how she'd done it. Dumb luck, no doubt.

The woman turned back to Ethan. "First, none of my girls would steal a kid. If any of them were into that sort of badness, I'd know. And the minute I did know, they'd be out on their asses."

"Figured as much."

"And second, I don't know a Bettina Carlton or a Mary Lou. But I can check around. Maybe somebody knows somebody who knows somebody." She drummed a flock of flamingos against the countertop. At least, Faith assumed the pink birds decorating Maudie's artificial nails were flamingos. Maudie noted her interest and fanned her fingers for Faith's inspection. "They're eagles."

"Huh." Embarrassed eagles by the look of them.

"I'm the patriotic sort, particularly when it comes to the Eighth Amendment." At Faith's blank look, she explained, "It's against the law to inflict cruel and unusual punishment on our nation's citizenry. Some poor schmo gets horny and can't get any, I consider that cruel and unusual punishment. So, I do my patriotic duty to make sure that doesn't happen."

Faith couldn't help it. She laughed. "Has the judge ever bought that one?"

Maudie winked. "I plan to run it by him the next time he drops in."

Ethan interrupted the girl talk. "If you have any information for me, give Jack a heads up."

"I'll do that." She tossed Ethan a flirtatious smile around her cigar. "You come back and visit soon."

"I'll do my best."

Maudie blew a stream of smoke in Faith's direction. "You make sure he doesn't, honey."

Faith grinned. "I'll do my best."

"And if you see Dinky, tell him to go screw himself." She released a raucous cackle of laughter. At Faith's puzzled expression, she explained, "Dink and me, we used to enjoy a relationship, if you catch my drift. Lasted a whole two years until I discovered I loved his cigars more than him. That's when we split. I went one way with the cigars, he went the other with my Marlboros. We've lived happily ever after ever since."

Ethan chuckled. "You can't argue with true love."

Maudie's humor faded and she turned serious. "No, you can't," she agreed, angling her head in Faith's direction in a not-too-subtle hint.

A minute later they were on the street. The temperature had dropped a notch, and though the rain came down in earnest, deepening the gloom, a hint of gray edged the buildings to the east. Dawn wasn't far off.

"We've done all we can for now," Ethan said. "Time to head home."

They walked back toward Dinky's, the bitterly cold rain making it an unpleasant process. Halfway there, Faith stopped dead in her tracks. A series of snapshots from Frankie's flashed through her head again, pausing now and again at key intervals. Then another series flipped past, scenes from the other bars they'd visited. Finally, the missing piece clicked.

"I know why Benny—or all of the others, for that matter—didn't want to tell us about the homeless man," she announced.

"Why?"

"Someone else is looking for our Homeless Harry."

Ethan frowned. "Who?"

"Someone who saw him there. Someone who doesn't want Harry telling the cops what he witnessed."

"The kidnapper."

Faith nodded. "Exactly. And I'll tell you one more thing."

"What?"

"The reason no one jumped at your offer for a reward? I'll bet my last nickel they were offering a larger one than you were."

ETHAN RELUCTANTLY turned off the pounding spray from the shower and grabbed the towel Faith had left for him. Exhaustion dogged his every step, but he'd needed the second shower to wash away the stench of cigarette smoke and cheap booze. His leg, pissed off at having been tortured by so much walking, sent a complaint screaming from his ankle clear up to his chin. He jerked open the medicine cabinet and grabbed a bottle of over-the-counter pain relievers. He popped a half dozen.

Wrapping a towel around his waist, he wandered into the bedroom. Faith had returned to Lily's bed and was sound asleep, a tattered stuffed lion clutched in her arms. No doubt it was one of his daughter's favorite toys. Ethan stood watching Faith for a long moment, his pain now as much mental as it was physical.

God, she was beautiful. Sexy. Funny. Intelligent. Helpful. More than helpful, if the truth be known. He'd never had a woman fit so perfectly into his life before. From the moment they'd left Dinky's, they'd worked together in total harmony. It made him hungry to experience that again. And not just while they hunted for Lily. He wanted to experience it in all aspects of his life with her—at home, at work, as a parent.

As a husband.

Yeah, right, Dunn. What were the chances of that happening? She wasn't meant for him. She never had been. Still…he couldn't resist her now, any more than he had five years ago. He glanced toward his bed and then back at Faith again. Lily's bed wasn't built for two. It was barely built for one. "Tough," he muttered. Right now, holding Faith outweighed any potential discomfort.

Easing onto the mattress, Ethan wrapped his arms around her, pulling her close. The top of her head filled the curve just beneath his chin. She didn't wake. But she did squirm closer, her sweetly rounded bottom pressing against his groin. She felt so good. Soft. Fragrant. Warm. Early morning sunshine streamed through the dormer window, bleaching her hair almost white. The long silky strands clung to the smattering of whiskers along his jaw and his chin sank deeper into the softness. *Heaven couldn't be this wonderful,* was his last conscious thought.

And then he slept.

THE NIGHTMARE CAME two hours later, fast and deadly, catching Ethan at his most vulnerable. A man's accented voice whispered its hateful message while his boot heel ground into a treasured photograph. A strap cracked against a wooden table and then came at Ethan, exploding through the air. He fought back, as he always did. And as always, he failed.

He awoke just as he crashed to the floor. The nightmare still rode him, clouding his mind. But this time he knew he wasn't alone. A woman was with him on the floor and they were entwined in a tangle of arms and legs.

"Ethan?" she said in a bewildered voice. "What happened?"

He scrambled away from her. It wasn't safe to get too close to him immediately after a nightmare. His confusion sometimes caused him to lash out. He sucked in a breath. Then another.

The woman crept closer. "Ethan?"

"Don't. Stay back." The guttural order stopped her in her tracks. Her voice finally registered. Faith. He was with

Faith. "Give me a minute, honey. I'll be all right if you just give me a minute."

She curled up on the floor a few feet away, a pool of white against the dark carpet. "What's wrong? What happened?"

"A dream."

"A dream? Or a nightmare?"

The pounding of his heart eased ever so slightly. "Does it matter?"

She blew out her breath in a sigh. "Oh, Ethan, what have you done to yourself?"

"Don't worry about it. It doesn't happen often. Call it an occupational hazard."

"That's quite a hazard." He could make out the graceful movement of her hands in the darkness and found that it helped center him. "You said it doesn't happen often. Are we talking once a year not often? Once a month? Once a week? Or are we talking about not often, like it happens every night?"

He winced at a tone that was half sarcastic and half compassionate. "Not often, like...every other night. Sometimes more."

"Oh, Ethan." The sarcasm vanished and she crept closer. The delicate give and take of her breath came from just inches away. Her hand settled briefly against his chest before fluttering again. "I'm so sorry."

"Don't."

"Don't be sorry?"

"Don't touch me. Not yet. It's..." It was a struggle pushing the words past his locked jaw. "It's not safe."

"Dear heaven, Ethan. Is it really that serious?"

"Yeah, it's that serious. Serious enough that I shouldn't have taken the risk of sleeping with you. I knew it the other night when you crawled into bed with me." He'd been a fool, more caught up in his own needs than in protecting those in his care. "To risk it again tonight—it was foolish. I shouldn't have. But I thought… I couldn't—"

Her hands cupped his shoulders. No fear. No hesitation. Just lightness and warmth and a loving determination. "You wouldn't hurt me. Not ever."

"Not on purpose, maybe. But by mistake. Without meaning to."

"It wouldn't happen."

She said it as though it were the simplest equation in the world, as though there weren't any other possible option. He closed his eyes. He'd led such a tough life, had fought so long and hard. And she felt good. Incredible. Just for a moment he needed some gentleness in his life. Some softness. A woman's touch. He leaned into her and her mouth collided with Lily's ring, resting in the hollow at the base of his throat. She kissed him with a featherlight caress.

And with that one simple touch, she decimated his self-control. His head arched backward and his throat worked, but no sound escaped. It was too much. Coming on the heels of his nightmare, it was way too much, too soon. He flung an arm around her, wrapping her in a band of steel. Feminine collided against masculine, pressing tight. It helped ease the pain, but still wasn't enough. Her hands left his shoulders to brush his hair, then along his jaw, next his shoulders and arms, sending sensations rioting through him.

He cupped her face, taking her mouth with bruising thoroughness. He was too rough. He knew it, but couldn't seem to figure out how to ease up. He'd forgotten how to be gentle—assuming he'd ever known.

But she didn't pull away. She held on, opening to him, quieting the raging emotions with a series of lingering kisses. And she spoke to him between each one. He had no idea what she said, but the words offered sustenance, as well as reassurance. The terrible pain that rode him eased, and he wrestled with his self-control, finally winning the battle.

And then he gave back to her. He found the gentleness he needed, a gentleness he'd never been capable of before. He caressed her mouth, slipping in with all the tenderness in his possession. To his amazement, he found he had an infinite supply, perhaps because it was Faith. A tiny moan rumbled deep in her throat and he inhaled it, exchanging it with one of his own.

His hands slid from around her back, seeking a more intimate touch. He cupped her breasts and stroked his thumbs over the tips. Once. Twice. A desperate need gripped him, spiraling rapidly out of control. He inhaled sharply, struggling with his baser desires. If he took this any further, he wouldn't be able to stop.

As though sensing his thoughts, she reluctantly pulled free of his embrace. "Are you all right now?" she asked.

"Some of me is."

It didn't take her long to figure out which parts were still in pain. "Sorry. But the rest of you is out of luck."

"Yeah. Figured you'd say that." He stood, stepping back a pace. "I'm sorry if I frightened you."

"You didn't." She followed suit and stood, as well. Matching his movements, she fell back a step, too. "I'm worried about you, Ethan."

"Don't be. You have enough to worry about without taking on my problems." Exhaustion was setting in and he jerked his head toward the bed across from Lily's. "I'll take the spare." To his disappointment, she didn't try and talk him out of it.

They retreated to their separate beds. After a moment, she called to him. "Ethan?"

"Yeah?"

"Sweet dreams, okay? Don't argue, just do it. For me."

He couldn't help it; he smiled. "Yeah, sure."

This time when he slept, there were no more nightmares. He did it for Faith.

CHAPTER TEN

THE PHONE RANG just as they were finishing brunch the next morning. Faith answered it, handing the receiver to Ethan. "It's Dinky," she mouthed.

"Yeah, Dink. You have some news for me?"

"I need you to get down here. Fast."

"What's wrong?" Ethan asked.

"I'll explain once you're here."

The line went dead and Ethan grabbed their coats off the back of the couch. He tossed Faith hers. "Time to roll. Something's breaking down at Dink's."

"What?" She stepped in front of him, forcing him to halt midstride. "You asked Dinky what was wrong. *Is* there something wrong? Does he have information about Lily?"

Ethan could tell she was struggling to maintain her composure, but stress fractures were developing around the edges. "I assume it has to do with her kidnapping," he replied calmly. "But he didn't give me any details. It can't be too serious or he'd have called the cops."

Judging by her expression, she didn't care for his response. Unfortunately, as much as he'd like to offer something better, he couldn't give her answers he didn't have. They piled into Lil and headed for the city. The trip seemed to take forever. Christmas traffic clogged their path, and pedestrians cut in and out of cars as they crisscrossed the streets. Forty-five minutes later Ethan pulled up outside of the End of the Road and parked. In daylight the bar looked far worse than at night, if that were possible. An unforgiving, winter-stark sun spotlighted each and every flaw. The place appeared deserted.

He rapped his knuckles against the dirt-streaked window and waited. A few minutes later, Dinky cracked open the door. He glanced nervously up and down the street before waving them in. "We gotta move fast."

"What's the problem?"

"The problem is...I found your homeless man."

Faith's breath escaped in an excited gasp. "That's not a problem. That's wonderful."

"Not really. Come on back and you'll see what I mean."

They followed Dinky into a room off the back of his bar. An emaciated man sat on a chair, staring vacantly into space. His hair was long and gray. A thick beard and mustache covered the lower half of his face. His clothes hung on him and he looked as if he hadn't had a decent meal in weeks. In his hands he clutched a paper bag.

Ethan swore beneath his breath. "Is he drunk, stoned or both?"

"Take your pick. Your guess is as good as mine."

"Huh." He crouched in front of the man, giving him a cursory examination. No reaction. He waved a hand back and forth. Still no reaction. Damn. Ethan stood and took a step back. "Dinky, rustle up some grub, will you? He could be diabetic. Maybe a decent meal will help bring him around."

"Can do." Dinky hesitated. "There's another problem you need to know about."

Something in his tone alerted Ethan. "What?"

"Not here." He jerked his chin toward the door, and Ethan followed. After checking to make sure Faith was out of earshot, Dinky said, "Word's out on the street."

"What word?"

"About the old-timer. You're not the only one looking for him."

That confirmed Faith's suspicions. ''We wondered.''

''Somebody's laying down serious money, Ethan. Twenty-five gees for the guy.''

''You gotta be kidding me. Twenty-five gees?'' That couldn't be right. He shook his head. ''No way.''

''It gets worse. It's twenty-five—dead or alive.'' Dinky's hands trembled as he lit a Marlboro. ''If something isn't done, and I mean soon, the streets are gonna be littered with dead bums.''

''Damn it to hell.'' Ethan shot a swift glance over his shoulder and then turned back to Dinky. ''Who would be willing to pay twenty-five thousand for him?''

''You say he witnessed your kidnapping?''

''Or was in on it.''

Dinky shook his head. ''Not likely. He doesn't strike me as the dependable sort. Who'd want him involved? Too risky.''

''So, if he isn't involved in the kidnapping—''

''Then your first guess is right and he witnessed it,'' confirmed Dinky. ''And if he's a witness, I'll give you one good guess who might put a bounty out on him.''

Damn. Ethan glanced at the old man again. It was looking more and more as though the scenario he and Faith had come up with at Bettina's apartment was right. Julian Black had, indeed, intended to kidnap Emily in order to keep Abby and Luke from testifying in the fencing case. It also meant Black had both the motive and the necessary cash to order the hit on any witnesses to the abduction. Ethan's hands balled into fists. That made it absolutely imperative that they find Lily, and soon. The minute Black realized his plan to silence Abby and Luke had no chance of success, he'd start eliminating everyone and everything that could tie him to the two crimes.

''Okay, Dink,'' Ethan said. ''Go ahead and throw together whatever you can spare from your fridge. In the meantime, I'll try and talk to our friend and see what shakes loose.''

''You got it.'' Dinky puffed out a cloud of smoke. ''But once you're done, you gotta get him out of here. Twenty-five grand in this neighborhood is serious money. Hell, you could buy half the homeless in Seattle for twenty-five hundred. If anyone suspects he's here, they'll rip my place to pieces looking for him.''

''I'll take care of it.''

Ethan reentered the room. Faith was kneeling in front of the man. She'd gathered his hands in hers and was speaking softly to him. ''...don't know if you have any children. But if you do, Harry, you must understand how frightened we are.''

To Ethan's surprise the homeless man nodded. Either he'd told her his name or she'd gone with Homeless Harry. Whichever, he seemed to accept the designation. There also seemed to be a light flickering in the attic. ''Harry'' listened intently, the vacant expression fading from his gaze.

''We'd do anything to save our little girl,'' she continued.

''Yes,'' the man whispered. ''You have to save her.''

''That's right. You were there. You saw the woman who took Lily. Do you remember? Do you remember Lily?''

His brow wrinkled. ''She was blonde?''

''Yes! She's a blonde. Lily was with another little girl who's also blond. They both wore their hair in braids.''

''A lady spoke to them.''

''Yes,'' Faith said eagerly. ''That's right. A woman spoke to them.''

''She had blue hair. Only...it moved.''

''Moved?'' It took Faith a moment to understand. ''You mean, it slipped? Like it was a wig?''

''Yes. A wig. And sunglasses.''

''Do you remember what else she was wearing?''

"Skirt. Blouse. Jacket. Nice jacket. Leather." He shivered. "It looked warm."

"And the car? Do you remember the car?"

"Yes."

"Do you know what make it was? Or the model?"

The questions came at him too fast and he tugged free of her hands, drawing back in confusion. "It was nice. It was a nice car."

"Okay. Do you know which way they went? Was there anyone else in the car? A driver, maybe?" She crowded closer. "Is there anything else that you remember? Anything else at all?"

Harry clutched his bag protectively in his arms, shrinking back from her, his confusion growing. Ethan placed a hand on Faith's shoulder and drew her away. "That's enough," he said.

She shook him off. "No. It's not enough. I have more questions. I need to know—"

He wrapped his hand around her arm and pulled her to her feet. "He's gone, honey. You're not going to get anything else out of him right now."

"You have to make him." Her voice rose. "You have to make him tell us what we need to know."

"Faith—"

"No! You're some sort of hotshot mercenary. You must have picked up a few tricks along the way."

He stiffened. "Tricks?"

Tears gathered in her eyes. "Yes, tricks. Tricks to get people to talk. Tricks to force them to give up their information. Someone has to find the woman who took Lily," she stormed. "Now, make him tell you."

The strap whizzed through the air, exploding against the rough wooden surface with an earsplitting crack. "Tell me who sent you and why, and the pain can end. Otherwise—"

Ethan stared stonily over her shoulder. "You want me to hurt him? Beat it out of him, maybe?"

"Beat...? No!" Her face crumpled and she covered her mouth with her hands. "Oh, God, what am I saying? I'm sorry. I'm so sorry. Of course I don't want you to hurt him. I just want Lily back. I just want her back safe and sound."

He tugged Faith into a tight embrace and rocked her while her tears dampened his shirt. "And we'll get her back," he murmured. "I swear we will. Just hang on a little longer."

"What's happening to me, Ethan? I'm not normally like this. I don't think like this. I don't talk like this." She clung to him, trembling. "I'm turning into someone I despise. This has to stop before I totally lose it."

He snagged her chin and tilted her face up to his. "Hey, it's all right," he said softly. He thumbed the dampness from her cheeks. "You're not alone. We're in this together. And that's how we'll find Lily. Together."

A smile broke through the tears. "You and me against the world, is that it, Dunn?"

"You've got it, sweetheart." He combed the curls back from her brow with his fingers. "Remember how you were last night? Tough. Courageous. Strong. Laughing, even when you hurt. That's the real you. That's the woman who'll help find Lily."

"Ethan, it was an act."

"True. But you looked really cute when you were acting tough."

Laughter overtook the tears. "You're crazy, you know that?"

"Yeah. Ain't it grand?"

Dinky cleared his throat as he entered the room, pretending not to notice Faith's tears. "I fixed some eggs and bacon. Toast and coffee, too."

"Thanks, Dink," Ethan said.

Faith stepped forward. "Please. Let me." She took the

heaping plate and carried it over to Harry. ''I'm sorry if I frightened you,'' she said. She crouched in front of him, holding out the plate as a peace offering. ''I hope you'll forgive me.''

He studied her for a long moment. ''You're scared, like me. Aren't you?''

''Yes, I'm scared,'' she admitted unevenly. ''Like you.''

''Don't cry. Lily will be okay.'' Tucking his bag inside his coat, he accepted the plate. He polished off the contents in short order, drank the coffee and then stood. ''Thank you for the food. I have to go now.'' He was polite and to the point.

''Why don't I give you a lift?'' Ethan offered.

''No. I can walk.''

''It's too cold to walk. Let me drive you.''

After a moment's consideration, Harry nodded, and they all made their way to the front door. Dinky motioned them back while he checked the street. As soon as it was clear, he snatched open the door. ''He was never here.''

Ethan held out his hand. ''No problem. I'll be in touch.''

Then it was Faith's turn. She gave Dinky a quick hug. ''Twenty-five thousand is a lot of money to pass up. Thank you.''

''You heard?''

''I heard.''

He shuffled uncomfortably. ''Couldn't put a child at risk. Don't matter the price.''

They didn't waste any further time. The three hurried to the Trans Am and Faith climbed over the seat into the back, leaving the front available for Harry. Ethan pulled out his cell phone, put through a quick call to Luke Sloan and arranged to meet him at the day care. He phrased it carefully so as not to alarm his passenger. When they pulled into the parking lot at Forrester Square, they found the detective leaning against a black SUV, waiting for them.

"Should I bother asking where you found him?" he asked wryly.

Ethan offered a grim smile. "No. But you should know there's a bounty on his head. You better find someplace safe to keep him until we straighten this out."

Luke's brows drew together. "A bounty? Are you kidding me?"

Faith joined them, holding Harry by the hand. "Hey, guys? There's a woman across the street trying to get our attention."

With a loud "yoo-hoo," the woman sailed into the street, holding up a regal hand to halt traffic as she came. She was a substantial-size matron, not fat precisely, but well anchored, and brakes screeched in her wake. "Are you the police?" she demanded the minute she joined them.

At the question, Harry pulled free of Faith's hand and shrank back in alarm. She patted him on the shoulder, murmuring quietly to him. "It's okay. No one's going to hurt you. See? We brought you home."

He shot a nervous glance toward the day care center and seemed to relax slightly. "Home," he repeated.

Luke approached the woman and flashed his badge. "Detective Sloan. What can I do for you?"

"I live over there." She stabbed a finger toward an apartment building on the same side of the street as the Emerald City Jewelry Exchange. "I just returned from a visit to my son's and heard about this kidnapping business."

"You have information?" Faith asked eagerly, stepping forward.

"I do. I saw the whole thing."

Luke stilled. "You *saw* the kidnapping?"

"And you didn't report it?" Ethan demanded.

"Back off, Dunn," Luke ordered, before switching his attention to the woman. "Ma'am, I'm going to need a statement from you. Would this be a convenient time?"

"It would."

"Could you tell me your name?"

"Mrs. Edna Kirk." She turned a forthright gaze on each of them in turn. "And you are?"

Faith spoke up. "The little girl who was taken—Lily—is our daughter." She touched Ethan's arm, linking them. "Detective Sloan's been trying to help find her. Could you please tell us what you saw?"

"That's why I'm here," she assured them. "Shall I begin?"

Luke pulled a notebook and pen from his pocket. "Please go ahead."

"Very well." She took a moment to think, then launched into her recitation. "I was going to my daughter-in-law's. She and my son needed me to baby-sit my granddaughter. I planned to spend the night, and then did so."

Luke flipped open the notebook and scribbled something on the page. "You didn't see the newscasts about the kidnapping during your stay there?"

"All that mayhem is inappropriate viewing for my granddaughter and I told my daughter-in-law as much. Ellen is only three. I switched off the set prior to the announcement. I didn't hear about it until my neighbor, Mrs. Clemmons, informed me, not one hour ago."

"Okay. I can understand that. So, let's discuss what you witnessed. Take me through it step by step."

"Very well." She laced her hands together, her back rigid, and spoke clearly, from the diaphragm. Mrs. Kirk had been well-trained to project. Ethan felt a momentary pity for her granddaughter, not to mention the son and daughter-in-law. Edna Kirk struck him as the type to project frequently and at great length. "I left my apartment building at precisely nine-fifteen in the morning."

"Which building is that?"

"I gave you that information earlier. If you're going to

be a successful police officer, you need to pay attention to details.'' She poked her finger in the direction of a large complex a few doors down from the jewelry exchange. The building had a couple dozen floors and a basement garage where an electronic gate secured the vehicles parked inside. ''I pulled out of the garage and stopped at the street. I checked both ways and put on my turn signal.''

''What did you see?'' Luke prompted.

''I saw a woman carrying a child. The woman had purple-colored hair. If she was trying for red, it was a very poor dye job. In my opinion, she should sue her hairdresser.'' As if suddenly aware she'd digressed, Edna cleared her throat. ''Anyway, her child was having a temper tantrum. I do not abide temper tantrums myself. I simply do not allow them. I remember thinking that the mother was doing the right thing, taking her little girl back to the car instead of indulging her behavior.''

''You saw the woman's car?''

Mrs. Kirk hesitated. ''I pulled out just then, so I wasn't paying close attention. I drove past it, though.''

''Do you recall the color?''

''It had two colors, I believe. Blue. Maybe gray. Do not quote me since I'm not certain of my facts.''

''You said two colors?'' Ethan interrupted. ''Like someone repainted the car and hadn't done a very good job?''

''Don't be ridiculous. This was an expensive car. Lavish. Too lavish. I do not approve of wasting money on vehicles of that sort. If you want my opinion, it suggests a serious lack of breeding.'' She risked life and limb by shooting Lil a disparaging glance.

Ethan opened his mouth to say something, then thought better of it. He needed to keep his focus on Lily, not worry about defending his car's reputation.

Luke flashed him a quick, understanding grin before resuming his questioning. ''Do you remember anything else about the woman?''

''I remember her clothing. Skirt up to her armpits. Heels. Pretty enough if you like those professional types.''

Luke tapped his notebook. ''Professional...like a hooker?''

Mrs. Kirk drew herself up, clutching her pocketbook beneath an impressive bosom. ''You will watch your language when you speak to me, Detective. I most certainly did not mean that sort of—of *creature.* I meant a city woman. An executive.'' She put verbal capitals on each word. ''The sort of young lady who spends more money on clothes and accessories than on intellectual pursuits.''

Ethan exchanged a meaningful glance with Faith. The description fit Bettina Carlton to a T. ''You're saying she was a wealthy woman? Good clothes. Good car. Good grooming?''

''Haven't you been paying attention? That is precisely what I am saying.''

Luke jotted down a few more notes. ''Talk to me about the car again. You say it was expensive?''

''Expensive and foreign. Apparently American-made wasn't good enough for the likes of her.'' The dowager's brow crinkled. ''And there was something else.''

''About the car or the woman?''

''The car. The front of it was...odd.''

''Odd, how?''

''The front part.'' She made a vague gesture with her hands. ''It was different.''

''The grill?'' Ethan pointed toward that area of the Trans Am.

She strode to the car and examined it. ''This is all wrong. The car I saw had one grill, not two like this one has. And it wasn't recessed, either. It extended outward, in a separate attachment. This car's also too low,'' Mrs. Kirk explained.

"The car I saw was more..." She made a vague shape in the air with her hands.

"Boxy?" Luke suggested.

"Yes. Boxy."

"Talk to me about the grill. You said it—" he checked his notes "—extended outward."

"Yes. It had vertical slats and was surrounded by chrome. Oh! And it had one of those creatures perched on top of the hood."

"A hood ornament?" Luke addressed Ethan. "Rolls?"

Ethan nodded. "Sounds like it to me."

"Mrs. Kirk, would you be willing to come down to the station and take a look at some photos of cars? That way we can confirm the make."

"Of course."

"Thank you. How about if I meet you there in half an hour? Would that be convenient?"

"It would."

Luke took down her phone number and address before handing over his card. "If you think of anything else over the next few days, please call me. Any detail, no matter how small, could help."

"I'll give it further thought." She checked her watch. "I'll meet with you in thirty minutes at your police station. You won't be late?"

"I wouldn't dare."

With a brisk nod, she swept back across the street, her hand raised regally to stop the flow of traffic.

"That is one scary woman," Ethan muttered.

Faith smiled. "You're just sore because she slammed your car." Then her eyes widened and she gasped. She looked frantically left and right. "Where's Harry?"

At some point during their conversation with Mrs. Kirk, he'd slipped away. The three took off in separate directions, searching the grounds and perimeter of the day care center.

Harry was nowhere to be found. They reconvened in the parking lot. Faith looked close to tears again and Ethan swore beneath his breath.

"I'm sorry, sweetheart. I really screwed up. I was so anxious to hear what Mrs. Kirk had to say about Lily—"

She waved his apology aside. "I was, too." She walked into his arms, resting her check against his leather jacket. "I'm scared, Ethan. If we were able to find him, someone else will, too." She didn't have to say the rest. Now that they'd lost him, chances were good they wouldn't be seeing him again. At least, not alive.

Luke shoved his notebook into his pocket. "You said there was a bounty on him? Were you serious?"

"Dead serious."

"Why the hell put a bounty on the guy?"

"At a guess?" Ethan replied. "Because he saw something he shouldn't have. Like a kidnapping."

"So now we have a woman in a two-toned Rolls kidnapping Lily, and a bounty out on the homeless man who witnessed the abduction." Luke's eyes narrowed. "What do you want to bet that Julian Black owns a two-toned Rolls?"

Ethan's mouth settled into a grim line. "And from what you've told me about him, he'd also have the sort of money to ensure the disappearance of any witnesses."

"It won't take long to find out. And once we do, it won't be long until we find him—"

"And find my daughter."

Something in his tone must have alerted Luke. His gaze sharpened. "I warned you to stay out of this."

"Right. Because that's just what you'd do in my position. That's what you'd be doing right now if Bettina hadn't mistaken Lily for Emily. You'd be staying out of it."

Luke didn't bother responding to that one. How could he argue with the truth? He'd be all over Julian Black, and they both knew it. Instead, he checked his watch. "I've got to get to the station and meet Mrs. Kirk. I also need to arrange to have her protected until we find Black.'' He crossed to his SUV and opened the driver's door. ''I'll call you as soon as I hear anything. In the meantime, sit tight.''

''Yeah, right. That has a familiar ring to it.''

With a shake of his head, Luke climbed in and gunned the engine. The minute he pulled out of the parking lot, Ethan wrapped an arm around Faith. ''Try not to worry, honey. We're getting close. It won't be long now.''

''How can you be so certain?'' she asked unevenly. ''All we have to go on is a car that Mrs. Kirk can't identify for sure and a woman who might or might not be Bettina Carlton. We don't know where Julian Black has gone or whether he's even the one responsible. And what if the kidnappers go after Abby and Emily?''

''Now, that's an easy one. They're going to be fine,'' Ethan assured Faith. ''Luke will make certain of that.''

Faith stared at him, silently begging for reassurance. ''How do you know?''

''Simple. I've met men like Luke before. Anyone who goes after his family is going down. And going down the hard way.''

A tiny frown pulled her brows together. ''You're like Luke.''

''Yeah.''

''Which means…''

He couldn't look at her. ''Don't bother going there. There was never any question about what would happen to the people who took Lily if I found them before the cops did.''

Faith started to argue, then changed her mind. Smart woman. Not that he was off the hook. Chances were excellent they'd continue this discussion at a future time of her choosing. ''What are we going to do about Harry?'' she asked.

''I'll call Dinky again. He won't be happy.'' That had to

be the understatement of the century. ''I'll also alert Jack. Other than having Luke put out a bulletin, there's nothing we can do.''

''Lily will be home soon, right?'' she asked. Or was she begging?

Ethan caught her in his arms and held her close. ''I promise you a Christmas miracle. That's one promise I plan to keep.''

But privately he was forced to acknowledge that Christmas miracles had always been thin on the ground where he was concerned. If this Bettina Carlton woman was responsible for the kidnapping and she was doing it to get at Abby, what would she do once she'd discovered she'd taken the wrong kid? And what would happen once Julian Black realized they were on to him? Ethan knew what was the most likely possibility—the smartest option if they hoped to cover their tracks.

They'd kill Lily.

CHAPTER ELEVEN

"YOU CAN'T DO THIS, Julian," Bettina begged, clinging to his arm. She spared a quick glance toward the cabin, where Lily was playing. Could she hear? Not willing to risk it, she lowered her voice. "Enough is enough. We screwed up taking this first kid. We don't need to make it worse by taking Abby's daughter. We have plenty of money. Let's cut Lily loose and make a run for it."

He shook her off. "Why should I run? The cops think you're the mastermind behind the fencing operation. You're also the one who kidnapped the kid. There's nothing to connect me to any of this."

"Except that homeless man. Crock thinks he saw us. *All* of us," she stressed.

"He won't be a problem. At least, not for long."

Her stomach cramped with fear. "You have Crock out there looking for him, don't you? Tying off loose ends?"

"I'm just being thorough, my dear. I don't like untidy details."

At what point would she become one of those untidy details? She needed to find a way to get out of here and fast. And she wouldn't get a more convenient window of opportunity than right now, while Crock was off running Julian's errands. Bettina had a far better chance of bending Julian to her way of thinking than Crock. Julian had vanity and ego she could play off. Crock simply did as ordered, without compassion or concern for his victims. There was nothing inside of him to reach, no connection to plug into.

She moved closer to Julian, forcing an understanding smile to her lips. "You're so clever, darling. You always have all the angles covered. But what if they figure out that we were after Emily and took the wrong kid by mistake? They could be using Emily as bait, waiting for us to make a move. Sloan is a clever cop. And you said he has a serious thing for Abby. That means he's going to be extra vigilant."

A hint of anger sparked in Julian's pale eyes. "No one saw us."

"Except the homeless man."

"Exactly."

"And you know that because Crock noticed him watching us."

"Yes, yes." Impatience gave his words a dangerous edge, warning her to tread carefully.

"That meant Crock had his attention fixed on the homeless man. But..." She moistened her lips. "What if someone else was watching *us* while Crock was watching the homeless man? What if they saw your Rolls and recognized it? After all, you said yourself that the Rolls is sometimes parked outside the exchange or in the parking lot, where anyone can see it. It's not a car they're likely to forget. What happens if this other witness notices it the next time you go to the exchange, makes the connection and calls the cops?"

She'd frightened him. She could see it in his eyes and in an odd tightness that gripped the muscles along his jaw and shoulders. He smoothed his pinky around his mouth. "I'll put the Rolls in storage and use the Mercedes."

"Good idea. After all..." She slanted him a quick look and pushed just a tiny bit harder. "Kidnapping is one thing, Julian. Murdering the kidnap victim... Well, that's the sort of crime that gets a needle stuck in your arm. Or would you prefer a good old-fashioned hanging? I think that's still an option in the state of Washington."

His eyes narrowed with the sort of calculating expression

that worried her. But the smile that came on its heels flat-out terrified her. "Not if you do it right," he murmured. "Not if you do it right."

"ETHAN?" Faith hovered in the doorway of Lily's bedroom. Early morning sunlight slipped beneath the shades and slanted across Ethan's slumbering frame. He came instantly awake, though nothing moved except his eyes. His gaze cut to hers and he lifted an eyebrow in silent inquiry. "We need to get to the day care right away," she explained. "There's been another development."

He lifted himself up on one elbow, the comforter falling away from the upper half of his torso. "What's happened?"

She forced herself to ignore his seminudity. "There's been a break-in at the day care. It happened last night while one of the owners was working late—Alexandra Webber. Do you remember her?" At his nod, she continued. "They don't know whether it's connected to the kidnapping, but Harry—our homeless man—is involved somehow."

"How?"

"I don't know. A police officer by the name of Griffin Frazier will meet us there to discuss the situation."

Ethan came off the bed in a single graceful move and reached for his clothes. "Who's he? And why isn't Sloan handling it?"

"Apparently Frazier took the call last night and he's volunteered to fill us in while Luke looks for Julian Black."

Ethan wasn't having any of it. "Screw that!" He zipped up his jeans. "Luke has the inside track on what's been happening. Get Sloan back on the phone and tell him to get his ass over to the day care."

She'd anticipated this—or rather, Luke had. "Luke says Frazier is an excellent cop and can give us the necessary information."

"Bull." Ethan yanked on socks and thrust his feet into

fleece-lined boots. ''This sounds like a perfect case of the left hand not knowing what the right's doing.''

''Luke also had a message for you. He said it won't be a case of the left hand not knowing what the right's doing.'' Not giving Ethan an opportunity to argue further, she plucked his shirt from the back of a chair and tossed it to him. ''Breakfast is ready. I want to leave as soon as we're done.''

He joined her in the kitchen five minutes later. In another fifteen, they were out the door. Traffic was particularly bad that morning, the streets clogged with Monday morning commuters and Christmas shoppers determined to get an early start on their spending.

''I'm surprised you didn't buy a house closer to work,'' Ethan commented as they inched along.

''Closer to work definitely wasn't in my budget. Even Ballard was a stretch.''

''Got it. Well, at least you're pursuing your dream.'' He slid a hand along the back of her neck in a whisper-soft caress. ''I often wondered...hoped, really, that you'd go for it.''

His unreserved pleasure made her smile. ''What about you? What will you do now that you're no longer mercenarying anymore?''

He shot her an amused look. ''Mercenarying? Is that even a word?''

''You know what I mean.''

''Yeah, I know.'' His smile died. ''To be honest, I don't know.''

''Well, what else are you qualified to do?''

Apparently, it was the wrong question to ask. His expression turned downright grim. ''Nothing,'' he replied after an endless minute. ''Not a damn thing.''

She tiptoed further into the discussion. ''Your training must have honed skills you can use in other arenas.''

"Sure. If anyone wants to hire me to fieldstrip a rifle, do reconnaissance work, put together a unit of mercenaries, track down gunrunners or dopers, I'd be perfect for the job. Or there's always working as a hired killer. Isn't that what you accused me of being?"

"What's going on, Ethan?" she asked quietly.

He downshifted and shot around a slow-moving truck. "I'm sorry," he finally said. "That wasn't fair."

"That's why you came looking for me, isn't it? You didn't know where else to turn." She didn't like the idea of being his last resort.

"No. There are plenty of places I could have turned. They're just not places I wanted to go." He spared her a quick glance. "I'm not your father, Faith. I didn't leave you because I was bored or because I had another family on the sly. True, I didn't reveal who or what I was when we first met. But the minute you told me what your father had done to you and your mother, I came clean. I didn't want you coloring me with the same brush."

"Still...you left." The stark words escaped of their own accord.

The harsh lines scoring his face softened ever so slightly. "You've had a lot of people leave you. Your father. Your mother when she died. Elizabeth. Me. It makes it difficult to trust. I understand that. The difference is that I came back. And now that I have, I'm not leaving. Not ever again. I'm going to be part of your life from now on. Yours and Lily's."

"Why?" The question was whisper-soft.

He pulled into the Forrester Square parking lot. "Because I love you." He made the statement with breathtaking simplicity and utter sincerity. "I've always loved you."

He didn't wait for her response. Thrusting open the door, he climbed out of the car. But she noticed his limp seemed more pronounced as he headed for the front door of the day care. She sat, stunned, trying to work through her reaction to his announcement.

When he'd first said he loved her, she'd been filled with such a fierce joy she didn't think it could be contained in one body. But almost immediately, a cautionary voice had issued a warning, dampening that joy. She'd taken this path with Ethan once before. It hadn't led anywhere she wanted to go. Losing him had been one of the most traumatic events in her life, almost as bad as losing Lily. The difference was she expected to have her daughter back in her arms at any moment, while five years ago, she'd believed Ethan's loss was for all time.

Now he'd returned. Part of her wanted to grab him and never let go. But another part was terrified of losing him all over again. And she didn't doubt that she would lose him. She couldn't help suspecting that his return was temporary, despite what he claimed. He'd lost the most important part of his life—his job and his friends—and now he was looking for fulfillment elsewhere.

He'd chosen her.

But how long would it last? Regardless of what he'd claimed, how long would it be before he decided that she didn't give him the edgy thrill he'd experienced in his previous life? How long before he got restless and went off looking for excitement elsewhere? She couldn't handle that. No way, nohow.

Better to lose him now, when the pain would be excruciating, but not soul-shattering, than risk loving him and having that love destroyed by an affair gone bad. One quick plunge of the knife struck her as less traumatic than slowly being cut to pieces over the ensuing months or years. At least she'd know he was alive, even if he wasn't living that life with her.

Satisfied, if not happy, with her conclusions, she climbed out of Lil and followed Ethan into the center. She caught up with him just outside the office and slanted him a swift look. Not two minutes ago he'd declared his love for her. But in those brief seconds since, he'd closed down his emotions, leaving his face an unreadable mask. She started to say something, but decided against it at the last instant. They didn't have the time to continue their discussion. And she didn't have anything to tell him that he'd want to hear. Not if he was hoping for some sort of fairy-tale ending for their relationship.

With a silent sigh of regret, she walked into the day care office. Alexandra was waiting for them, as was a Seattle police officer she assumed to be Griffin Frazier. He wore an SPD uniform and was running through some notes on a pad while the other two owners, Hannah and Katherine, sat quietly in the background. He kept his attention fixed on Alexandra, his solicitous attitude slightly more than mere professional courtesy. Watching him, Faith caught a glimpse of pure masculine interest in his calm brown eyes. How intriguing.

Alexandra hadn't picked up on it, and Faith frowned when she took a good look at the petite woman. She was pale and drawn and lacked her normal vitality. Deep circles ringed her green eyes and even the bright red of her hair seemed to have lost its vibrancy.

"Are you all right?" Faith asked in concern.

"I'll live."

"What in the world happened last night?"

"I assume Luke Sloan phoned you?"

"He said there'd been a break-in and that Harry—that's the name I gave the homeless man—that Harry was involved, somehow."

"I asked Officer Frazier if he'd stop by and speak with you about the incident, because of the situation with Lily." Alexandra wrapped her arms around her wiry frame. "We believe it was a burglar. I guess he didn't realize I would be here on a Sunday night, and I surprised him. He came after me. I think...'' Tears sparkled in her eyes. ''I think he might have attacked me if Harry hadn't come charging in. He scared off the man and carried me to safety.''

The police officer interrupted just then. He offered his hand to Faith. ''Griffin Frazier, Seattle Police Department. Sloan said you had a conversation with this homeless man just yesterday.''

''Yes,'' she confirmed. ''He witnessed the kidnapping of my daughter, Lily. He couldn't tell us much, but I gave Luke what details there were.''

''You don't think he was an accomplice in the abduction?''

Ethan handled the question. ''Not a chance. There was something wrong with the guy. He wasn't all there.''

''Any chance he was faking it?''

''No.''

''Okay. Do you have any idea why he's been hanging around here?''

''I think he feels a connection with the place,'' Faith volunteered.

Griffin regarded her with interest. ''Why do you say that?''

In the quirky manner typical of the way her brain worked, the time she'd spent with Harry appeared to Faith in a series of snapshots. She mentally rearranged them, selecting details to support her theory. ''For one thing, he likes to hang around here. He's also intimately familiar with the area, which suggests he might have lived near here at one time. When we were distracted yesterday, he vanished in a matter of minutes. He also feels a strong attachment to Lily, and another little girl, Emily. It was clear that the kidnapping upset him, and that he wanted to help.''

''Do you think there's a connection between the kidnapping and this break-in?'' Ethan asked the cop.

Griffin hesitated. ''My gut instinct says no. But anytime you have a string of crimes in an area that hasn't had any before, you start looking real hard at how the unconnected connects, if you know what I mean.''

Ethan nodded. ''I know just what you mean.''

The officer handed over his card. ''If you hear anything else, or something occurs to you, give me a call.''

''Sure.'' Ethan pocketed the card. ''By the way, what was the burglar after? There's no money on the premises, is there?''

''We think it may have been a random break-in. Bust a window and snatch and grab whatever can be converted to fast cash.''

''Got it. We can go then?''

''Absolutely. If you have any more contact with this homeless man, please let us know.''

As Faith started to leave, Alexandra came over and gave her a quick hug. ''Hang in there,'' she said. ''They'll find Lily and she'll be fine. She's strong. And smart. She'll be home again soon.''

Faith responded with her most confident smile, although it felt a bit shaky around the edges. ''I'm sure you're right.''

With that, she and Ethan left, and Alexandra escorted Griffin Frazier to the door. ''Thank you for your assistance, Officer,'' she said.

He shook hands with her. ''Call me Griff.'' He hesitated for a moment, her hand trapped in his. ''Listen, I know this might seem a bit...I don't know. Sudden. But would you like to have dinner with me tonight?''

Alexandra blinked in surprise. Where had that come from? She scrutinized him more closely than she had earlier. Before, all she'd noticed was the uniform and the air of authority. Now she saw the man. He stood calmly, allowing her to look her fill. He was a comfortable height for a woman on the short side, and had light brown hair, a neatly trimmed mustache and pleasant features with appealing brown eyes. Under other circumstances she'd have been interested, though hesitant. Free spirits and authority figures rarely mixed well.

As though he were picking up on her ambivalence, his mustache twitched to one side and he gave her a half friendly, half chagrined smile. "No strings."

No strings. A free meal. Congenial company. Well, why not? Her friends had been urging her to get out more. One dinner date couldn't hurt. And maybe it would help get her mind off her problems. "Sure. That sounds great."

"I'll pick you up at seven?"

"You have the address to my apartment on the report. I'll see you then."

When she returned to the office, Katherine and Hannah looked at her expectantly. "Yes," she said before they could pepper her with questions. "He asked me out. And yes, I accepted."

"Only because you knew we'd say something if you didn't," Hannah retorted.

Alexandra grinned. "That might have played a part in my decision." Her grin became a yawn.

"You're exhausted," Katherine stated, assuming the mother hen role. "Have you seen the doctor we recommended?"

Alexandra shook her head. "Not yet."

"The insomnia hasn't gone away, has it? And you're still having nightmares." It wasn't a question.

"Yes to the nightmares, no to the insomnia." She hesitated. Throwing herself into the chair behind her desk, she decided to confess all. "I told you that I think the nightmares are related to the fire that killed my parents when I was little."

Concern reflected in Hannah's pale blue eyes. "And we

told you that if you're still dreaming about a fire that happened twenty years ago, you have to get help.''

''I will. But...'' Alexandra grabbed a pen off her desk and rolled it between her fingers. ''I think there's a reason they're becoming more frequent. Since I've been back in Seattle, I mean.''

Katherine studied her intently. ''You think something's sparked them?''

''It's this homeless man.''

Hannah released a groan. ''Not him again.'' She tucked a swath of honey-blond hair behind her ear. ''I swear, Alexandra, you're obsessed with him. First, you won't let us call the cops when we catch him hanging around. Then you give Marilyn hell for confronting him when she should have been watching Emily and Lily. And now he rescues you from a burglar. What gives?''

Alexandra shrugged. ''He reminds me of someone.''

Hannah started to say something more, but Katherine waved her to silence. ''Who, honey? Who does he remind you of?''

She hesitated a long minute, then whispered, ''My father. There's something about him. Something that makes me think... Makes me wonder—''

''Your father is dead, Alexandra,'' said Hannah with typical practicality. ''He died in that fire.''

''Rescuing me. I know, I know.'' She jumped to her feet, pacing between the desks. ''Sometimes I can hardly remember Dad, but this man reminds me of him. The tone of his voice, the way he moves. His gestures.''

''There's something else, isn't there?'' Katherine asked. ''You're giving off vibes.''

Alexandra paused, struggling to put her sensations into words. ''It's how I feel around him,'' she reluctantly admitted. ''When he carried me out of the building, it was like the night of the fire all over again. There's only one other person who's ever made me feel that safe. That secure.''

''Your father,'' Katherine stated.

Alexandra's throat was too tight to respond. She simply nodded.

Her father. A man who had died twenty years ago. A man who haunted her dreams and was a weight on her heart.

Jonathan Webber.

ETHAN AND FAITH spent the rest of the day checking with various contacts and comparing notes with Luke. Not that it did much good. As each hour passed, it became increasingly difficult not to lose hope. If it hadn't been for Ethan, Faith suspected she'd have done just that. But he had an uncanny knack for staying calm and positive, which kept her anchored, as well. Whenever she began to doubt, she'd catch a glimpse of his firmly set jaw and the flinty determination in his blue eyes, and her hope would be renewed.

Late in the afternoon Luke phoned and spoke to Ethan at length. ''There's one piece of encouraging news,'' he announced as soon as he hung up.

Faith fought to contain her eagerness. ''Luke's found Julian Black?''

''Not yet. But he's been able to build more of a case connecting Julian and Bettina outside of a work venue. Apparently, they have a favorite restaurant where they always request the same discreet booth in the back. According to the waiters and the maître d', the encounters have all been highly romantic. And one of the employees at the jewelry exchange has admitted that she caught them enjoying a rather passionate kiss right before Bettina's arrest.''

''Plus, the security guard has seen Julian at Bettina's apartment on a regular basis,'' Faith reminded him. ''That's something, right?''

''Absolutely. On top of which, the lawyer who handled

Bettina's case just added Julian Black to his client list, *and* the company who put up her bail money is a dummy corporation that snakes back to—''

''Julian Black?'' Faith interrupted eagerly.

''You got it. Added together, all of that's enough for Luke to suspect that Julian may actually be the mastermind behind the fencing operation, not Bettina. And it's enough for him to look at both of them in connection with Lily's kidnapping, particularly—'' he flashed Faith a triumphant grin. ''—particularly since Julian drives a two-tone blue-on-blue Rolls-Royce, our kidnappers' car du jour.''

''Mrs. Kirk confirmed the make?''

''Mrs. Kirk confirmed the make.''

Emotion gripped Faith's throat and it took her a minute to get her questions out. ''Then we were right? Julian and Bettina took Lily by mistake?''

''Sure looks like it.''

Tears filled her eyes. ''We're getting close, aren't we?''

''Very close, sweetheart.''

She needed to move, to act, to focus her nervous energy in a positive direction. ''So what next? Where do we go? Who do we talk to?'' She glanced around for her purse and coat. ''I'm ready to head out as soon as you are.''

''Great. I thought we'd drive down to the waterfront and have dinner.''

She shook her head. ''That's not what I meant. Besides, I'm not hungry.'' Impatience edged her words. ''I want to do something to find Lily. Come on, Ethan. We need to act.''

''There's nothing we can do right now.'' His voice had taken on a soothing tone that grated on her nerves. ''We have to be patient and let the police try and find Julian.''

''That's not what you said before.'' Her jaw crept out. ''You told me you were going to make something happen. Well, what are you waiting for?''

"I haven't needed to make anything happen," he argued. "Things are doing that all on their own without any interference from me. Right now our best choice is to sit tight."

He wasn't telling her everything. "Why? Why do we have to sit tight? Why can't we go look for our daughter?" she demanded.

"Because we know who has her—or at least we're pretty sure we know. That means we have to let the police handle it. If we interfere in their case, the kidnappers could get away. How would you feel if our actions caused something to go wrong?"

She took a moment to digest that. It made sense. Unfortunately. She certainly didn't want to do anything that would hurt Lily or prevent her from being safely returned. Some of Faith's nervous energy dissipated, leaving her feeling frustrated and depressed. "Okay. I understand." She thrust a hand through her hair, shoving stray curls off her forehead, and considered their options. "You want dinner, so let's get dinner. Why don't we order pizza and have a quiet night in? That way we won't miss any calls."

Ethan shot her a questioning look. "Are you sure? We've been stuck in the house a lot recently. Hell, I'm wearing out the carpet with all the pacing I've been doing. Luke has my cell number. He'll call if anything important happens. And we could use the break."

They did need a break from the trauma of the past few days. If they stayed home, she'd only obsess over Lily. That would lead to a crying jag and— She broke off her train of thought before she burst into tears. "Where do you want to go?"

"Elliott's on the Bay," he answered promptly. "It's quiet and casual. Very low profile."

"I've heard of it."

"They also offer to-go if you can't handle eating out."

His gentleness almost proved her undoing. She cleared her throat. ''Thanks, Ethan. Elliott's sounds perfect.''

The traffic into the city was heavy, but not horrendous. They parked without too much trouble and walked the short distance to the restaurant. Christmas lights gleamed up and down the street, the cheerfulness at direct odds with her somber mood. If it weren't for Lily being missing, it would have been a perfect setting.

As though sensing the direction her thoughts had taken, Ethan clasped her hand in his. ''I made a promise to you, sweetheart, and I plan to keep it,'' he told her. ''Our daughter will be home by Christmas. I swear it.''

He didn't give her time to reply, but pulled open the door to a rustic restaurant that extended out onto Elliott Bay. The decor had a nautical motif, with old timber and planking decorated with evergreen swags and white twinkling lights for the holidays. The only touch of modern elegance was the floor-to-ceiling glass walls that allowed diners to watch the comings and goings of the ferries and commercial barges plowing a path across the sound. Outside the windows, pedestrians braved the wintry cold and wandered along a boardwalk that surrounded the restaurant. And overhead a huge moon, just shy of full, hung in the western sky. It illuminated the snow-capped peaks of the Olympic Mountains, while the rest of the mountains dissolved into velvety darkness.

The hostess greeted them pleasantly. ''You've caught us at a busy time. But we should have a table available in twenty minutes or so. Would you care to wait?''

Faith could feel Ethan's gaze on her and forced her most cheerful smile. Not that he bought it. With a quick shake of his head, he turned back to the hostess. ''We'd like to order a meal to go.''

''Certainly.'' She handed over a pair of menus. ''Why

don't you have a seat in our lounge and the cocktail waitress can turn in your order when you're ready.''

''That sounds perfect,'' Ethan said. They were escorted to the lounge, which enjoyed a postcard view of part of Elliott Bay, Magnolia Bluff and a generous sweep of the city skyline. ''Would you like a drink while we wait?'' he asked Faith. ''Another single-malt like you had at Dinky's?'' He was rude enough to grin at her shudder of distaste.

''A glass of Chablis,'' she hastened to request. They took a seat at one of the small tables grouped around the bar. After examining the menu, they gave their drink and food orders to the cocktail waitress.

Ethan spotted Jack sitting at a window table a split second ahead of Faith. ''Why don't you invite him over?'' she suggested.

''You don't mind?''

''No, of course not. I like him. He's one of the good guys.''

Jack joined them with alacrity. ''Did you get my message about your homeless guy?'' At their bewildered expressions, he said, ''I called a little while ago and left a message. Dinky has him again. He promised to keep him stashed for a couple days until this bounty business is cleared up.''

''That's a relief,'' Faith said. She'd been so worried about him. So had Alexandra. Faith made a mental note to pass on the good news. ''So are you waiting for someone?'' she asked Jack.

''Nah. Got stood up,'' he grumbled, signaling the waitress for a refill on his beer.

Ethan laughed. ''Again?''

''Shut up, Dunn.'' He turned hurt, puppy dog eyes on Faith. ''I think I scare women. When we first meet, they're all, 'Oh, you hunk, you,' and 'Show me your gun.' I mean, what's a guy to do? I invite them out and they say yes—''

Ethan interrupted. "Then they go home and think about all those muscles and that great big gun."

Jack nodded morosely. "And they bail."

"So ditch the gun and just flash the muscles," Faith advised. She waited until the waitress had deposited their drinks and departed, before asking a question that had plagued her for years. "You know, there's something I've always wanted to know...."

CHAPTER TWELVE

THE TWO MEN EXCHANGED meaningful glances. ‘‘Let me guess,’’ Ethan said. ‘‘Why a mercenary?’’

‘‘Okay, so it’s not the most original question. It’s just… It’s not exactly the type of occupation little boys dream about. I can’t see a bunch of five-year-olds saying, ‘Someday I want to grow up and become a mercenary.’

Ethan pulled back an inch. ‘‘What, are you nuts? Excitement. Guns. Blowing up bad guys. Next to girls, it’s a little boy’s hottest dream.’’

‘‘Mmm. Like that, is it?’’

‘‘Oh, yeah,’’ Jack confirmed.

‘‘Got it. But even so, most little boys outgrow that particular dream. What happened with you two?’’ Okay, judging by their expressions, maybe that hadn’t come out quite the way she’d intended. ‘‘You know what I mean.’’

Ethan fielded the question. ‘‘Unfortunately, I do. In our case, it’s pretty simple. Fighting was the only thing we did well.’’

‘‘There are other options if you wanted to see action. Law enforcement. Military service. Various government bureaus.’’

‘‘I wasn’t interested in anything that organized.’’

Jack froze, his glass half raised to his mouth. ‘‘You haven’t told her, have you?’’

‘‘Drop it.’’

‘‘No, man.’’ He returned the beer to the table. ‘‘Tell her.’’

Faith looked from one to the other. ''Don't keep me in suspense. Tell me what?''

Ethan's face lost all expression. ''You want to know? Okay, fine. I didn't qualify for any of your suggestions. They require a better education than I received.''

''Don't you just need a high school—'' Her eyes widened. ''Oh.''

''Yeah, oh.''

He had to give her credit. It took her a single sip of wine to come up with a new tack. ''You can do something about that.''

''I did. Five years ago. I had a lot of time to kill in that hospital bed. I spent most of it working toward my GED.''

He could see her analyzing the various reasons he'd have felt compelled to earn his high school equivalency diploma. She collared it on the first try. ''You wanted your GED so when you returned to me, you'd be able to earn a living doing something other than soldiering?''

''Something like that.''

''Then you really were going to walk away from your former life.''

She seemed intent on pushing his buttons. And Jack didn't help any. He sat there ready to jump right in with an excess of information should Ethan fumble the facts. ''Yes, I really was. Not that it matters now. I'm too old and beat-up for either police or military service.''

''There are other choices, Ethan. It's up to you.''

''You never give up, do you?''

''No.'' She fixed him with a direct look. ''And neither do you. It's one of the qualities I've always admired about you.''

''There are times when you remind me vividly of my grandmother,'' he said, and saluted her with his tumbler.

She accepted the compliment with a smile, the tension

draining out of her. ''What a sweet thing to say. I know how much you loved Lily.''

''I flat-out adored that woman. I'd have done anything for her. I gave up street fighting, for one thing.''

''Hell,'' Jack interjected, ''even I gave up fighting. That's the kind of lady she was. She inspired you to better yourself.''

''I know she died, but—''

Jack shook his head at Ethan. ''Man, don't you two talk?'' He filled Faith in. ''There was a burglary while we were at school. She was killed in the scuffle.''

''Oh, no!'' Jack had shocked her, and Ethan plucked her wineglass from between her fingers before she dropped it. She then nailed him with an accusatory look. ''You never told me about that.''

Jack stepped to the plate again and smacked another homer into left field. ''That's because he blames himself.''

Ethan tossed back his whiskey, showing little respect for the quality, and allowed the tumbler to strike the table with a pointed crack of glass against wood. Not that it did any good. Neither of them was paying any attention to his preferences. ''It isn't something I like to discuss,'' he stated in no uncertain terms.

She didn't take the hint. ''Why do you blame yourself?''

Jack jumped right in. ''He thinks if he'd been there, he could have prevented it from happening. Popped the guy or something.''

''Do you mind?'' Ethan interrupted.

''Yeah, as a matter of fact, I do. How come you never told Faith any of this stuff?''

''I didn't want to get stood up. Try it. You might actually keep a woman long enough to get laid.''

Faith laughed as though she thought he was joking. ''Somehow I don't think Jack has a problem in that area, despite this evening's lapse.'' Her smile faded. ''But I wish

I'd known Lily. She sounds grand. What happened after she died?''

Ethan didn't wait for Jack to run interference. ''Foster homes.''

''What about your parents?''

He shrugged.

Jack sighed. ''Tell her,'' he insisted. ''She's gonna get it out of you one way or another.''

Ethan limited himself to a single word. ''Unfit.''

''Unfit?'' Jack snorted. ''Hell, they beat the sh— 'Scuse me, ma'am. Crap. Is it okay with you if I say crap?'' At her nod, he rattled on. ''They beat the crap out of him. State took him away and handed him over to Ms. Lily. First she tucked Ethan under her wing, then me right along with him. God rest that woman's soul. Her death was quite a blow, let me tell you. Ethan and me, we figured she was our one shot at making it in life.''

Faith patted Jack's hand as though he alone had suffered the loss. ''And then she died.''

''And down the tubes we went.'' Jack heaved a deep, pitiful sigh. ''Side by side, straight to hell.''

Straight to hell. Sheesh. By the look of her, Faith was eating it up, buying into every exaggerated word. ''We made out all right,'' Ethan argued. ''We met up with other loners. Made a career for ourselves. Now, do you think we could change the subject? I'm getting seriously depressed here.''

His comment didn't earn him so much as a twinge of sympathy. He just didn't have the eyes for it. Jack, with his big brown soulful gaze, wriggled into every female heart in King County. Women all wanted to mother him. Ethan had never been able to pull that off. His were bedroom eyes, and only good for one thing. And lately, they weren't even good for that.

''So, what about you?'' Jack asked Faith, obediently

changing the subject. "I understand you were raised by your grandmother, too."

"Elizabeth. She and Lily would have adored each other, I suspect."

"You lose your parents in an accident?"

It was Faith's turn to offer a noncommittal answer. "Something like that."

Ethan wouldn't let her get away with it. "Not a chance, sweet pea. You can't put me through the wringer and then not climb in there yourself. Tell him the truth."

She lifted her chin. "Fine. The truth is, my father took off when I was ten and my mother died not long after. Elizabeth was mother, father *and* grandmother to me."

Jack grimaced. "Tough break." He took a long swallow of beer, then inclined his head in Ethan's direction. "How did you meet this no-good bum?"

Her gaze sought Ethan's and she smiled in a way that ignited a slow burn, way down low in his gut. "A scuzzy little thief grabbed Elizabeth's purse and took off running. Ethan just stood there and watched, leaning one shoulder against the doorway to a florist shop. At the last possible second, he stuck out his arm as the purse snatcher ran by. Clotheslined him. The little runt hit Ethan's arm, bounced off and slammed onto his back. Never knew what hit him. He didn't stir until the cops came and hauled him away."

"Love at first punch, huh?"

Ethan waited to see how Faith would answer that one. Before she could, the waitress approached. Enticing aromas issued from the large plastic bag she carried. "Here's your dinner."

Faith pushed back her chair and the question slipped away. "Would you like to join us?" she asked Jack. "I think we ordered enough for an entire football team."

"No, no. Appreciate the invite, but you two go ahead.

I'm gonna find somebody else to stand me up. Maybe that cocktail waitress.''

''Remember, Jack,'' she admonished. ''Don't show her your gun.''

He scuffed his size sixteens like a recalcitrant schoolboy. ''I won't.'' His big brown eyes went into action. ''Unless she makes me.''

As they headed for the door, Faith noticed Alexandra Webber walking along the boardwalk outside the restaurant. With her was a familiar-looking man. Faith pointed them out to Ethan. ''Isn't that the policeman we met this morning?''

''Yeah. Frazier. Griffin Frazier,'' Ethan confirmed.

''Huh. I *thought* he was attracted to Alexandra. Looks like I was right.''

''Too bad it doesn't go both ways.''

Faith craned her neck. ''How can you tell? I'm too short to see what you're seeing.''

''He's grinning like an idiot and she's smiling. Politely. That's not a relationship that's going anywhere fast.''

''What a shame. I'd hoped it might come to something.''

''Hope all you want. It isn't going to happen.'' They left the restaurant just in time to see the couple pause by the railing and exchange a kiss. ''Definitely not interested,'' Ethan murmured.

''No,'' Faith was forced to agree. ''He is. But she isn't resonating.''

''Resonating, huh?'' His arms closed around her and he pulled her into a tight embrace. Their dinner bumped against her thigh, the heat from their meal mirroring the heat generated by Ethan's touch. ''What would they see if they watched us kiss, I wonder?''

And then he lowered his head and took her mouth with explosive passion. Faith groaned, wrapping her arms around his neck. It never failed to amaze her how, with one simple touch, she went up in flames. Time became a blur. It could have been mere seconds that passed, or hours.

She clung to him, opened to him, greedy for what he had to give her. It had been like this from the beginning. It was as though all of her senses were attuned to him and him alone. Without even looking, she knew his scent, his touch, his taste. On some primitive level, she'd imprinted his essence on her very soul. He belonged to her, just as she belonged to him. They were mated in every way possible, except by law.

A crisp wind blowing in from the northwest finally drove them apart. When Ethan reluctantly released her, Alexandra and Griffin were nowhere to be seen. "Well?" he asked. "Any resonating?"

"There might have been a tiny twinge resonating there somewhere," she admitted.

"Yeah? Like where?"

She cleared her throat. "You name it. It resonated."

THEY RETURNED to Faith's house and consumed their meal without a word, though the tension building between them spoke volumes. Immediately after dinner, Faith closeted herself in the bathroom, doing whatever women seemed to need to do for hours on end. Splashing water. Dusting the place with a layer of talc. Plucking at various parts of the body, while creaming others. The various activities also involved a lot of muttering and tisking and sometimes an exclamation of serious pain.

The first time he'd heard that, he'd rushed to the door, ready to bust it down. His efforts had been greeted with an annoyed, "I'm fine. Leave me alone," and a glimpse of a pair of tweezers the size of plyers. It had had a lasting effect, striking terror deep into his poor, innocent male psyche. Whatever secret ritual went on, it defied both description and understanding, but inspired the utmost caution.

Shortly after she'd disappeared into the bathroom, Faith's phone rang. "Dunn here."

"It's Luke."

"One sec." Ethan padded onto the back deck with the portable, oblivious to the chill. Overhead an endless sweep of stars glittered down on him. He doubted Faith would have heard the conversation even if he'd elected to remain inside, but he'd rather not take the chance. "Go ahead. What have you found out?"

"The official word is that Julian Black is still on vacation. Indefinitely."

"And the unofficial word?"

"He's in town. Incommunicado."

"Does he know you're looking for him?"

"I kept it very low-key. Just told the woman I spoke to at the jewelry exchange that we had some questions regarding Bettina's movements before she was arrested. I implied we were trying to tighten up our case."

"Did she buy it?"

"Seemed to."

"If Julian realizes you're on to him, you know what will happen."

Luke was silent for a long minute. Then he said, "I know." The comment held a painful finality.

Ethan punched the Disconnect button and returned to the house. He hadn't been totally frank with Faith. Events were fast reaching the crisis point. If they didn't find Lily soon, the chances of getting her back alive were next to nil. Either panic would set in and the kidnappers would act on that panic. Or, if Lily's kidnapping had been done with cold, rational deliberation, they'd want to tie up loose ends.

Lily would be one of the first loose ends they tied.

If he and Luke were right about Julian being the actual mastermind behind all this, there was an excellent chance he could get away with it, too. They had no definitive proof of his involvement. If rescue efforts arrived too late, Bettina would get the blame for the kidnapping as well as the fencing operation. All Julian would have to do was wait a short time and he'd be back in business, no one the wiser. But Lily would be gone. And Ethan didn't doubt for a minute that Bettina would meet with a regrettable accident, as well.

He closed his eyes, the refrain running through his head growing louder by the minute. *There were details missing.*

"Ethan?" Faith appeared at the foot of the steps. "Did I hear the phone ring?"

"Luke called."

She shoved a tousled mess of damp hair from her brow. Her fingers were shaking. "What happened? Did he find Julian?"

"Julian's still on vacation."

Her gaze met his with a directness he couldn't avoid. "That means he's gone, doesn't it?"

"He's on vacation until the cops can find him."

"But they're looking, right?"

"Quietly."

Tears gathered in her eyes. "Quiet is important, isn't it?"

"Yeah. It is."

"Lily..." Her voice broke.

"Don't go there, Faith." He joined her at the foot of the steps. "And don't you dare give up. We'll get her back. I promise."

She fisted her hands in his shirt. "You can't promise that. You know you can't."

A reckless determination filled him. "I'm doing it, anyway. I won't lose my daughter. Not after I've just found her." He wrapped his arms around Faith. "I'm not losing you, either. You don't know what it's like to have a family and then suddenly lose them."

"Yes," she whispered. "I do."

He closed his eyes. "Of course. Your parents and Elizabeth. I'm sorry, sweetheart. I wasn't thinking.'' But her loss only made it all the more urgent that he get through to her. ''You lost those closest to you, the same as me, so you should understand the importance of family. You should understand why I'd do anything to keep mine intact.''

''Stop it, Ethan. You're moving too fast.''

Didn't she get it? ''I moved too slow last time,'' he countered. ''And I lost you to another man. I'm not going to make that mistake again. You're expecting too much if you think I'll back off. Or maybe I'm wasting my breath explaining. Maybe I should just show you. Maybe then you'll agree with me.''

Without another word, he swept her into his arms and carried her upstairs, seemingly oblivious to the damage he could be causing his bad knee. Faith opened her mouth to say something—anything—to convince him he was making a terrible mistake. Not a single argument came to mind. Sure, there were plenty of reasons why they shouldn't make love. There were even more reasons why they shouldn't be together.

He didn't fit into her lifestyle—or at least, the lifestyle she'd determined would be best for her. He was rough and hard and had a red Trans Am named Lil. Far worse, he'd lied to her about his background. Of course, she'd also lied to him, she realized with a tinge of discomfort. Or at least, she'd omitted a few pertinent details about her background.

He'd climbed five steps and she still hadn't uttered a word.

And then it came to her. She didn't want to say anything that might stop him. She'd loved Ethan since the day he'd first rescued her grandmother from the purse snatcher. If Faith was honest with herself, she'd admit that she'd suspected from the start what sort of man he was. Anyone who could take down a petty thief with such casual efficiency couldn't be a simple businessman. He exuded danger. And passion. And excitement.

And she'd fallen without a moment's hesitation.

Just a few hours ago, while sitting outside Lily's day care center, she'd told herself she wouldn't get involved with him again. That it wasn't worth the heartache. She'd been so careful over the past five years to protect herself from being hurt again. But holding Ethan at a distance hadn't worked. It certainly hadn't lessened her pain. And she knew why. He was a part of her, a part she couldn't deny. She could no more cut herself off from him than she could cut herself off from her heart and soul.

''Oh, God.'' She buried her face against his shoulder. ''If you want me, you can have me.''

He paused at the top of the steps. ''In the biblical sense of wanting and having?'' he asked cautiously.

''Yes, yes! How many ways do you want me to say it? Just do it. I'm yours. Damn it, Ethan. Just *take* me.''

''Absolutely.'' He entered the bedroom and lowered her to her feet. He didn't bother turning on the light. The moon lit the room with a soft glow. ''Why don't we start by getting rid of our clothes,'' he suggested.

''Sounds good to me.''

Neither of them moved, and Ethan sensed the beginnings of an Awkward Moment. Taking a deep breath, he made the first move, stripping out of his clothing in short order. And then it was her turn. The pace slowed as he dealt with buttons and zippers and hooks, removing one garment after another. The pile of clothing at their feet grew until there was nothing left to remove. Moonlight poured over them, revealing all their secrets. Too many, if the truth be known. He sensed her gaze taking in the network of ridges left from his various injuries.

''I'm scarred.'' The words escaped of their own volition.

She didn't appear disturbed by the confession. "War wounds," she insisted. "Badges of honor."

"Not everyone would agree."

"I'm not everyone."

"That's true enough." He drew her onto the bed, sprawling across the soft cotton sheets. "You know, you scare the hell out of me, sweetheart."

"Me?" She sounded shocked. "Why?"

"Lots of reasons." An endless number. He popped off the top three. "I'm afraid you're a figment of my imagination. I'm afraid I'll let you down again. I'm afraid I can't give you what you want."

"Have I done that to you?" she questioned, concerned. "I'd hate to think I've added more pain and grief to your life."

"And joy. And happiness. I'm never happier than when I'm with you."

"Then allow me to correct a few of your misconceptions, Mr. Dunn." She came up onto her knees in front of him, totally unselfconscious in her nudity. "First, I'm not a figment of your imagination."

He smiled. That was for damn sure. "No?"

Moonlight cascaded over her, turning her hair to silver and her skin to alabaster. "No." She reached for his hand. "Here, touch me and see for yourself."

Who was he to argue? He started at her head and chased the path the moonlight took, tracing the exquisite planes of her profile, down the length of her neck to her breasts. They were heavier than before, fuller since the birth of their daughter. He'd missed seeing that, missed seeing her ripen with child. Missed her labor to bring their baby into the world. Missed watching her nurse Lily. He didn't intend to miss another moment in either her life or Lily's.

The moonlight beckoned to him, drawing him farther along his path of exploration. He slid his fingers across the tip of each breast, watching them pearl with excitement. Then he ran his hand downward, across her belly to the juncture of her thighs. He swerved off the path and delved into shadow.

"Are you still afraid I'm a figment of your imagination?" The question escaped in a husky whisper.

"I have to admit you feel real enough." His voice echoed the raw desire quickening within. "Give me a minute to make sure."

She shivered. "What else were you afraid of? Letting me down? Not giving me what I want? There's only one way you could do that."

She didn't need to clarify further. "That's not too likely," he hastened to assure her.

"Then what are you waiting for?"

The provocation worked. He shifted into a patch of moonlight, which revealed features gritty with tension. No one seeing him now would ever call him a "pretty boy." The taut lines revealed a man pushed to the brink. His eyes were indigo in the darkness, the blue barely discernible. They glittered in the subdued lighting, flaming with desire, his hunger a physical force straining for release.

Her own passion leaped in response. It was time to close the door to a painful past and open another that would lead them toward a new life. Tonight would do just that. It had been an eternity since she'd last had him in her bed like this, but she remembered each and every occasion as though it were yesterday.

Their times together had been amazing, one night soft and gentle, another time hard and urgent. Still another, playful. Tonight she wasn't interested in either gentle or playful. She wanted him hard and urgent, with a little desperation thrown in for good measure. The need lashed through her, turning her tidy, white-picket world into sheer chaos.

Somehow their limbs became entangled, locking them in

an inescapable embrace. His mouth found hers and he slid inward, their tongues dueling in a ritualistic mating dance. The moment was achingly familiar, one they'd shared countless times in the past. It brought back memories, most good, some bittersweet. He must have felt the same way. He stirred above her.

"Don't go there, Faith. Don't remember."

"They're good memories," she protested. "It's only later that they became something else."

He took her mouth with a hint of contrition. "I would have come back if I'd known," he told her between each hungry kiss. "I wouldn't have left you to handle it all alone."

"I'm not alone. Not anymore." She shielded him in a protective circle of arms and legs. "And neither are you."

The words impacted harder than she'd intended. Or he felt them harder. He bowed his head, his forehead resting against hers. His breath came in deep, painful gulps. "You don't know what it's been like these past five years."

Did he really believe that? "What part don't I know, Ethan? Feeling like you're all alone? Feeling like your life has taken a whole series of turns you never intended? Feeling like your life's been ripped apart and put together again, only put together wrong?"

"Fair enough. I guess you do understand."

"Yes, I do." She cupped his face, forcing him to look at her, and willing him to believe this time as she repeated, "You're not alone, Ethan. Not anymore."

Something shifted in his face and in his eyes. A lightening. An easing. A gentling of whatever turmoil smoldered beneath the surface. He turned from an inward focus to an outward one, concentrating on her. Determination solidified. "We're in this together," he said. "You and me."

She smiled. "You and me against the world. Isn't that what we always said?"

Without taking his gaze from hers, he slipped his hand between their bodies. His downward movement was so slow and deliberate that she began to squirm before he was halfway there. He reached the apex of her thighs and cupped her, his middle finger barely touching the tiny bud hidden within the folds. If his weight hadn't kept her pressed against the mattress, she would have shot off the bed.

"Easy, honey."

She turned her head from side to side. "You're killing me."

"Not yet." His fingers splayed, dipping inward, then withdrawing. Teasing. Stroking. He scraped the painfully sensitive flesh with his fingertips. "But soon."

Too soon. If he didn't stop now, it would be all over before it had begun. "No, Ethan. Wait."

He hesitated. "You want me to stop?"

"Yes!"

He pulled back in concern. "Honey—"

"It's not what you think. I just want to slow down a little."

She reversed their positions. Holding his gaze, she let her hands drift downward in an imitation of the path he'd taken. Her fingertips traced along the whorls of hair matting his chest, before following the narrow band arrowing across his belly. Just as he'd teased her with a gradual downward spiral, she teased him. She inched ever lower until she found him, cupped him, wrapped him up in a gentle fist. He tried to say something, his throat working frantically. He managed a harsh sound that combined threat with demand, and she released a laugh of sheer joy.

"Welcome home, darling."

"You will pay for this, woman."

"Don't you like it?" she asked with mock innocence.

"What do you think?"

In a quick, practiced move, he tossed her onto her back

and forced her hands above her head. Their fingers meshed, clinging together. ''If you knew how long it's been since I've made love to a woman, you wouldn't take risks like that.''

''How long has it been?''

''Take Lily's age and add seven months. That's how long it's been since I left you, isn't it?''

Her breath caught in her throat. ''Oh, Ethan,'' she whispered unevenly.

''You were a once-in-a-lifetime sort of love, sweetheart. After you, I didn't want anyone else.''

He didn't give her a chance to say anything further. Lowering his head, he captured the tip of her breast between his teeth. It blossomed beneath his touch. At the same time he released her hands and parted her thighs, intent on further exploration. Fires that had been banked burst into flame again. Moisture gathered around his fingers and he followed it inward, dipping to the very core of her. She tensed, helpless to control her reaction. A painful knotting began, a tightening that grew more critical with each passing second. She needed more. Much more. The tantalizing touch came again, dipping and stroking. She dug her fingers into his shoulders, teetering on the very edge.

''Ethan!'' The warning exploded from her. She was close. So close.

He kissed her, a quick, biting kiss. ''I love you, Faith,'' he told her. ''I always have and I always will.''

She was too mindless to do more than whimper his name.

Kneeling between her widespread legs, he mated her body with his, his actions every bit as hard and thorough as she needed. He'd made an impossible trip home, one that had defied the years—even defied death itself. And she wanted to feel him totally. Completely. With every fiber of her being. The urgency built between them, a primal demand that frustrated all resistance.

"I want to go slow," he said through gritted teeth. "I want to enjoy every second."

She bucked beneath him. "No, fast. Slow later. Fast...now."

They moved together, uncertainly at first—an orchestra warming to its music. Arms collided. Legs kinked before finding the perfect spot to entwine. Hands fought for supremacy. Mouths miscued only to try again, this time with astonishing results.

And then the concerto began, the music in perfect pitch. The give and take, the drive and slide, the thrust and parry came together as nature had always intended. She moved with him, called to him. And he responded, his voice harmonizing with hers, his movements an elegant match. It was as if they'd never been apart.

The music lashed them, soaring and graceful, driving toward an exquisite culmination. They fought their way to a crescendo beyond anything they'd ever known. Long ago there had been love, there'd been a mating of minds and bodies. But with every moment that passed, every movement that sealed them as one, Faith knew this bonding was far more. This time their souls mated, as well.

Ethan must have sensed it, too. "I told myself I could live without you. Without this."

"You were wrong." The words were absolute and undeniable.

Then she couldn't speak, could scarcely breathe. Contractions rippled through her, a direct counterpoint to the song they were singing. The counterpoint grew, overtaking the song. He drove inward and she peaked, closing around him like a velvet fist. He sheathed himself within her and they clung to each other as the climax rushed over and through them, singing an unearthly song of completion.

The silence that followed was eerie, shattered only by their ragged breathing. It was a long time before he could speak. "It's always been like that with you," he murmured against her throat. "I can't explain why. I just know you make me whole."

"We were always good together...at least in bed."

"No. It was more than that and you know it."

She started to respond, but a huge yawn interrupted her. "I think you've worn me out," she murmured.

He decided not to push. As usual, his timing was off. But at least their relationship was moving in the right direction. The rest would come, given time. "I *know* you've worn *me* out," he responded lightly.

He reached down and snagged the covers. Before he'd finished tucking them in, Faith was asleep. He lay awake for a long while, finding a simple pleasure in watching her, wondering what miracle had allowed him to reenter her life. So many things had gone wrong in his past. It felt good to have one thing go right. All that remained was finding Lily. He touched the ring strung around his throat, which served as part talisman, part compass. And he would. No matter what it took, he'd have his daughter home by Christmas.

He yawned in turn, his eyes drifting shut. But right now, he'd take the gift fate had bestowed—a peaceful night's sleep with Faith in his arms.

CHAPTER THIRTEEN

THE NIGHTMARE CREPT into his subconscious, stealing all hope. All trust. He smelled the cigar, felt the bitter bite of leather against flesh. And he heard the words that he'd ultimately believed, instead of keeping faith with what he knew in his heart to be true.

"Not Faith," he muttered. "She'll wait."

But she hadn't waited, and in the dream he knew she wouldn't, knew that all hope was lost. Still, there was a way out. A way that would end his pain. All he had to do was tell them what he knew, and his torment would be over. But he couldn't. If he told, he'd lose everything—not just Faith and his self-respect. He'd lose his very soul.

"Ethan?"

A bedside light flared to life, temporarily blinding him. "No, don't!" He bolted upright in bed, the breath shuddering from his lungs. "I don't know! I don't know...."

Gentle hands crept across his chest. "You don't know what, Ethan?"

"I...I don't know anything."

Her voice was low-pitched and soothing. "You were dreaming."

He thrust a hand through his hair. "Yeah. Dreaming."

"Another nightmare?"

"You could say that."

"About Lily?"

"No." He bowed his head, struggling to shake off the aftereffects of the dream. "Not Lily."

''About your experience in South America? When you were captured?''

''I don't want to talk about it.''

She ignored him. ''You mentioned my name. You said, 'Not Faith. She'll wait.'''

''Did I? I don't remember.'' Awareness of his surroundings slowly crept into his consciousness. It was the deepest, darkest part of night, his least favorite time. Terrifying creatures stirred in these dead hours, stalking through thoughts and dreams. Only daylight brought salvation. ''What time is it? How close to morning?''

She disregarded the question. ''What was I supposed to wait for?''

He closed his eyes, trying to distance himself mentally. But the dream still held too tight a grip. He couldn't shut down. Couldn't compartmentalize. Couldn't shove the memories and emotions into that dark, untouchable place. ''Don't go there. Please.'' His throat worked. ''Don't.''

But she kept going anyway, chipping away at a time and a place and an event he'd do anything to keep from her. ''I was supposed to wait for you? Is that what you meant?''

''Yeah, I guess.''

''But I didn't wait, did I?''

''No. You married your rich banker. You were pregnant with his son.''

She cupped his face and forced him to look at her. ''I didn't marry Christopher. The baby wasn't his. She's yours.''

''He said…'' Ethan struggled to separate reality from fantasy, to differentiate between here and now versus what had once been. ''Aw, hell. It doesn't matter.''

''It does matter. What did he say?''

Ethan took one look at her and was lost. The words came of their own volition. ''That you wouldn't wait for me. That you were married to some rich banker. That you were having his baby.''

"And when you returned home..." Her gaze remained locked with his, her eyes a brilliant gold, full of rich, clear light. He could see compassion reflected there, but without the cloying sympathy that would have allowed him to push her away. "I was marrying someone else. Christopher. A banker."

"Yes."

"So you did the honorable thing."

"I walked."

"But you didn't stay away."

The muscles along his jaw tightened. "I tried. God help me, I tried. But I couldn't. I needed to see you one final time. I just wanted to know if you were still married to him. If you were happy."

"Your nightmares...they're memories of your time in captivity?"

He brushed aside the question. "I answered that already."

"Fair enough. Answer this instead. After you were rescued, you ended up in the hospital. You said it was because you were injured. Did that happen when you escaped?"

He fought free of her hold and abandoned the bed. "Yeah. When I escaped."

She followed him, dogging his steps. "What about before then? Were you hurt before you escaped?"

He shrugged, but she kept pushing. Pushing. Always pushing.

"Look at me, Ethan. Stop pacing and look at me." She caught his arm. Did she have any idea how dangerous that was? How dangerous *he* was, especially in the throes of that dream? "How were you injured? Why were you in the hospital so long?"

"It has nothing to do with you."

"I think it does. Maybe Jack can tell me."

"*No!* Leave Jack out of this."

"Then you tell me."

"You don't want to know."

"Yes, I do."

"No!" He exploded then, getting in her face and allowing the emotions to rip loose. It felt good, pounding out the words. Letting them spill free after years of being shoved down. Punctuating the air like a punch-drunk boxer. "You don't want to know what happens when a man gets taken. When they have questions that he can't answer. When he's honor bound to keep his silence. You don't want to know the methods they use to try to get him to talk."

"What did they do to you?" she whispered.

"I got off easy." His voice cracked and he slammed his fist against his chest. "Look at me. All my parts intact. Ten fingers. Ten toes. All the vital equipment a man should have. Some broken bones. Maybe a lot of broken bones. But hey. I'm alive, right?"

Her eyes were bright. Too bright. It hurt to look at them. "They tortured you. That's why you were in the hospital. That's why it took six months to recover."

"Yes, damn it! They tortured me." The words howled from him. "Are you happy now? Is that what you wanted to hear?"

"No." The tears spilled over. "It's not what I wanted to hear. But it's what you had to say. It's what you needed to tell me so I'd understand."

"You don't understand," he shouted. "Not one damn thing. How could you?"

She came right back at him. "Yes, I do. I understand that your love for me kept you alive for six months while you were beaten and tortured. I understand that you should have died and didn't because you wouldn't give up, not as long as you had me to come home to. I understand that when you finally crawled out of that hellhole, you found your worse nightmare had become reality. I'd failed you."

His darkest secret came screaming out. "Yes, damn you! You *failed* me. You were supposed to wait. You were supposed to love me as much as I loved you. I made a choice.

I went on one last mission. And I saved Davis, but I lost you. There are nights when I wake up wishing I'd let him die. There are times when I hate him, hate the choice I made—''

''And hate me?''

That stopped him. He sucked in a great, shuddering breath. Then another. ''Not hate. Anger? Yes. Betrayal? Absolutely. But never hate.''

''Jack told me you were dead,'' she tried to explain.

Ethan had gone beyond rational thought. ''You should have known I wasn't! You should have felt it. Instead, you were going to marry Christopher and become Mr. and Mrs. White Picket Fence. Have you any idea how much that hurt? I've seen that world you're part of and I don't fit into it. God knows, I've wanted to. You have no idea how badly I've wanted to. But men like me, we're always on the outside looking in. And all I want…'' He threw back his head. ''All I want is for someone to let me in.''

''I'll let you in.'' She slid her arms around his waist, risking life and limb with her touch. ''The gate's open, Ethan. Just walk through.''

''And then what? Hide inside with you?''

''Hide?'' He felt the tiny leap her heart gave. ''I'm not hiding.''

''Don't lie to me. Don't you dare. Not now. Not after you've sliced and diced every inch of me.''

She leaned into him, resting her head against his chest. The breath sighed from her lungs. ''I'm not hiding. I'm trying to create—create something different from what I had growing up.''

His arms stole around her without conscious thought, his hold entirely protective. ''What are you talking about? You've always had the perfect world. I mean, I know your father left you, but your mother…''

It was time for total truth. Total honesty. To share her darkest secret the way he'd shared his. ''My mother walked out of the house shortly after my father left, and she never came back.''

He swallowed, taking a moment to absorb her words. ''What do you mean…never came back?''

''I mean I never saw her again.''

The single word that escaped him was shockingly coarse. Then he added, ''What did you do?''

''I kept it a secret for a couple of weeks. At first, I thought she'd return. Every day, every minute of every day, I expected her to walk back through the door. Then the money ran out. So did the food. And still she didn't come. I was desperate. Eventually my teacher caught on and called social services. Elizabeth arrived within hours. From that point on, she became my anchor in a stormy world.''

''And you've been chasing your own picket-fence lifestyle ever since.''

''Yes. That's why I was so angry when I found out you'd lied to me about being a businessman.''

''And why you wanted boring. And safe.''

''No Rambos need apply.'' A bittersweet smile crept across her mouth. ''So what did I get?''

''Rambo with attitude.'' He tucked a wayward lock of hair behind her ear. ''We're one hell of a pair, aren't we?''

She lifted her luminous gaze to his. ''I do have a suggestion.''

''And what's that?''

''We can create our own world, Ethan. It might not have the most perfect picket fence. At least, not the sort we dreamed about when we were kids. Maybe it'll be a hot pink or a bright orange instead of white. But it'll suit us.''

''And Lily.'' He hesitated, his voice turning gruff. ''And Lily's brothers and sisters.''

Her mouth trembled, curving into a shaky smile. ''It's a start. As for the rest…'' She shrugged. ''We can make it up as we go along, can't we? Figure out what suits us best?''

''Works for me.'' He gave her a serious look. ''And I'll

start with a promise. I swear to you, Faith, on my honor. I won't leave you again. Not ever. No more soldiering, no more trying to save the world and everyone in it. I'm through with that life. I don't know what I'm qualified to do instead. But I'll find something."

She smiled the sort of smile women do when they want to leave a man baffled and bewildered. He hadn't a clue what it meant. Before he could ask, she caught his hand in hers and tugged him toward the bed. "Come on. We can worry about that some other time."

He allowed himself to be dragged onto the mattress—a man could resist for only so long. Then he kissed her. And with that one kiss, he discovered something quite amazing. When he was held within Faith's arms, the ghosts from his past were locked out of their world, leaving the two of them sealed safely inside. After that, there was no more time for thinking, or worrying about ghosts, or the past, or even the future.

There was only Faith, open and loving and constant.

He gave to her, anointing her with tender words and reverent touches until he felt her desire wash over her in ever increasing waves. He cupped her breast, filling his palm with the life-giving beat of her heart. There wasn't an inch of her body he left untouched or unappreciated. He reveled in every dip and curve and slope, lingering until he'd mapped it all. By the time he was done, slow and leisurely had become urgent and hungry.

She lifted herself to him as he came down on her, their hips meshing, locking in frantic need. He thrilled to it, free for the first time to give himself without the past shadowing his every impulse. Their lovemaking turned demanding, hard and driven on one hand, soft and fluid on the other. He eased into her, but it wasn't enough for either of them. He drove in, the taking swift and wild and aggressive. She twisted beneath him and he angled her hips upward, melding the two of them together.

They moved in concert, duplicating the timeless rhythm they'd perfected earlier, mated in mutual need and desire. The tension built, moment upon moment, storming through them, devastating barriers and defenses and artifice, until all that remained was an expression as honest as it was glorious. When their release came, it was beyond anything they'd experienced before, an unstoppable storm of such power they were helpless in its path.

The aftermath left them both shaken.

And then, in those timeless seconds of total vulnerability, Faith did something that almost destroyed him. She looked at him. Looked at him with eyes of pure gold, eyes filled with something he never thought he'd see again. Love. Honest and faithful and absolute. It was a love that promised she'd wait, even if it meant a lifetime. That she'd believe, even against all odds. That she trusted, even when everyone else doubted.

It was a love that promised forever.

ETHAN AWOKE, feeling strangely contented. Faith lay snuggled in his arms, her profile peeking out from a fluffy blond cloud. The nightmare that had haunted him for so many years was gone. Something deep inside had loosened and finally let go. The anger and fear, even the feeling of grief and betrayal had faded, slipping away within the healing balm of Faith's embrace.

The clock read almost noon, and he realized with a start that Christmas was just two short days away. He fingered the ring suspended from his neck. A certainty built, gaining hold with each passing moment. Lily would be home when Christmas morning dawned. Somehow, some way, he'd make it happen.

There were details missing.

The words slipped through his mind, driving him from the bed. Faith muttered a protest, but he simply scooped her up and limped into the bathroom. Turning on the shower, he walked into the stall, still holding Faith.

When the spray hit her, she gasped, burrowing deeper into Ethan's arms. "You're cruel," she accused. "You didn't even wait for it to get hot."

He simply laughed. "Better than coffee for getting your engine revved."

"I'll take the coffee," she informed him.

"Yeah?" He cupped her bottom with soapy hands. "I'll take you."

It was a long time before they left the shower. The water had gone from cold to hot and back to cold again, the sudden drop in temperature chasing them from the stall. After they'd dressed and eaten, Ethan hit her with his announcement. "I'd like to go back to Bettina's apartment."

Faith took it more calmly than he'd anticipated. "Why?"

"Ever since we left, I've had this nagging feeling we overlooked something. Something important."

"What are we missing?"

He smiled. "If I knew that—"

She cut him off with a wave of her hand. "Right. Silly of me to ask. So, how do we get inside?"

"I want to avoid asking for Luke's help. For one thing, I don't think he'd let us go through the apartment again—we were pushing our luck last time. And for another, if I warned him ahead of time that I want in, he might try and stop us."

"How *do* you plan to get in?"

He offered his most charming grin. "I was thinking we'd try a simple frontal assault."

"Ah, got it. Plan A." She wrinkled her nose at him, a teasing gleam in her eyes. "We ask the manager to let us in."

"Exactly. I'm hoping he'll remember us from our visit with Luke and assume we're with the police department. If we're really lucky, he won't ask any awkward questions."

"And if that doesn't work?"

"We go with Plan B. We find a way to slip in unnoticed."

She shook her head in mock disapproval. "Why do I get the feeling Plan B involves Jack, somehow?"

Ethan lifted a shoulder. "He does know his way around a lock."

Fortunately, Plan A proved such an unmitigated success they were able to skip Plan B altogether. The building manager did remember them from their previous visit, and let them into the apartment without asking so much as a single question or requesting identification. He clearly assumed they were with the police, and they didn't bother disabusing him of the notion, although Faith almost broke down under the weight of sheer guilt. Realizing how close she was to confessing all, Ethan whisked her into the apartment and closed the door in the manager's face.

"Take a deep breath and remember why we're doing this," Ethan told her. "If you have to confess, you can do it later, after Lily's home."

Faith twisted her hands together. "I wouldn't have made a very good mercenary."

"You're right. And you have no idea how happy that makes me. Come on. Let's get a move on."

Once again, they drifted from room to room, simply looking. "I don't see anything we might have missed last time," Faith said after twenty minutes of unproductive activity.

"Neither do I. But it's here."

"What I don't get is why Bettina was so certain Abby would understand the reference to Mary Lou."

Ethan shook his head. "Beats me. There isn't anyone named Mary Lou on the payroll at the jewelry exchange. We know that much for sure."

"Could she be a customer?"

"Luke already thought of that. He's checking."

Faith wandered into the living room and studied the paintings on the wall again. Ethan trailed behind, his hands stuffed into his pockets. "Could it be someone she met socially with Bettina?" he asked.

"Abby says she never socialized with the woman."

"What about with Julian?"

"No. He was into a whole different scene that catered to the rich and famous-in-their-own-minds. Fancy cars. Yachts. Lavish parties. Probably a flirtation with drugs. Gambling."

"I get the picture."

Faith circled the room, pausing by the ornate glass-and-chrome table, decorated with its silver-framed photos. She studied them again—Bettina draped in white fur, Bettina asleep on the couch, Bettina Sports Girl.

Ethan reached past her and snagged the sailing photo from the table. "She does look good in that getup."

Faith muttered something uncomplimentary beneath her breath. Taking the photo from him, she started to return it, then hesitated. "Huh."

"What?"

"Just a thought." Going with her gut instinct, she flipped over the frame and carefully removed the backing so she could get to the photo. "Check this out. What does that look like to you?"

"Where?"

Faith tapped the bottom of the photo. "This part here that was covered by the frame."

Ethan squinted. "A name?"

"Hang on. I might have something we can use." She handed Ethan the photo and rummaged through her purse. "Come on, come on. Where are you?" A minute later she came up with a velvet drawstring bag that held a round glass magnifying disk. Ethan handed her the photo and she ran the disk across the bottom of the photo. "Oh, God."

"What?" She didn't say a word, simply handed him the photo and magnifier. He peered through the glass. The name painted on the boat swam in front of his eyes for an instant before coming into focus.

It was the *Mary Lou.*

"CAN YOU SEE WHAT THEY'RE doing, kid?"

"Yes. They're being very, very naughty."

Bettina fought to remain calm. "Naughty, how?"

"Crock's giving Julian a gun." The girl flashed wide blue eyes in Bettina's direction. "Now can I be a snake? I need to bite them very bad."

Oh, man. This couldn't be good. "Soon, kid. Soon," Bettina said, her thoughts racing. Time was fast running out. "We'll make our move soon."

Lily settled cross-legged on her bed. "Are they going to shoot us?"

The question shocked Bettina, more so because Lily asked it so matter-of-factly. "No! Absolutely not," she lied.

"Are they going to shoot Emily's mommy?"

"Why do you think that?"

"I heard Julian say so to Crock. I pretended to be asleep. Julian wanted to steal Emily. But Crock said no, Detective Sloan wouldn't let that happen. But maybe they could shoot Abby instead, 'cuz Detective Sloan couldn't stop a bullet. Then they were going to run away."

"Try not to worry, Lily. We'll get out of here and warn them."

"Okay. But then I'm going to bite Crock and Julian really, really hard for being so bad."

"You scare me, kid."

"Yeah, that's what my mommy says, too." An engine rumbled beneath them and Lily scrambled off her bed and into Bettina's arms. "What's that?" she asked fearfully.

Bettina closed her eyes. "They're moving the boat."

Time was up.

ETHAN DROVE AS FAST AS he dared, at the same time punching numbers into his cell phone. As soon as Faith realized what he was doing, she snatched it from his hands. ''Give me that,'' she snapped. ''You could kill someone that way.''

He didn't argue. ''Get hold of Sloan. Fast.'' He fumbled with the detective's business card. ''His number's on there. Try his cell if he's not at the office.''

He wasn't, and Faith left a voice message for him before calling his cell phone. Once again they were routed to voice mail. ''No good,'' she said. ''He's out of reach.''

''Are you sure the *Mary Lou* is berthed at Sunset Marina?''

''Positive. It's along Seaview, on Shilshole Bay.''

''You can tell all that from the photo?'' he asked doubtfully.

''In this instance, yes. Sunset Marina has this huge pelican statue near the boat slips, and Lily and I took a picture of it when we walked along there one day, looking at all the boats.'' She tapped the photo, speaking with such limitless patience he felt like a total heel for questioning her. ''I can see a piece of the statue in the background.''

It seemed to take forever to get to the marina. ''It's because of the Christmas Ship Festival,'' Ethan said, frustration edging his voice. ''Everyone's headed for the marina either to take out a boat or to watch the decorated ones leave.''

Twenty minutes later they arrived. Ethan left Lil double-parked and raced into the office, with Faith right behind. He cut to the front of the line and addressed the kid behind the counter, a skinny youngster with a name tag that read Timmy. ''This is an emergency, Timmy,'' he explained. ''I need to know if you have a boat moored here by the name of *Mary Lou*.''

Timmy wasn't impressed. ''Dude. Like, wait your turn—''

Ethan snagged the kid's shirt, knotting his fist just beneath Timmy's frantically bobbing Adam's apple. He half dragged the boy across the counter. "Answer the question, dude. Like *now.*"

"Ethan." Faith stood at his elbow, her calming voice washing over him. "Let him go."

The minute Ethan released the boy, Faith stepped forward. "You probably heard about the recent kidnapping that's been in all the papers?" At Timmy's apprehensive nod, she said, "The little girl who was taken is our daughter. We believe she may be on the *Mary Lou.* Do you have a boat by that name moored here?"

That got through to him. "Let me look it up." He shot a nervous glance in Ethan's direction, careful to stay out of arm's reach as he hurried to a computer terminal. Rapid key tapping followed. After what seemed an interminable wait, he pointed toward the pelican statue on the north side of the marina. "The *Mary Lou.* Slip 241."

Ethan and Faith took off at a run. They chose the wrong boardwalk on their first attempt, pelting to the very end before they discovered their mistake. By the time they found the right one, Ethan was limping badly, hopping more than running. They finally reached the correct slip.

It was empty.

Faith took one look and threw herself into Ethan's arms, bursting into tears. He stood there for an endless moment, his arms wrapped around Faith, staring in crazed disbelief at the empty berth. They'd come so close, he could practically feel his daughter's essence, catch the little-girl scent of her, hear her voice whispering across the water in a desperate plea. He couldn't contain himself.

"Lily!" he bellowed.

Her name reverberated off the lapping waves before being swept up by the northwest wind and carried away.

LILY LIFTED HER HEAD. "What's that noise?"

"Just the wind, kid. Now, pay attention. I've drawn a picture for you." Bettina tapped it with one of the crayons

Julian had reluctantly provided for Lily's entertainment. "Take a look and tell me the truth. Are you sure you can be a snake?"

"Yes."

"Next problem. Do you know how to unlock a door?"

An abashed expression drifted across her face and she squirmed. "Promise to keep it a secret?"

"I promise."

"Sometimes I get a chair and unlock the door at home," she said in a rushed whisper. "Promise you won't tell my mommy?"

Bettina gave her a quick hug. "Cross my heart. Now, listen up, kid." She picked a different colored crayon and began to draw. "Here's what I need you to do."

THE NEXT FIFTEEN MINUTES passed in a blur. The owner of the boat in the slip next to the *Mary Lou* was able to describe the missing yacht and reassure them that it had left the marina less than a half hour ahead of them. They then managed to talk Timmy into renting them a speedboat, a sleek eighteen-foot Sea Ray.

Parking Lil, Ethan rummaged in her trunk for a blanket and a long black carrying case. "Let's go."

"Have you ever driven one of these things before?" Faith asked.

"Yeah, as a kid." He hopped onto the swim platform at the back of the boat and then to the vinyl carpet covering the fiberglass floor of the cockpit. Turning, he helped Faith aboard. "I figure it's like riding a bicycle."

"Uh-huh." She stepped gingerly off the platform and staggered to the passenger seat. "You have ridden a bicycle, right?"

"Hey, no sweat." Taking the helm, he threw the speedboat into reverse by mistake and nearly slammed into the yacht tied up behind them. He swerved with inches to spare. "We're okay. No need to panic. I think I've got the hang of it now.'' His expression revealed a touch of chagrin. ''But just to be on the safe side, let's get the hell out of here before Timmy changes his mind about renting to us.''

They exited the marina at a sedate ''no wake'' speed and headed south toward the city. ''Where do we look?'' Faith asked over the drone of the engine. It was chilly in the boat, even though she was wrapped up in her winter coat, and she huddled low in the seat behind the windshield. ''They could be anywhere.''

Not anywhere. Julian needed some specific conditions for what he'd have planned. ''I've been thinking about that,'' Ethan said. ''I'm almost positive they'll be with the Christmas boat parade.''

Faith had read about the parade. Boaters from all over the area decorated their vessels with Christmas lights and then cruised the waterways along a given route. Luke had said that some of the ships, particularly the sailboats, were a truly magnificent sight. ''How do you know that's where they'll be?''

''Because they can hide in the crowd. They'll be just one more boat decked out for the parade.''

Another concern struck her. ''Do you know the route?'

''They'll be between Lake Washington and Lake Union. Timmy gave us a map of the waterways. Take a look at it for me. I want to take the ship canal through the Ballard Locks and catch up with them somewhere between the two lakes, though I'm guessing we'll find them closer to Lake Washington.''

''Why would the *Mary Lou* go there? What are they planning?'' She could tell Ethan didn't want to answer. She caught his grim look and began to tremble. ''No. They're not going to kill Lily.''

''Honey—''

''*No!* How can you even think that? Why now? Why tonight? Why there?''

He answered reluctantly. ''Because this is the last night

of the parade. In all the Christmas confusion, they can sink the *Mary Lou* and make it look like an accident. Without proof to the contrary, the authorities will assume that Bettina—probably due to inexperience—made a critical error and the boat went down.''

''I don't understand. Why do they need to make it look like an accident? Why not just kill Bettina and Lily outright?''

''Because then the authorities will know that there's another party involved, namely Julian,'' Ethan explained patiently. ''He needs Bettina to take the blame for both the fencing operation and the kidnapping. Alive, she can turn on him. Dead, she can't. Dead with Lily, alone on a boat, she's silent and guilty.''

Comprehension set in and Faith grabbed Ethan's arm. ''If Julian can pull off an accident, there won't be any proof he was involved in any of this. He'll walk.''

A deadly light gleamed in Ethan's eyes. ''No, honey. He won't. One way or another, he's going down.''

CHAPTER FOURTEEN

"ARE YOU READY?" Bettina asked.

"Yes."

"You sure you can do it?"

Lily looked scared, but determined. "I think so."

"Okay. Let me get these screws the rest of the way out."

Bettina pulled a silver nail file from her purse—one Julian and Crock had overlooked, thankfully—and carefully removed the four Phillips head screws holding the access panel in place. Setting the upholstered piece of plywood to one side, she studied the engine compartment. It was dark and deafeningly loud and absolutely terrifying.

She closed her eyes. If she found it that bad, how would a kid react? One quick look gave her the answer. Lily appeared on the verge of panicking, and Bettina sucked it up, knowing what she had to do. She caught the little girl by her shoulders.

"Now, listen up," she barked in her best drill sergeant voice. "You're the only one who can do this. I'm too big to fit in there. The only way we win is if you're brave enough to crawl in there and save us. What's it going to be, kid? A big, brave lion, or a scared little mouse?"

Lily's bottom lip poked out. "A big, brave lion won't fit in there." Tears welled up in her eyes. "But a scared little mouse might."

ETHAN TURNED TO FAITH. "Heads up, honey. We're going to drift in and out among the various boats. Give a shout if you spot the *Mary Lou,* but do it quietly. We don't want Julian to realize we're on to him.'' Ethan pulled out his cell phone. ''I'll keep trying to raise the authorities.''

The phone chirped before he could place the call, and he thumbed the Connect button. ''Dunn here.''

''Ethan?'' Static blasted through the line. ''Damn, I...hardly...you. It's Luke.''

''Sloan? Where the hell have you been? I've been trying to reach you for hours.'' He grimaced. ''Never mind that. We found the *Mary Lou.* It's not a person, Luke. It's a boat. Did you get that? It's a boat.''

Luke cut him off. ''Listen, listen! We've got problems. Julian's driver...is dead. He came after Abby with a gun and I...take him out. We...able to get any information...about Lily. Did...hear? No information...''

Ethan swore, trying to piece together the conversation. This wasn't good. Not good at all. ''Okay, okay. We think we know where Lily is, but I need help. Now. We're in the Lake Washington ship canal. We've just left the Chittenden Locks.''

''Where? Speak up. I...hear you. There's...static.''

''The Chittenden Locks,'' Ethan repeated. ''We just came through and are heading for Lake Union.''

The signal cleared briefly. ''Listen to me. If Crock's in on this, Julian must be, too. Be careful. He could be armed.''

''Can you get the Harbor Patrol looking for the *Mary Lou?*''

''I'll call it in. Do you have...sort of boat she is?''

The signal faded. ''A Bayliner yacht. White. Thirty-five to forty foot.''

''Got it. Will call...in.''

With that, the phone went dead, and Ethan relayed as much as he'd been able to understand to Faith. Hearing about Crock, she turned pale and her expression closed down. But she didn't say anything, just set her chin and kept scanning the boats they passed. Ethan could only hope that Luke had caught all the information and would pass it on to the patrol.

He kept their speed slightly under the posted seven knots, sliding delicately in and out of traffic. Night had fallen, along with the temperature. He leaned over and tucked the wool blanket he'd brought around Faith. Even with a blanket and coat, the wind cut through her, he could tell. Not that she complained.

When they reached Lake Union, he throttled back on the motor. From here, the lake dipped down to the south, forming a long, thick finger between Queen Anne and Capitol Hill. Dozens of brightly lit boats cruised the shoreline, showing off their Christmas finery. Directly across from them and looping to the north was the canal that led to Portage and Union Bays. Beyond that was Lake Washington.

Faith checked the map and gestured toward Lake Union. "If we go that way, we've got more than a square mile of water to check. Do we search there, or keep going toward Lake Washington?"

Ethan thought about it for a minute. "Lake Washington. If they plan to scuttle the boat, that's where they'll do it."

"OKAY, LITTLE MOUSE. In you go."

"Don't forget the scared part—it's a scared little mouse," Lily corrected.

"Right. A scared little mouse who's going to scamper through that hole quick as can be and out the other side."

Lily nodded and Bettina turned her toward the engine compartment. She felt like pond scum, but if they had a hope of getting out of this alive, Lily would have to work her way past the two engines and out the other side.

"I know it's noisy, but the engines are covered. There aren't any parts that can hurt you. Just squeeze through that little space. When you get past them, turn this way—" Bettina pointed to the left "—and you'll be in a storage area.

Remember the picture I drew you? There'll be a tiny door you can push open and you'll be all done with the scary part. Once you're out, sneak back toward our room and unlock the door. We know Crock's not back yet, and Julian will be way up on top, driving the boat. If you're careful and stay against the wall, he won't see you. Okay? You should remember how to get back here from the times you've gone to the bathroom. You ready?''

Lily nodded, a tear escaping down her cheek. But she didn't back away. Taking a deep breath, she crawled into the engine compartment, inching her way between the twin diesels. When she reached the back of the engines, she turned to the left, out of sight. An instant later she poked her head back around and actually grinned. The mouse had transformed into a lion. Then she disappeared.

The wait was endless, so long that Bettina was afraid Julian had caught the poor kid and tossed her overboard. Then she heard a faint scratching at the door, followed by the dead bolt snicking home. An instant later, the door swung open and Bettina grabbed the little girl in a tight hug. ''You are the smartest, bravest, most incredible kid I've ever met,'' she crowed.

Lily dimpled in pleasure. ''Come on. Let's run away. We can bite Julian some other time.''

''Now, why would anyone want to bite me?'' a congenial voice asked from behind them.

''WEBSTER'S POINT IS DEAD ahead,'' Ethan said, indicating a peninsula jutting out near the entrance to Lake Washington. He frowned. If the *Mary Lou* had already gone past the point, their chances of finding her in time would drop significantly.

''There!'' Faith grabbed Ethan's arm and gestured toward a sleek white Bayliner yacht, drifting deep in the shadows away from traffic. ''Doesn't that say...? Yes, it's the *Mary Lou!*''

He scrutinized the boat. Sure enough, he could just make out the elegant lettering scrawled across the stern. The next moment the name dipped beneath a wave. "Aw, hell. He's already doing it. He's sinking her."

Faith shot out of her seat. "Ethan, there's a struggle going on. You have to get over there—fast!"

He angled the motorboat toward the yacht and hammered down on the throttle. The Sea Ray shot across the bay. They could see two figures struggling at the back of the yacht—a man and a woman. A little girl stood behind the man, beating at him with her fists and shrieking at the top of her lungs.

"It's Lily!" Faith grabbed the windshield for balance. "Dear God, Ethan. Hurry!"

The struggle continued. Then the man on the yacht backhanded the woman—it had to be Bettina Carlton and Julian Black—and yanked something from beneath his coat. "Gun," Ethan shouted. "Faith, get the case I brought."

She fell to the floor and scrambled to retrieve the case from the storage compartment where Ethan had stowed it. Yanking at the locks, she ripped open the lid and gaped at the Smith & Wesson .357 Magnum. It was a wicked piece, over a foot in length with an extended barrel that glinted blue-black in the subdued lighting. Grasping the burl wood handle, she tugged the weapon loose. It weighed a ton and she lobbed it awkwardly in Ethan's direction. He caught it in a one-handed move that struck her as far too experienced.

On board the yacht, Bettina regained her feet and lunged toward Julian and the gun, screaming at Lily over her shoulder. *"Jump!"*

Lily hesitated for a split second, long enough for Julian to slam a fist into Bettina's jaw and knock her down the companionway. Then his gun came up and arced in Lily's direction. It was all the encouragement she needed to scramble to the railing and fling herself overboard into the frigid waters. Without even thinking, Ethan marked the spot where she went in.

Faith came out of her seat and would have hurled herself into the water after Lily if Ethan hadn't caught her around the middle and wrestled her back. "What are you doing?" she screamed. "She'll drown."

He didn't react to her panic. A familiar iciness overtook him, and he suppressed every ounce of emotion, intent only on his goal. "You'll get shot. How will that help her?" He shoved her toward the bottom of the boat. "Now stay down and don't get in my way."

As Julian crossed to the railing and took aim at the water, Ethan stood, balancing himself the best he could, and squeezed off a round to get the man's attention. The reverberation boomed across the water like cannon fire. Julian's head jerked in Ethan's direction. So did his gun. An instant later, bullets came screaming at them like a horde of angry bees. They sizzled as they hit the water around the boat, some pinging against the hull. Faith's head bobbed up and Ethan knocked her down a second time, planting a foot on her back to hold her there.

He could hear her muffled shrieks as she called to Lily. Far in the distance, a siren blared from a blue-and-white Harbor Patrol boat. Horns blew from nearby boats. He ignored all of it. He ignored the sirens and the shouting and his own rising panic, as well as the frantic pleas of the woman he loved more than life itself. Worst of all, he ignored his drowning daughter. He ignored everything but the man with the gun. He continued to stand dead center in the lurching boat, positioning himself at an angle so Julian would have as narrow a target as possible.

A bullet tore through his leather coat, just beneath his armpit, missing him by less than an inch. Another nearly parted his hair. Lifting his arm, he took careful aim. And then he pulled the trigger, squeezing off round after round in a smooth, practiced rhythm. The shots thundered across the bay. With the extended barrel, his bullets covered more distance than Julian's, and with far greater accuracy. His .357 also had better fire power over his opponent's 9 mm. With one to spare, Ethan's seventh bullet hit its target and Julian crumpled to the deck.

Without hesitating, Ethan dropped the gun, stripped off his jacket and shoes and dived into the water. *Lily.* She couldn't drown. Couldn't die. Not now. Not when he'd finally found her. The exchange of gunfire felt like it had taken an eternity, but in reality he knew that less than a minute had passed. Lily had, at most, nine more before the cold killed her—assuming she didn't drown first. He swam to the spot where she had gone in and then he heard it. A tiny voice.

"Help," she whispered.

Somehow, perhaps because the yacht rode so low in the water, she'd managed to grab on to one of the rubber fenders that protected the sides of the boat when moored. He swam to her, terrified by how weak and blue she looked. "Hang on, Lily. You're safe now."

"Are you going to save me?" she asked through chattering teeth.

"Yeah. I'm going to save you." He pried her hands off the fender and pulled her into his arms. "That's what daddies do. They save their little girls."

She clung to his neck. "My daddy's dead." She shook so hard he could barely understand her. "He can't save me."

"Yes, he can. Look at me, Lily. Look at what I'm wearing around my neck." He worked his way through the water toward the Sea Ray. "Stay with me, now, honey. Can you see what I'm wearing?"

It took her a few seconds to focus, and then a few more to respond. "That's my ring."

"That's right. I found it in your room and I've been wearing it ever since those bad people took you. Your ring helped me find you. I'm your daddy and I came back for you, baby. I came home just so I could save you."

"My daddy? My real-life daddy?"

"Your honest-to-goodness, real-life dad."

Dimples flashed for a brief instant. "We've been missing you. Sometimes Mommy cries for you."

The icy conditions must have affected his vision. His eyes stung and he blinked rapidly to clear them. "Yeah. I've been missing you, too."

Faith had figured out how to work the throttle, and nudged the speedboat alongside them. She grabbed Lily first, pulling her aboard, then helped Ethan in. An instant later, Faith had stripped Lily of her wet clothing and wrapped her in the coat, as well as the blanket. Both of them were weeping. Ethan crouched in the bottom of the boat and watched their joyful reunion. He wanted to join in, hungered to be part of their loving circle. But a painful uncertainty held him in place.

"Mommy, I got stolen," Lily said between her sobs. "The bad people took me. I tried to be a brave lion, but I was a scared little mouse."

"I know, baby. I know." Faith tightened her hold on Lily, rocking back and forth. "And I tried to find you. I tried to get to you. I'm so sorry it took me so long. But you're safe now. Do you hear me? You're safe. And I'll never let anyone take you away again."

"Promise?"

As Faith opened her mouth to reply, her gaze collided with Ethan's. Something in his expression must have given away his feelings of estrangement. Did he look like the stereotypical starving orphan boy with his nose pressed up to the window of the local confectioner's shop? He must have, because her comprehension was instantaneous. So was her response. She nudged their daughter in Ethan's direction.

"Ask your daddy, Lily. He'll tell you."

There was a momentary hesitation on his daughter's part.

Then she reached out to him. What had been a magical circle of two expanded, welcoming him into the inner warmth. It was everything he'd dreamed it would be...and more. "Do you promise, Daddy? No one will take me away again?"

"I promise, sweetheart," he whispered. "No one will take you away from us ever again."

The three of them huddled in the middle of the boat, wrapped tightly together. They were a family. Cold. Wet. Still frightened. But a family, nevertheless. After an endless moment, he eased Lily back into Faith's arms.

"Take her. I'm too wet to hold her. I'll only make her colder."

Lily gazed anxiously up at her mother. "Did I miss Santa?" she asked with chattering teeth. "Did he come when I was stolen?"

Faith choked on a laugh. "No, Lily. You didn't miss Santa, honey. He comes tomorrow night, I promise. He'll know you've been a very good girl this year."

"No coal in my stocking?"

"Definitely no coal."

Ethan watched as Faith cupped her daughter's face and drank in every blue-tinged inch. The joy and love between the two was unmistakable. An intense gratitude filled him. He was part of that now, and nothing would separate him from his family. Not ever again.

Lily shuddered in Faith's arms and she turned to Ethan. "We have to get her to a hospital, fast. She's freezing."

The Harbor Patrol cruiser was approaching at a rapid clip, and Ethan inclined his head in its direction. "The police are on their way." After waving at them, he bent double in an effort to conserve body heat. "They won't get to *Mary Lou* in time, though. She's going down fast."

"No!" Lily struggled within Faith's hold. "You have to save Bettina! She's still on the boat. Julian hit her. She's hurt. She's going to drown."

Ethan shot an uncertain glance toward the yacht. ''The police will be here any minute.''

Faith kept her arms wrapped around Lily. ''Ethan, she'll be gone before then.''

Lily fixed him with a frantic gaze, her eyes eerily similar to his own. ''Please. Save Bettina. If you're really my daddy, you would. Mommy said he was very brave.''

He closed his eyes. He'd heard something similar years ago. Another woman and child. *Ethan. Please. Save Davis. You're the only one who can.*

Faith must have recognized the hideous decision he faced, and understood its significance. ''Go, Ethan,'' she whispered.

He stubbornly shook his head. He had what he wanted right here in this boat. He wouldn't put it at risk. Not again. ''Not a chance. Last time I made this choice, I lost everything I held dear. Besides, I promised. I promised I wouldn't try and save the world and everyone in it. Not anymore.''

''You won't be able to live with yourself if you don't save Bettina.'' Faith smiled with such sweetness it robbed him of breath. ''Don't you get it? It's who you are. It's what you do. That's never going to change. If I can accept that, so can you.''

He glanced over his shoulder. It was now or never. He turned back to Faith. ''I'll be back. I promise.''

''You better be, or I'm going to be really, *really* angry. You hear me, Dunn?''

''I hear you, sweetheart.'' He managed a tired grin. ''Hell, half of Union Bay hears you.''

He dived back into the water, praying his strength would hold out, that hypothermia wouldn't get him before he could reach Bettina. There was a ladder at the stern of the *Mary Lou* and he dragged himself up it, flopping onto the deck and gasping for air. A scant foot to his left, Julian lay sprawled on the deck in an awkward heap. He was quite dead. If he hadn't been, Ethan decided without compunction, he would have finished the job. He hadn't met many men who deserved to die, but this one did in spades.

Struggling to his feet, Ethan crossed to the companionway. He found Bettina unconscious at the bottom of the steps, the water rapidly rising around her. He slipped on his way down to her, landing heavily on his bad knee. Searing pain knifed through him, and he knelt in the bitterly cold water, fighting to breathe. The crippling agony held him immobile while precious seconds ticked by.

"Move, Dunn," he finally muttered. *"Move!"*

Just as he grabbed hold of Bettina, the boat listed to starboard. Before he could react, it rolled onto its side, groaning a hideous death knell. Water rushed in, swirling around him like a whirlpool and slamming him against the wall. Then the world turned upside down. He had one final thought as darkness descended. Once again he'd broken his promise to Faith.

Damn, was she going to be pissed.

IT SURPRISED ETHAN to discover that death held no pain. There was even the darkened tunnel he'd heard so much about, with a bright light at the far end, beckoning him onward. He tried to get to it but found, much to his annoyance, that he wasn't making much progress. Something held him back, pulling him toward the blackness of hell. That infuriated him, making him all the more determined to go to the light. After all he'd been through, he damn well deserved heaven. He fought harder than he'd ever fought before, dragging something behind as he approached the bright glow ahead.

Excess baggage. It had to be excess baggage from his former life. Baggage he should dump.

But he couldn't. For some reason he felt he had to bring it with him. So he did. Kicking and clawing, he burst into heaven's light, dragging Bettina along for the ride. He expected an outpouring of joy and warmth and a kindly reception when he reached heaven's gates. At the very least a "How's it going?"

Instead he was hit with an icy wind, drawn weapons and a spotlight square in the eyes. Worse, instead of the kindly reception, he heard his least favorite voice in this world or the next.

"By the time I'm through with you, Dunn," Luke Sloan informed him, "you're going to wish you'd drowned."

THEY WERE ALL GATHERED around the Christmas tree—Ethan, Faith and Lily, as well as Dinky, Maudie and Jack. Luke, Abby and Emily had come and gone, letting them know that Bettina might be given a lighter sentence thanks to what Lily had revealed about the kidnapping. In the hours following the rescue, Ethan, Lily and Bettina had been transported to the nearest hospital and treated for hypothermia. By the time Luke had finished with him, Ethan didn't wish he'd drowned, but he'd come close—especially when Luke learned about their second trip to Bettina's apartment.

On a brighter note, Ethan had finally been able to keep one of his promises. Lily had returned home in time for Christmas. And now the presents had been opened and a twenty-pound turkey squatted in the oven, working on acquiring a crispy golden brown tan. Lily took turns perching first on Jack's knee, then on Dinky's. But her favorite place to roost was in Ethan's arms, hugging him for all she was worth. Around her neck was suspended a ring, held in place with a bright blue ribbon identical to the one Ethan wore.

"Faith's right, you know," Dinky said. "You should be looking into a job doing something helpful. You're better at helping people than anything else."

"Except maybe fighting," Jack couldn't resist adding.

Faith plunked herself down beside Ethan and snuggled into his embrace. "Well, I've been giving it a lot of thought, and I have a suggestion for a job."

Ethan smiled agreeably. He didn't care what sort of employment she had in mind for him. He'd take it. Nothing mattered more than Faith and Lily—and living the sort of safe and secure white-picket-fence existence his family required. "And what job would that be?"

"You can start up a private eye business. We'll call it White Picket Fence Investigations."

She had to be kidding. "What happened to safe and secure?"

"I kind of liked walking the wild side with you. Parts of it were fun."

"Ooh! Ooh! How about White Picket Fence Security?" Dinky interjected. "We protect your hearth and home."

Faith nodded enthusiastically. "Good one. You and Jack can be Ethan's partners, and Maudie can run the office and keep you guys in line."

"And what will you be doing?" Ethan asked dryly.

Her bright gold eyes assumed an all-too-innocent expression. "I thought we'd already settled that at Frankie's. I'm your hired gun, remember?"

"Not a chance."

"What do I get to do?" Lily interrupted. She rested her elbows on his knee and cupped her chin, staring up at him with those startling blue eyes of hers. "I want to help, too."

"She does have a way with locks," Jack offered. "A little training and—"

"Have you lost your fu— da—"

"Dang?" Faith supplied helpfully.

"*Dang* mind?"

Jack held up his hands. "Okay, okay. It was just a thought. So are we going to do it? Are we going to be White Picket Fence Security? I kind of like the idea myself."

Ethan sighed. "It's better than the Loners, I guess."

"What's the Loners?" Faith asked curiously.

"Our old unit."

"Your unit was called the Loners?" Her brow puckered in a frown. "That's just sad."

Ethan shrugged. ''It's what we were.''

''It doesn't matter,'' she maintained stoutly. ''Now we have a new unit. White Picket Fence Security. Or Investigators. And it's not a unit anymore. It's a family.'' She smiled at Ethan, held safe within his arms, their daughter clinging to his knee. Then she turned to the others, her smile widening to include them. ''What about you guys? You want to sign up? Families always have plenty of room to expand.''

Her offer was greeted with unanimous enthusiasm, and she smiled in satisfaction. She'd always wanted a home and a huge family, and that was precisely what she'd gotten. Maybe, once Ethan became accustomed to the idea, she'd suggest he get in touch with some of the other Loners and see if they wanted to become family members, as well.

The rest of the evening flew by as they made plans for their new business, the subject preoccupying them throughout dinner and dessert. The party finally broke up not long after, and Faith and Lily hugged each of their guests before closing the door on a cheerfully squabbling Dinky and Maudie.

Taking a deep breath, Faith turned to gaze uncertainly at Ethan. ''Well?'' she asked.

''Well what?'' He folded his arms across his chest. ''It sounds like you've got everything all planned out.''

Her uncertainty grew. ''Only if it's a plan you can live with.''

He frowned. ''What about your job at the newspaper? It's always been your dream to be a photojournalist. I don't want to destroy that.''

''Dreams change.'' She took a step closer. ''Or, in this case, dreams come true.''

His expression softened. ''Is that what you consider me? A dream come true?''

''Yes.'' There was no hesitation. No doubt. Just endless love.

He pulled her close. ‘‘You have it all wrong, Faith. You’re the dream, a dream I thought I’d lost.’’

‘‘We came close, didn’t we?’’

He shuddered. ‘‘Too close.’’

‘‘No more nightmares?’’

‘‘They’re all gone,’’ he assured her. He cupped her face between large, callused hands. ‘‘And what about you? Any more fears that I’m going to leave you like your parents did?’’

‘‘None,’’ she replied with absolute certainty. ‘‘You’re here to stay.’’

His expression eased, a smile replacing his frown. ‘‘In that case, we only have one option.’’

She offered a matching smile. ‘‘Which is?’’

‘‘That we get married and live happily ever after.’’

Tears gathered in her eyes as a fierce joy filled her. ‘‘I can’t think of anything more perfect.’’

Ethan lowered his head and took her mouth in the sweetest of kisses. Faith wrapped her arms around his neck, her lips parting beneath his. He’d promised her a Christmas miracle and he’d delivered. Lily was home. And so was the man Faith loved more than life itself. Whether he knew it or not, he’d given her one other gift, as well, the most miraculous gift of all. With his return, he’d renewed her trust and faith, qualities she’d thought she’d lost long ago. The fear that had haunted her for so many years had disappeared as surely as Ethan’s nightmares.

She had no idea how long they stood there before a flash of light broke them apart. Faith turned toward the living room, dazed. ‘‘What…?’’

Lily grinned at them from across the room, Faith’s camera clutched between her hands. ‘‘I took your picture. I took a picture of my mommy and daddy kissing.’’ She ran over to Faith and thrust the camera in her direction. ‘‘Now you take one, Mommy. Take one on top of the sticks so you can be in it, too.’’

Faith laughed. ''Okay, okay. I'll set up the tripod. How about we stand in front of the Christmas tree? I'll set the timer so we're all in the photo together.''

''And then we'll put it on our family picture wall, right?''

Ethan ruffled his daughter's hair. ''I'd like that.''

It took only a moment to set up. He and Faith crouched in front of the tree with Lily between them. The three of them smiled self-consciously at the camera while the red warning light blinked endlessly.

''This was my best Christmas ever,'' Lily chattered as they waited. ''I got a daddy for Christmas. I bet none of my friends got a daddy. 'Cept Emily. Her mommy's giving her a new daddy, too. And I already know what I want for Christmas next year.''

''Smile, sweetie. Almost time,'' Faith warned.

Ethan glanced at his daughter. ''So, what do you want?''

''A brother.''

The flash exploded, perfectly capturing their first ever family photo. Lily mugged for the camera, laughing gaily, her dimples flashing. And her parents bracketed her, both staring at their daughter and wearing identical expressions of stunned bemusement.

They didn't know it then, but it was an expression they'd wear on a regular basis, particularly when Lily teamed up with the brother that arrived—as requested—the very next Christmas.

EPILOGUE

THE INSISTENT RINGING of the phone pulled Hannah Richards from the spreadsheet on her computer screen. She lifted the receiver and tucked it between her shoulder and her ear. "Forrester Square Day Care," she said.

"Hi, Hannah. It's Dylan Garrett."

She instantly recognized the private investigator's slow, reassuring drawl, and knew with an instinctive certainty that he was calling with news of her son. "Hang on. Let me save this file."

Dylan had seemed the perfect person to turn to when she'd decided to hire a P.I. to find the baby she'd given up for adoption nine years before. For one thing, the adoption agency she'd used all those years ago was located in Texas, as was Dylan. And for another, his specialty was reuniting families. She'd met him a couple years before her pregnancy, while attending college in Dallas. Dylan had been with the local police department, and they'd kept in touch over the years, even after he'd left the force to start up his agency, Finders Keepers.

It took two tries to successfully close out her accounting program, perhaps because her fingers were shaking so hard. "Okay, I'm finished. Talk to me. Are you as good as you've always led me to believe?"

"I have a belated Christmas present for you. Is that good enough?"

Hannah closed her eyes, vacillating between intense joy and a nervous dread. In the past nine years, not a day had gone by that she hadn't wondered about her son, worried about him, ached to see him. And not a day had gone by that she'd wondered if she'd done the right thing by giving him up for adoption. Now she'd find out, and she was terrified to learn the truth.

"Where is he?"

"You're not going to believe this, Hannah. He's right there in Seattle."

"Here!" She sat in stunned silence. All this time, and he was living right under her nose? How was that possible? "What's his name? How is he? Is he happy? Healthy?"

Dylan's baritone chuckle eased down the line, providing a warm touch of Texas in the middle of a cold Seattle January. "Slow down, Hannah. One thing at a time. First off, his name is Adam."

"Adam." She savored the name. Strong. Solid. Simple.

"There's more. And I'm not sure you're going to like this next part."

Her hand tightened around the receiver. Had something happened to Adam? Was he ill? Lost? In trouble? After the recent crisis with Lily Marshall, Hannah was more than ready to anticipate the worst. "What? What is it?"

"Are you sitting down?"

"Yes, yes," she replied impatiently. "For crying out loud, Dylan. Just tell me."

"Okay. Your son was adopted by a single parent. A man."

A horrible tension seized her. "Who is he?" Dylan didn't answer immediately. And then she knew—knew it as certainly as two and two added up to four. "It's Jack McKay, isn't it?"

"Adam's biological father. Yes."

Dear heaven, how was it possible? *Jack McKay.* Images of the man crowded her mind. Long, jet-black hair. Striking blue eyes. Crooked, come-to-bed smile. A cowboy's solid, muscular build. And a bad-boy attitude that kept him teetering on the edge of the law—when he wasn't actively falling over that edge. He'd been her first love, a mistake that should never have happened.

A mistake that had landed her pregnant and alone.

"I don't understand." She fought to keep her emotions in check, with only limited success. "What sort of reputable agency would give an innocent baby to an unreliable cowboy? And why would Jack take on that sort of responsibility? He could barely take care of himself."

"You'll have to ask Jack those questions."

Her focus switched to her primary concern. Her son. "What about Adam? Is he okay? Is he healthy? Is he..." *Is he safe?*

"All your questions will be answered shortly. I've made an appointment for you to meet with Jack."

She flipped open her calendar book and snatched up a pen. "When and where?"

There was another significant pause. "Next week. At his parole office."

Hannah closed her eyes. That was no surprise. A parole office was the second place she figured she'd find Jack McKay—the first being in jail. Despair ate at her. She'd spent the past eight years picturing her son living an ideal existence with Ozzie and Harriet type parents. And it had all been a sham. She hadn't given him to a loving family who'd raise him to make smart choices in life. She hadn't done what was best for her son at all. Well, someone had to look into the situation. And there was only one person in a position to do it.

No matter what it took, she had to make things right.

* * * * *

Harlequin® Historical
Historical Romantic Adventure!

Imagine a time of chivalrous knights and unconventional ladies, roguish rakes and impetuous heiresses, rugged cowboys and spirited frontierswomen— these rich and vivid tales will capture your imagination!

Harlequin Historical . . . they're too good to miss!